What the critics are saying...

ख

4 Stars "This delicious tale is quite a treat...filled with sexual tension, a bit of mystery and the gift of love." ~ *Romantic Times Magazine*

4 Cups "Once again Ms. Hunter makes a story snap and sizzle." ~ *Coffee Time Romance*

"Cabin Fever ...is a tasty winter treat full of tension and hear-warming tenderness...worthy of being kept around for another read or five..." *Ecataromance*

4 Stars "Hunter's characters leap off the pages." ~ *Just Erotic Romance Reviews*

"From the very beginning CABIN FEVER is addictive, I read the entire story in one sitting." ~ *Romance Junkies*

4 Hearts "The tension is high and the sensuality is abundant. The love scenes are steamy and will leave readers breathless." ~*The Romance Studio*

DIANA HUNTER

CABIN
Fever

ELLORA'S CAVE
ROMANTICA PUBLISHING

An Ellora's Cave Romantica Publication

www.ellorascave.com

Cabin Fever

ISBN # 1419955047
ALL RIGHTS RESERVED.
Cabin Fever Copyright© 2005 Diana Hunter
Edited by Pamela Campbell.
Cover art by Willo.

Electronic book Publication October 2005

Trade paperback Publication September 2006

Excerpt from *Table for Four* Copyright © Diana Hunter 2004

Warning:

The following material contains graphic sexual content meant for mature readers. This story has been rated E–rotic by a minimum of three independent reviewers.

Ellora's Cave Publishing offers three levels of Romantica™ reading entertainment: S (S-ensuous), E (E-rotic), and X (X-treme).

S-ensuous love scenes are explicit and leave nothing to the imagination.

E-rotic love scenes are explicit, leave nothing to the imagination, and are high in volume per the overall word count. In addition, some E-rated titles might contain fantasy material that some readers find objectionable, such as bondage, submission, same sex encounters, forced seductions, and so forth. E-rated titles are the most graphic titles we carry; it is common, for instance, for an author to use words such as "fucking", "cock", "pussy", and such within their work of literature.

X-treme titles differ from E-rated titles only in plot premise and storyline execution. Unlike E-rated titles, stories designated with the letter X tend to contain controversial subject matter not for the faint of heart.

Also by Diana Hunter

About the Author

୫୦

For many years, Diana Hunter confined herself to mainstream writings. Her interest in the world of dominance and submission, dormant for years, bloomed when she met a man who was willing to let her explore the submissive side of her personality. In her academic approach to learning about the lifestyle, she discovered hundreds of short stories that existed on the topic, but none of them seemed to express her view of a d/s relationship. Challenged by a friend to write a better one, she wrote her first BDSM novel, *Secret Submission*, published by Ellora's Cave Publishing.

Diana welcomes comments from readers. You can find her website and email address on her author bio page at www.ellorascave.com

Cabin Fever

જી

Dedication

ɛɔ

To my husband,
who helps me understand the male sexual point of view.

Trademarks Acknowledgement

The author acknowledges the trademarked status and trademark owners of the following wordmarks mentioned in this work of fiction:

Styrofoam: Dow Chemical Company

Charlie Brown: United Feature Syndicate, Inc.

Emerald City: Turner Entertainment Co.

MG: MG Rover

Ritz: Ritz-Carlton Hotel Co.

Chapter One

🍂

"No, Eddie, stop it. I mean it!"

Isabel slapped Eddie's hands away as she tried to back away in her seat. Damn MG — no place to go to get away from her date's roaming hands. She had surreptitiously unbuckled her seat belt as soon as he'd made his first overture. The date had been no more than bearable and she did not intend to let it go farther. Why had she let Beth talk her into going out with this jerk?

"Oh, come on, Izzy, just kiss me. You know you want to."

That pushed her button. She hated that nickname. Isabel's eyes flashed but Eddie was too much of an egotist to see his danger and he leaned toward her again, grabbing her bare, white shoulders.

"That's it, bucko." With a swift movement, Isabel brought her hands up through his reaching arms and slammed the back of her forearms into his. The force of her blow caught him off-guard and he let go of her shoulders, one hand banging into the dash. In a flash, Isabel got the door open and climbed out of the car.

"Ow! Hey, Izzy! I thought we had a good thing going! Get back in the car."

The top was up on the little car so Isabel could not see his face, but she could see his fingers grasping for the hem of her light summer dress. Taking a step farther back, she slammed the door.

"Sorry, Eddie. I know you as well as I'm going to know you. You need to learn when a girl says 'no', it means 'no'!"

"Oh, come on, Izzy, it's miles back to the city. Come on, get in and I'll drive you home."

"No, Eddie. I can't trust you. I told you I didn't want to drive up here in the first place and you did anyway. I told you I wasn't interested in making out on the first date and you tried anyway. You blew your trust with me. Go away, Eddie. We're done."

"But..."

"We're done, Eddie. Go. Away."

"Fucking little cock-teaser. Fine. Get back to the city yourself. Bitch." With a squeal of tires, Eddie threw the MG into gear and sped down the mountainside, leaving Isabel alone on the old mining road.

The lights of the MG illuminated the woods until the car turned around a curve of the mountain and disappeared. The sudden darkness blinded her and Isabel needed several deep breaths to regain her composure. Her "date" had made her so angry that she was shaking in her summer shift.

"Well, that didn't exactly go very well, Isabel-girl." She shook her head and rocked on her heels while surveying her predicament.

The summer had lingered this year, the warm nights extending almost all the way through October. The first frost had finally settled one night last week. Had the sun been out instead of the moon, the view around her would have shone with the peak colors of autumn on a lazy Indian summer day. But only moonlight lit the trees now, and a few scuttling clouds skimmed their way across the night sky.

The darkness of the night swallowed Isabel's wry grin. Inhaling deeply as her eyes adjusted to the dim moonlight, she turned, surveying the woods surrounding her. This old road wasn't traveled very much anymore and the chance of catching a ride to the city, ten miles distant, was pretty slim. A breeze blew over her skin and she shivered.

"Oh, blast it, but you've gone and done it, girl. So he wanted to grope you, you couldn't let him cop a feel and be done with it?" Shaking her head again, Isabel took a few steps along the dirt road and stumbled over a patch of pebbles, her thin, high heel catching between them to roll her forward.

"Damn heels." Continuing to mutter under her breath, Isabel kept up her running conversation as she kicked off her three-inch-heeled sandals. "No, you need to be in control all the time, don't you, woman? Well, Independent Woman, get walking. You've got three miles to go before you reach a phone."

Grateful for the faint moonlight that lit the dirt road, Isabel hooked her finger through the straps of her shoes and started off again, only to come to another halt a few feet farther along the road.

"These stockings need to go, too. They're just going to catch on every rock and twig in the road. Might as well go barefoot like the old days." The nearest town was a little more than three miles down the mountain, but there were scattered farmhouses before that. Still, a three-mile hike was best done in sneakers, boots, or barefoot.

Stepping to the side of the road, she set her shoes down and then, out of habit, looked both ways before lifting her dress to remove her stockings, laughing at her modesty.

"Okay, girl. Just who do you think is going to see you out here taking off your stockings? 'Course, this is a whole lot easier when you have a chair to sit on." She hopped on one foot and tugged at the stockings, then yanked them off the rest of the way, turning them inside out in the process. Sitting on a rock in her brand-new, thin summer dress was not an option as far as she was concerned. Having high hopes for this particular date, Isabel had indulged in a new outfit. But she'd known she was in trouble from the moment Eddie had picked her up and couldn't take his eyes off the stretch of fabric across her rather well-endowed breasts.

With a melodramatic sigh that helped mask her sudden loneliness, she threw her long black hair over her shoulder and, with a resolute step, started down the mountain once more.

At least she was fit and trim. Isabel prided herself on the fact that she kept in shape—if walking three blocks to work was any exercise. She never had time for the gym, so she compensated by walking just about everywhere she needed to go. As a result, her full-bodied figure with its rounded curves and deep valleys was not daunted by a mountain hike. She sighed. Would a man ever look at her for something other than her breast size or full hips?

Now in her thirties and still unmarried, she had given in to her married friend Beth, whose husband's brother had a friend, who—Isabel shrugged away from where her thoughts were taking her. She had accepted the date because Beth had bugged her so much, not because she was a desperate, dried-up old maid. Not yet. Not until she hit forty—and that was still three years away.

A howl deep in the woods brought her up short and for a moment her heart beat faster. But then reason set in again and she continued to find her way along the road. At least the only predators here were four-legged and probably as scared of her as she was of them. Still, if she could find a good, stout stick, it would make her feel better. Her eyes scanned the sides of the road as she stepped along, thankful that the dirt road seemed to be in relatively good repair.

Unfortunately, the moon chose that particular moment to go behind the clouds. The breeze picked up and several leaves skittered across the dirt road, their dry rustle sounding ominous in the darkness. Isabel squinted up at the narrow band of sky she could still see. How big was that band of clouds?

"Did I just feel a drop? Tell me it isn't going to rain." She stopped in the middle of the road and held out her palm. Sure enough, one drop, two drops, then several gently landed on her skin. "Figures. Maybe Eddie has enough gentleman inside him to come back and get me."

Starting off again, her face twisted in a wry grimace. "Nah, not him. He won't be back."

The rain started coming faster and Isabel tried to pick up her pace. But without the small light provided by the summer moon, the night was now pitch black and she stumbled headlong into a tree. Catching herself only at the last minute, she swore again. "Shit, but I'm about done with this." She scolded herself, as if talking to herself would keep the fear at bay. "So, Mistress Isabel, just how many wrong decisions *did* you make tonight?"

The rain pelted her now and her vision was all but gone. Feeling her way tree-by-tree, her progress slowed to a crawl. She dropped a shoe and spent several moments feeling around the ground for it before giving up and returning to the tree she *thought* was the last one she'd touched.

How long had she walked? Why was the road going up again? "You just didn't pay enough attention when he was driving you up here, that's the problem. You were too busy arguing with him." Her voice was a whisper against the fierce wind that now howled through the treetops, whipping branches into her face and lashing her arms and legs.

She was cold. Wet and cold. Too cold to be angry anymore. If Eddie showed up, she would swallow her pride and accept a ride with him—and thank him afterward. And what had made her leave without a jacket? The late fall night had been deceptively warm earlier, but now definitely moved to the winter side of fall. Shivering, she grabbed the stockings still wadded in her remaining shoe and wrapped them around her neck like a scarf. They offered little protection or comfort, but Isabel grasped at every small amount of warmth.

Why hadn't she worn a watch? And her purse? Damn! Her purse was still in Eddie's car. Along with a cell phone that was useless this far from town, anyway. Cursing at her predicament, Isabel tripped and fell full-length into a wet pile of old leaves. Fighting back tears, she righted herself and tried to brush off her new dress, but knew she was just spreading around the dirt.

She staggered on, the iron core of stubbornness that ran through her spine refusing to give up and admit that she was hopelessly lost. "Downhill, girl. Go downhill." Already soaked through, Isabel tried to ignore the scared feeling that sat like a rock in her stomach.

And yet the ground rose before her again. Why could she not keep her bearings? And where was that blasted road? It couldn't be more than a few feet from where she was. "To your left, Isabel-girl. Come on, keep yourself moving."

Her eyes closed against the stinging rain, she turned into the storm, feeling her way with her fingers and toes only to stumble again, bashing her leg against a log that had no right being anywhere near the road. This time Isabel could not stop the tears that first fell from the sudden pain, then fell because she was lost and continued to fall because she was alone, and then fell just because.

For several moments, she knelt, holding her shin, rocking on her heels in the rain that poured down her face to mingle with her tears. Sobs racked her body as Isabel gave in to her despair. All of her recent frustrations — the nagging of her mother because she was thirty-seven and unmarried, the awful date with Eddie, his abandonment of her—just as she had been left by every other man she ever dated. What was wrong with her? Her mother kept telling her that her standards were too high and Isabel sobbed all the more for fear her mother was right.

The component of her brain still capable of rational thought tried to tell her that she needed to move—she would catch cold just sitting there. Staggering up, Isabel ignored the shooting pain in her calf as she moved through the trees. All sense of direction was lost now, she didn't care where she was going. Nor did she have the strength to give voice to her thoughts. *Shelter. I just need to find shelter.*

Prying open her eyes, Isabel squinted into the dark night. The wind had abated but the rain fell steadily, giving her no respite. Was that something that glinted off to her right?

A low growl close by froze her where she stood. Was she too near a wolf's den? A bear? Fear choked her and she could not breathe. Conflicting emotions ran through her as her mind fought for control. *Run; don't run. Scream; don't scream.* Her instincts for survival warred with her panic.

Leaves rustled to her right and she spun before she could stop herself. Again the animal growled, but the sound was now to her left. Her head snapped to the side and a whimper of fear and indecision escaped in spite of her attempts to keep control.

With a feral snarl, the animal leapt. In the darkness of the night, she only imagined she saw the sharp fangs as she screamed, fleeing from the wild monster she could not see. Blindly she crashed through the trees, branches slashing at her dress, ripping through the thin fabric to leave welts and thin lines of blood on her skin. Mindless, panicked, she ran to escape her fears.

Her body slammed into something hard. Isabel cried out, more in surprise than pain, as she recoiled. And when the lightning flashed, giving her a momentary glimpse of the man before her, her breath caught in her throat and fear strangled her cry.

Solid. Huge. Menacing.

Isabel turned to flee, her heart lodged in her throat. A strong hand caught her wrist and she struggled to get loose. She still had enough presence of mind to bring the shoe in her other hand up to slam down on the powerful grip that held her. And when the hand let her go with a garbled oath, she ran again into the night.

She took only three strides before the wolf tackled her, knocking her to the ground, snapping and growling at her face. Throwing an arm up to protect herself, her fear of the wolf superseded her fear of the powerful man and she cried out for help.

And then the wolf was gone and the rain fell on her face and the man leaned over, shouting something at her. It was too much. Isabel did something she had never in her life done before. She fainted.

Her body stood poised upon the edge of a cliff, wearing a flowing gown of seafoam green. The soft fabric of her dress caressed her legs as the light wind caused it to billow and swell where she stood just feet away from the edge. The gentle breeze lifted her hair to fall back again in waves as graceful as those that lapped on the shore far below. Out to sea, a light mist clouded the sun. Her gaze could not pierce the gloom to find…to find…what? What was she looking for?

"I'm here, Isabella, come to me now."

She peered into the gloom. Who spoke? It was a man's voice, deep and resonant and she wanted to answer. But only a yearning whimper came from her throat and she could not move.

"Come to me, Isabella. You are mine."

She closed her eyes and took a single step as the cliff disappeared into the mists. Echoes of the rich voice resounded in her head, vanishing as her consciousness faded into darkness once more.

* * * * *

Daniel Fox tucked the covers around the inert form of the woman he had found wandering in the rain. Her cuts had been tended to and the dressing changed on her left knee where she had scraped it raw. Only one long cut worried him. Along the upper part of her right arm, a thin line of red slashed down where a branch had dealt her a vicious blow. Daniel knew he was no surgeon, but had done the best he could to close the gaping tissue with five small stitches. He nodded as his brawny hand brushed against her forehead — her fever had broken. Good. He could get some rest now.

Rising to his full height, the huge man stretched his arms over his head, his fingers brushing against the rough wooden beams that stretched the width of the room as he did so. There was not much room in the old hunter's cabin, only enough for his own needs.

Except now a fool of a woman lay in his bed.

For the past day and a half Daniel had pondered why such a beautiful woman would be wandering, obviously lost, in his woods. If it hadn't been for Sasha pawing at the door, the woman might still be out there. Daniel had raised his pet from the tiny abandoned pup he'd discovered this past spring, to an almost full-grown wolf. Still, a wild animal is a wild animal, and Sasha chose to live outside no matter what the weather. Having no pack, the animal stayed close to the cabin Daniel had acquired as a family inheritance. He snorted. Not that the family had ever expected him to actually live in the thing.

More of a shack than a cabin when he had first set eyes on the place, its very remoteness touched a chord in his soul. Built by his great-grandfather in the days when men hunted for food for the family table, it had mostly been abandoned by recent generations. Daniel's grandfather had told him stories about the place, but Daniel's father was a city-boy who wanted no part of such rural surroundings. In fact, the two of them had quite an argument when Daniel had quit a lucrative law career and dropped out of the rat race.

He grinned as he looked down upon the sleeping form of the woman. No doubt she would think him as crazy as his father thought him.

Massive by virtue of good food and good genes, Daniel's broad-chested, muscular frame stood him in good stead out here in the wilderness. He cut his own wood and cooked his own meals on a small two-burner woodstove that also served to keep the place warm. The privy was still a small hole in the ground several yards away from the cabin—that was next spring's project. Water had to be hauled from the stream that ran beside the cabin to prime the cabin's one luxury, an indoor water pump that ran into the kitchen sink. He'd seen the stream almost dry in August, only to become slightly swollen now with the late fall rains and the soft snowfall that had begun that morning.

He sighed as he stretched again. A yawn escaped and he rubbed his eyes. After thirty-six hours of watching over her, he was very, very tired.

The cabin boasted only two chairs—one straight-backed caned chair that sat neatly tucked under a shelf that served as Daniel's desk, and one overstuffed, rounded armchair that had last been recovered in the 1950s. Big, faded maroon roses on a gray background swarmed over and around the padded arms and back of the piece, and with a sigh, Daniel dropped into the chair and stretched out his legs. He was asleep in seconds.

* * * * *

He woke to a changed world. During the night, winter had arrived with a whisper of snow that muted all the noises of the forest. The wooded area outside the cabin's many-paned windows was now bedded down with a beautiful white carpet of snow. His patient still slept...would that woman ever wake up? He laced his feet into warm winter boots and stepped into a crisp, white fairyland.

Small ice pellets clung to the black branches, twinkling as daylight shimmered through them. But the sun itself remained hidden—the clouds would not allow her to show her radiance today. Indeed, a darker band of clouds moved into sight and Daniel recognized the signs that there was a real winter storm on the way.

A dip in the snow showed him the spot he had dug for his privy. Rather than dig it out again, he simply aimed in the general direction and relieved himself, enjoying the sound his warm piss made on the cold snow. His cock was thick, as big around as some men's fists, and as long as the handle on a hammer, but the frigid air of winter threatened to shrivel him where he stood.

The color of those clouds bothered him. He needed to get that woman home soon or it would be too late. With a last shake, he tucked his chilled cock back into his trousers, zipping his pants before turning again to the cabin. Next spring he would dig a proper outhouse. And find a way to heat it.

Cold air followed him in and he saw her stir in the bed. It was about time. He put the kettle on for tea and waited for her to wake up.

* * * * *

Isabel first noticed the softness of the sheets as her mind began the slow waking from her dreams—dreams that disturbed her, though she could not remember why. For a moment, she drifted, simply enjoying the feel of flannel sheets on her naked body. Flannel sheets? A soft bed? Her bed was firm. And she didn't own flannel sheets. Where was she?

Opening her eyes to a warm and gentle light, she blinked several times, trying to resolve the image before her. Rough beams overhead held up a honey-colored, tongue-and-groove ceiling that rose to a peak over to her left. The light flickered—was that candlelight? A faint odor of burning pine filled her nose. As her senses returned, her mind tried to understand what she was seeing, but she had no memories of this place. With a furrowed brow, she struggled to sit up, but found herself held fast.

"Don't panic. I put those there when you were thrashing in your fever."

A man's face hovered into view and Isabel gasped. She remembered that face. It was the man in the woods—the man she'd seen in the rain when Eddie had left her. She would never forget the glimpse of shaggy beard, nor forget the rock wall of his chest. The beard was trimmed now, showing his high cheekbones, but he was still as broad as a barn door. She attempted to sit up again as her mind recalled Eddie's behavior and the storm and the wolf. But straps held her pinned to the bed.

"Let me go. Why am I tied down? Let me…"

"Yes, woman, I intend to let you go. You just need to stop squirming around. You'll pull your stitches and get that knee bleeding again as well. That was why I had to strap you down to begin with."

The man's gigantic hands pulled back the covers and the cold air hit her body. "Put those back! Where are my clothes? What have you done to me?"

Fear grabbed at her throat. What was happening to her? What did this mountain of a man want from her? Or had he taken it already? Stifling a scream and trying to push down the panic, she thrashed about on the bed, trying to get her hands free to cover herself. For answer, the man just leaned back on his heels and watched her from where he squatted next to the bed.

There was no denying he had thought the thoughts that he knew ran through her mind. As he had tended her over the past two days, he'd had plenty of opportunity to admire the woman before him.

Isabel's full breasts figured prominently in his line of sight at the moment and Daniel enjoyed watching them bounce from side to side as she struggled to escape. The woman's tight round nipples pointed to the wooden beams above. True, tasting such treasures and fondling such exquisite white globes might be a firm fantasy he held, but in reality he had not touched her except to clean her up. Oh, he'd applied cold compresses to her head and wrists to bring down her fever, and he had cleaned her cuts and scrapes, but he'd kept control of himself.

His gaze drifted downward and a smile carved deep dimples into his cheeks. Yes, even though his cock wanted nothing more than to take a plunge into the tight hole guarded by the tuft of dark hair he'd glimpsed when he had first put her to bed, he hadn't taken advantage of the situation. Despite his surroundings and the rough exterior he cultivated, Daniel hid a deeper secret regarding what he wanted from a woman.

This one certainly had a temper. The fever had put her so out of her head that she had talked nonsense and constantly moved about. But when, in the grip of a fever dream, she had tried to get up to walk, Daniel knew he needed to restrain her lest she do that beautiful tanned skin any farther harm. Using a little Yankee ingenuity and four straps of a wide woven belt he usually used for hauling, he had cinched her body to the bed. One belt across the top of her chest and over her arms; one across her waist with her hands tucked in tight; another across her thighs — that had been the hardest to attach, since the sight of her naked mound and the musky scent which wafted from that hidden spot distracted him. But he had finished tying her down with one last woven belt across her calves.

"You can stop your moving about whenever you're ready." His calm voice finally sank in through her panic. He wondered if she'd ever been naked in front of a man before, the way she was carrying on. A blush reddened her cheeks and he realized her embarrassment.

Panting from her exertion, Isabel quieted. Like pools of black water, her wide, dark eyes showed her fear, and yet Daniel detected a hint of defiance behind them. Tempted as he was by her nakedness, he knew it was imperative that she begin to trust him. Now that her breasts had stopped their intriguing bounce and her breath was steadier, he would let her go.

Unfolding from his stooped position, Daniel bent over the belt at her calves, loosening the device he had used to cinch the strap. Immediately, Isabel tried to pull her knees up, but the next binding still held her in place. Tossing a reprimanding glance at her, his fingers undid the second belt.

As each restraint loosened, Isabel gained more possession of her panic. The mountain man made no move to touch her in any way. In fact, it seemed as if he were trying not to come in contact with her skin. But still she held herself rigid. After the look of reproach he'd given her when she'd moved the first time, she had decided it might be best to play by his rules for the moment. She did not exactly have the upper hand.

The last belt came loose and he threw the end across her—she was free to move about. Gathering her strength, Isabel started to flex her knees. A stab of pain in her left one stopped her.

"You scraped that up pretty bad. Go a little easy on it."

Not deigning to answer, Isabel simply stretched her right leg and gingerly moved the left one. But she lay too flat to see the damage. She needed to sit up.

That was another mistake. Pain shot through her right arm as she tried to raise herself onto her elbows and she fell back onto the bed with a small whimper. Immediately Daniel reached for the covers and tucked them tight around her shoulders.

"You have a pretty bad cut on your arm, too."

The warmth of the blankets was welcome and Isabel tried to voice the questions that swirled around in her head. The effort was too much, however, and the bed too comfortable. Fighting the exhaustion that threatened to overtake her, she blinked several times as the image of the mountain man blurred. In a few more heartbeats, Isabel fell asleep once more.

Chapter Two

એ

Isabel's surroundings startled but did not frighten her when she next awoke. Only a few seconds passed before she remembered where she was—and who was there with her—and what he had done to her. She didn't even know the man's name. There was no light flickering on the walls this time, casting the eerie shadows. Now the light was dim, as if the light that filtered through the windows came from a cloudy sky.

Gingerly Isabel rose on her left elbow, glad that it held her up. Remembering the restraints, a momentary panic clutched at her stomach. But her body was unfettered, although still nude. Instead of trying to stand, a feat she doubted she could accomplish, she took a moment to take in her situation.

With slow movements, Isabel tried sitting up, pulling her bottom up so that she could lean against the pillows and pull the blankets up to cover her nudity. Her bandaged right arm hurt if she put pressure on it, so she managed with her left. But her left knee ached when she tried to use it to push herself up. How did she get to be so weak? Had she lost a lot of blood? And how long had she slept? What day was it now? Where was the man who had been here before? Her eyes flickered around the room, trying to find answers.

Judging from the peak of the plank ceiling as it ran along the center of the room and the lack of doors, this one rectangular room appeared to be all there was to the cabin. A cast-iron stove along the short far wall provided the heat. A faint shimmer surrounded the black box giving proof to the fire within.

From this vantage point in the corner of the long, rough wooden wall, Isabel realized she lay in the room's only bed. Tucked away in the corner of the room, this must be the cabin's sleeping area. While the bed was large, a small guilt told her she had slept alone. Her eyes swept around the cabin again, noting the oversized, out-of-date, comfortable chair with a small wooden stool in front of it. Pulled up close to the stove to take advantage of the fire's heat, a carelessly thrown blanket over the back was testament that her mountain man had slept there while she had been ill.

Speaking of him, where was he? Her eyes narrowed as she searched the room. A large trestle table sat almost in the middle of the room with wooden benches on either side neatly tucked up underneath. The door to the cabin was on the wall opposite her, but down near the stove. Her eye tried to measure the distance. Perhaps thirty feet by twenty, give or take a few inches, she decided. The small cabin held few secrets. She was alone.

Idly, her hands drifted over her body as she surveyed the room, lightly brushing her breasts and feeling the raised nipples. Despite the fire, this corner of the room was chilly. While a part of her was shocked and outraged that this huge bear of a man had undressed her and put her to bed, she was surprised to discover that she was also gratified. Lost and alone, battered by the rain and whipped by the branches as she ran, this man had taken her in, tended her wounds and cared for her the best way he knew how. In spite of her concerns, there was something sweet about that.

But it was time she was getting home. And she needed to use the bathroom. Her eyes swept the room again. Just where might the door to the little room be? The only door she saw had to be to the outside. A kitchen curtain from the 1950s covered the window in the upper half. A large antique wardrobe blocked her view along the wall the bed lay against. Craning her body around, she glimpsed another door on the same wall as her bed, opposite the other.

That must be the bathroom, she decided. Swinging her legs over the edge of the bed, Isabel gathered the top blanket to wrap around her nudity. She found she could stand on her wounded leg, as long as she didn't try to bend it. But it still took several tries before she could stand long enough to wrap the cloth around her even once. Only having one arm to use didn't help. Her right arm ached if she tried to lift it too high, so she held it up as far as she could and used her other hand to wrap the blanket. Leaving the end trailing, she held onto the bed to steady herself as she took a few tentative steps toward the door that she figured must hide the bathroom. She made it almost to the overstuffed chair when a blast of cold air hit her naked shoulders as the door she headed for opened. She stumbled to her knees, wincing as her injured left leg banged on the rough wooden floor.

"What do you think you're doing, woman?"

The rough voice sent all her charitable thoughts fleeing and she braced herself on three limbs, gritting her teeth against the pain in her knee and cradling her arm. "I need to use the facilities."

Daniel gave the door a firm push and closed out the winter storm. With an oath, he dumped the armful of wood he carried and picked up a worn metal pail he normally used for ashes. Putting it by the back door, he turned to help her to her feet, but to his surprise, she was already pulling herself up, desperately trying to avoid stepping on the trailing blanket. He surveyed her as she stood and saw the unsteadiness and the independent spirit. Daniel shook his head. This type of woman would not take the news he had for her with calm acceptance. He pointed to the pail.

"There you go. You can use the pail and I'll dump it outside later."

"What are you talking about? Why can't I use the bathroom?" She eyed the solid door opposite the one with the kitchen curtains on it. Daniel had come through it with a load of wood in his arms and snow on his boots. Suspicion dawned in her eyes. "Are you telling me this place doesn't have a bathroom?"

"No indoor plumbing at all." He grinned at her shock and affected a country hick twang. "No electricity neither. I like my life simple."

"Simple? What could be easier than flipping a light switch or flushing a toilet?"

The burly man shook his head. He didn't think she'd understand. Not when she had been dressed in that slinky little dress he'd found her in. "Use the pail. I need to go get water."

"Can't I just use the outhouse?"

He saw her remark was meant to be sarcastic and took it as such. "Ain't got no outhouse, ma'am." He grinned and bowed in his best country manner. "All's I gots is a hole in the ground. A man don't need much more'n that." Two could play the sarcastic game.

Isabel knew she was defeated. Desperately trying to remain still and not do what her mother called the "potty dance" she gave the metal bucket a disgusted look. "All right, fine. I'll use the stupid pail."

Pointedly she waited until he turned and left the cabin through the same solid door. Now there was nothing for it but to drop the blanket she hugged around her. Squatting over the pail, her pee hit the metal in a strong stream of liquid. In the quiet of the cabin, it seemed as if the sound echoed, but there was no way Isabel could silence the stream. Pent up too long, her body craved relief and would not be denied. A roll of unopened paper towels sat on a ledge by the door and Isabel decided that would work as well as anything else. At least it wasn't a corncob.

Her needs taken care of, she felt suddenly weak. As her knees buckled again, she caught herself on her hand for the second time. Leaving the blanket where it was, she eased up and dragged herself across the floor on her hand and one good knee back to the bed, still holding her right arm protectively to her chest. The arm she used to steady herself shook under her and she wondered again how long she had been in that fever.

A blast of cold air hit her body once more as Daniel reentered, two water buckets in his hands. But she didn't look up or acknowledge his presence. Instead, her hand groped for the bedsheets so that she could pull herself up and onto the bed.

"Damn." Quickly setting down the buckets, Daniel hurried over to Isabel's almost inert form. "Here." Bending to scoop her in his arms, he was taken by surprise at her sudden strength as she fought him off.

"No. I can do it. Don't touch me."

He put his hands in the air and stepped back. This was taking independence a bit too far. Still, as a former lawyer, he knew the law intimately. The woman had told him to back off, so he backed away. Daniel watched with concern at first, then amusement as she managed to get herself into a kneeling position beside the bed. From here he got a very nice view of her ass—round and firm, pink in the cold air. One cheek would probably fit perfectly into his palm. For several moments he allowed his thoughts to roam, imagining his hands cupping those warm and inviting cheeks, spreading them wide to finger her tiny hole. He turned his snort into a cough to cover the direction his mind had taken.

Daniel had to give the woman credit. She was no shrinking violet. Just the way he liked them. Proud and independent, not looking to him to answer every single question. If he'd been looking for a relationship, he'd much rather have an independent woman to tame to his wishes than one who was just a doormat. More challenge that way. Except he wasn't looking for a relationship.

By the time the woman made it into the bed, it was obvious she was once again utterly exhausted. He heard her stomach growl and watched as she clutched feebly at the covers without the strength to pull them up over her. When Daniel leaned over her, again tucking the covers around her shoulders, she did not protest.

"You need some soup. Sleep now, it'll be ready when you wake up."

Daniel watched her for several moments as her eyelids fluttered and then remained closed, afraid he had let her get away with doing too much too soon. But her breathing was steady and strong. She would be fine.

Satisfied as to his patient's health, Daniel pushed aside a small scatter rug with his foot and reached down to tug on the trapdoor to the cellar. This was part of the original design of the cabin. Underneath, a foundation had been dug out and lined with fieldstone. Among the stories his grandfather had told him was one about this place being the main room of a much larger place his father intended to build. The back door was supposed to lead to another room. But then something had apparently happened and no additions were ever built.

The deep basement left from the original design was a great place to keep canned goods and other supplies. A steep, rough-hewn wooden staircase descended into the darkness below. Picking up a kerosene lantern from the table, Daniel lit it and went down to find what he needed.

He examined the shelves that lined one wall of the cellar and chose the ingredients for the soup. Several cans of store-bought soup marched on one shelf, of course. But homemade was always better and it would help her get her strength back more quickly. And the quicker he was rid of her, the better. His cock rose as the memory of her naked form sent warmth cascading through his limbs. Slender as a reed, the saying went, and now that he had seen her swaying from chair to bed, unsteady and beautiful, he understood the simile.

She was ill and he had no right to be getting excited by her nudity. And yet he was. Most definitely. Easing his cock out of his pants, he absently rubbed his palm along the thick shaft, allowing the memory of her to fuel his need to come, for the flame was lit inside and would not be dampened until it consumed him. He thought of her perfect breasts, large enough to fill his huge hands and still spill out between his fingers as he squeezed them 'til she moaned. Closing his eyes to the realities of the basement, his took a firmer grip on his cock and imagined her as he watched her through the long hours of her fever, strapped down to the bed so she would not harm herself, her damp hair clinging to her tanned skin, the Mediterranean coloring pale in the lamplight.

He had looked, but not touched. Not then and not now. But he sure could dream. Unconsciously, he ran his finger over the smooth tip of his cock, teasing along the rim as he fantasized about her strapped to the bed, unable to prevent him from giving her a trail of kisses from the little hollow in her throat, down between her beautiful breasts, stopping only to taunt a perfect, round button in the center of her belly, kissing and dipping his tongue into her navel to tickle until she begged him to move lower. He would listen to her pleas for release from the urgent need he built inside her helpless, bound form, power flowing strong in him — not giving her release until he was ready.

His cock, throbbing with the rhythm of his heartbeat, grew warm beneath his fingers as he pumped more rapidly, his breath ragged and uneven in the dim light. But his mind was elsewhere, imagining the kisses he would plant on the soft skin where her thigh met her hip, a spot virginal in its appearance, holy and sensitive. His tongue flicked against the soft skin, tasting her sweetness before mounting her, plunging his hard cock deep into her ready pussy.

In the darkness of the cellar, Daniel pumped his cock now with frenetic desperation. He let his head fall back and his fingers tighten around the tip of his cock. As they became a tight "O" he imagined himself taking possession of the woman who slept upstairs. Faster and faster he slid the skin at the rim of his cock back and forth until, with loud groans, he came hard, his cum squirting out to fall onto the dirt floor. He let himself empty, his mind still focused on the woman's dark patch of hair, wondering what wonderful secrets it hid.

Taking a deep breath, Daniel hovered a moment before releasing the pent-up air and letting himself ease back to reality. The basement was chilly now that he no longer had thoughts of a beautiful naked woman to keep him warm. Grabbing a rag, he wiped his hand, then kicked dirt over the seed wasted on the floor.

"Next time she needs to be tied up, we'll find out what's under that patch of hair, shall we?" Daniel grinned at his cock as he cleaned and then tucked himself neatly away.

Looking around the basement, he remembered what he had really come down here for before getting distracted. After choosing a sprig or two from the herb bunches hanging from the rafters and rummaging through the potato bin to find the ones he wanted, he climbed the stairs to the relative warmth of the cabin.

* * * * *

Isabel's stomach woke her. Its rumbling and gurgling forced her into consciousness as the aroma of spices filling the small cabin made her stomach ache with hunger.

Her small movements under the covers alerted Daniel immediately and he came right over with a bowl of vegetable and potato soup. The lack of food these several days had taken a toll on her slender body and Isabel had little strength left even to sit up. Setting the bowl on the desk, he leaned forward to put his arm around her to help her sit.

"Here, you used up all your strength earlier. Hope now you'll accept a bit of help for a while?"

His warm hand slid around her back and stopped under her arm. A tingle ran through her at his touch, a touch not sexual in any way, and yet somehow innately sensuous. With ease, he pulled her body up and Isabel held onto the covers as he did so. Somehow it seemed silly to be so modest in such a situation. After all, hadn't the man tended her while she recovered from her night out in the storm?

And yet, her modesty was all she could control at the moment. Betrayed by the weakness of her body, she could not run, indeed, she could barely summon the energy to argue with him. The least she could do was cover herself. So she did.

Pulling the desk chair to the side of the bed, Daniel sat, holding the soup bowl and filling the spoon with something that smelled delicious.

"You're going to feed me?" Too weak to be shocked, indignant, or even grateful, Isabel settled for wonderment.

"I am." A simple statement of fact. He brought the spoon toward her and after a moment's hesitation, Isabel opened her mouth. As she accepted the first mouthful, she closed her eyes, the better to savor the glorious liquid. A smile crossed her lips as she felt the swallow of soup trace all throughout her chest to fill her belly with warmth. Her sigh was deep and contented.

Damn, but the woman was beautiful. A radiant expression of pleasure filled her face and Daniel readied another spoonful. Once again, the woman obediently leaned forward and opened her mouth, apparently accepting that he fed her as one might feed a child.

Another spoonful carefully carried to her incredible mouth. Heart-shaped lips, he decided as he watched them close around the bowl of the spoon. Perfect for Valentine's Day greeting cards, or lipstick commercials. Or for kissing.

He shook his head. Might as well get rid of those thoughts right now. He'd take her down the mountain, drop her off at the bus station in town and be done with her. The snow was starting to accumulate, but now that she was strong enough, he could just put her on the sled he used for hauling and take her down before dark. That way, he could pick up a few more perishables and be back before the cabin snowed in for the winter. The woman's voice interrupted his reverie.

"My name is Isabel."

"Nice to meet you, Isabel. Open up." Daniel watched her kissable lips open for another swallow and imagined his spoon as an arrow piercing that graceful "O". Then he remembered how she had pushed him away when he had tried to help her into bed and decided to be thankful she had decided to be compliant for once. "I'm Daniel."

"Hello." A blush crept up her cheeks in spite of herself. Why on earth did she suddenly feel self-conscious telling this stranger her name? Okay, so he had washed her naked body, given her a pot to piss in, and now spoon-fed her like a child. But there was something more that made her heart give a little jump. This mountain man held an air of quiet authority…as if he were used to giving instructions that were obeyed without question.

She swallowed more soup, deciding there was a certain comfort in leaning back against soft pillows while a good-looking mountain man fed her. Now that she had the chance to look, she realized he was more than just a large male with an anonymous face. Dutifully swallowing each spoonful he gave her, she studied the incredibly handsome man who sat beside her.

What struck her most was his face. Not the rugged look one might expect from a man who lived alone in the mountains. Daniel's face reflected more of the jungle of the boardroom than the wild of the forest. While Isabel did not normally go for men with beards, she had to admit, the closely trimmed reddish-brown beard Daniel sported was quite attractive. As she sat poised, her mouth open for another spoonful, she wondered what it might be like to be kissed by a man with a beard. Would those hairs tickle her lips? She watched his mouth open slightly each time he raised the spoon in an unconscious mirror to her own, and she smiled.

She was rewarded by his self-deprecating grin. Small wrinkles creased at the side of sea-blue eyes and Isabel wondered how old he was. She had seen similar crow's feet in her own mirror. Guessing, she decided he certainly hadn't hit forty.

"How long was I out for?" Her strength coming back as the soup warmed her, her practical nature began to reassert itself.

"This is the fourth day since I found you in the rainstorm."

"*Four days*?" She shook her head against another bite as she struggled with this new information. The date with Eddie had been on Friday night. No one would have missed her on Saturday, or Sunday for that matter. But if today was Tuesday and she hadn't reported or called in to work for the past two days…

"I need to go home. Now." She fumbled at the bedclothes, remembering her nakedness at the last minute. "I would like my dress, please."

"Hang on a minute. I fully intend to take you down the mountain today, but you can't wear that dress. Even if it weren't anything but a rag now, it's still not warm enough for today."

Isabel continued to fumble at the sheets, clearly not listening to him.

Setting the soup aside, he strode to the old-fashioned wardrobe at the foot of the bed and pulled open the double doors. After rummaging a moment, he pulled out a gray hooded sweatshirt and came back. "Here. You can wear one of my shirts, to start with. You'll swim in any of my clothes, but at least you'll be warm."

Accepting his help, Isabel held up her hands as he slipped the shirt over her head and onto her outstretched arms, being careful not to pull her stitches. When her hands did not appear at the far ends of the sleeves, she giggled, then laughed outright to see just how much more material there was.

Grinning broadly, Daniel held out his hand. "Can you stand? Let's see if it covers your tush."

"My tush? Do you think you should be looking at my tush?" Isabel teased, feeling much better for having food in her stomach and knowing he had seen much more of her than that.

He had the grace to blush at least and look away as she came out from under the covers. The sweatshirt dropped down to cover not only her rear end, but her thighs almost to her knees.

"Um...I think you're safe now, Daniel. You can look."

Seeing that she was steady enough on her feet, he let go of her hand and stepped back to give her a critical look. "Definitely the latest in winter fashions. Everyone will be wearing them in the city this year."

His words about the city sobered her. "My boss must be ready to fire me...not calling in for two days. Why didn't you take me home the night you found me?"

"It was raining...and you were already out of your head."

"So? All the more reason to get me to a hospital or something."

"In what? I don't have a car here, and strong as I might appear, I don't think carrying you down the mountain in a freezing rain would have done you any good."

"You don't have a car?" Isabel shook her head in disbelief. "You live all the way up here and have no way to get down the mountain in an emergency?"

"Well, I thought about buying a horse at some point, but I'd have to build a stable first. And that just didn't get done this summer."

"Like the outhouse."

Daniel grinned. "Like the outhouse."

"So how do you propose we get down today?" She held up a hand to forestall any objections he might have. "I'm strong enough now that I have food in my stomach. I've made my boss mad enough at me. And the sooner I'm back in the city, the sooner I'll be out of your hair."

Daniel gave her an appraising glance that did more than just assess her fitness for travel. Isabel blushed at the look in his eye. There was more than one wolf on this mountain.

"I do want to get you down the mountain today. Soon. The weather's picking up and if you don't go down today, I think you might be here a lot longer than you want to be."

"I don't suppose you might have a pair of pants I could wear?" She grinned with a self-confidence she didn't really feel and looked down at her bare legs. Four days ago, walking down this mountain in good weather hadn't daunted her. Walking down today with only a bowl of soup in her stomach, through several inches of snow and wearing only a sweatshirt…did.

"I have a pair of sweatpants you could wear, but they'd be way too big on you. I don't know how you'd hold them up."

She said nothing, leaning against the bed in sudden weariness. "I never thought going four days without food would wear me out so quickly. Did I lose a lot of blood?" With her chin, she gestured to her bandaged arm as Daniel went back to the oak wardrobe at the foot of the bed.

"I don't think so. The rain washed away most of the blood, so all I had to do was stitch it up. Ah ha!" Daniel pulled out a pair of gray sweatpants that matched the sweatshirt she wore.

"You stitched it?" She stared at the bandage. No wonder it hurt like hell when she tried to move it. "How many?"

"Five."

Her eyes narrowed. "What did you use? Are you a doctor?"

Daniel sighed. "No, I'm not a doctor, but I learned how to put in stitches years ago. I managed to have enough of them put in me over the years. And I used sewing thread. It was all I had. So yes, you'll probably have a scar."

He threw the words out with a challenge and Isabel realized she was being rude. She had been wounded and unconscious and the man had done what he could for her. She had no right to be angry.

"Thank you."

"You're welcome. Now, let me help you put these on." Kneeling in front of her, he waited with patience as she lifted first one foot and then the other.

Isabel's sense of humor returned when she realized how big the pants were. "Daniel, I think both my legs might just fit in one leg!"

She was right. A light going off in his head, he instructed her to take her legs out. With a deft fold, he put one leg inside out and pushed it into the other one. Then he had her slide both feet into the one casing. Sure enough, the pants formed a perfect bunting for her legs...as long as Isabel didn't try to walk.

"Now I know how mummies feel...or mermaids!" She laughed as she flapped her legs.

"Just sit there while I go get the sled. Be right back."

In moments Daniel was bundled against the cold and had slipped out the back door.

Isabel wasn't sure how she was going to sit on a snowmobile with her legs wrapped together, but then decided sidesaddle might not be too hard, especially if Daniel were driving. And a sled sure beat walking. Although, if he had a sled, why hadn't he taken her down earlier?

Probably because you were so weak, she thought to herself, wishing she had a comb to run through her hair. She felt grimy and dirty after four days without a shower...and was sure she smelled bad as well. It was nice of Daniel not to mention it.

"All right," Daniel announced as he reentered. "All set. Let's wrap a few blankets around you, though, since you have no coat and the wind is picking up. I'm afraid we're in for a blizzard soon and I'd like to get you to town and get back up here before that happens."

Isabel nodded as he wrapped a blanket around her shoulders. Then, handing her a second one, he bent over and scooped her up as if she weighed nothing at all. Ignoring her startled cry, he carried her outside.

It was the first fresh air she'd breathed since the night she had come here and Isabel found it refreshing. Closing her eyes and taking several deep breaths, it wasn't until he set her down on the long sled that she realized the sled was just that—a sled. Not a snowmobile, but a sled.

The old-fashioned transportation was designed for hauling, not for sport, she realized as she snuggled into the upright back and sides of the contraption. She'd seen pictures of just such sleds in books about the Victorian age, though they were much smaller versions and were usually being pulled by children. This one was long enough for her to stretch out her legs while reclining against the back.

Taking the second blanket, Daniel tucked it in around her legs, pulling the pants legs down to cover her feet as well. Satisfied that she was warm and mostly comfortable, he pulled a knit hat out of his pocket and jammed it on his head.

"'If your head and feet are warm, the rest of the body will follow,' my grandfather used to say." He grinned at her and bent down to tie the strings of her hood so that only her face showed. With a final tuck of the blankets around her chin, he slid on a pair of ski gloves, picked up the rope and tugged. The metal runners of the sled bit into the snow as Daniel leaned forward against the rope and they were off.

But as they came around the front of the cabin, they came into the wind. Sheltered in the lee before, she had not realized the extent of the snowfall. Here the drifts were already beginning to pile against the door of the cabin. Daniel ignored them and started for the woods.

Isabel had no idea if there was a trail there or not…she could see nothing that indicated a drive of any sort. Bare trees bending in the strengthening wind surrounded the back and sides of the cabin. No wonder he didn't bother with a car. There was nowhere to park it.

The way passed through a double row of pines and Isabel wondered if this perhaps had once been the drive to the cabin. For a moment, the wind died and white, cottony flakes floated down, piling up against the drifts between the trees. Only the crunch of Daniel's boots and the soft gliding of the sled broke the peaceful silence of the scene. She settled back into the sled and pulled the covers closer as she pondered the man who pulled her.

Shoulders broad as a door, her grandmother would say. Strong, too. He pulled her along as if the sled were empty. Yet there was simple grace in his movements. A part of her had noted the ease with which he'd carried in the wood and water earlier. And now, as he leaned into the ropes and towed the sled without difficulty, his grace and strength made her head swim and her thoughts turn decidedly naughty.

But before she could get farther than imagining those muscles flexing under his thick winter coat, the two of them had cleared the line of trees and met the wind full blast. No drifting snowflakes here, these traveled parallel to the ground. The gusting wind stung Isabel's face and turned her exposed cheeks pink. Even pulling the blanket up over her nose didn't stop the deep cold of the wind from biting deep. Unable to see much, it felt as if he pulled her up the mountain, then leveled off. It made no sense to Isabel, so she simply accepted it and faced her head out of the wind to watch the scenery slowly pass. In moments, however, she could see little but the snow that swirled around them, closing off the world in ever-narrowing swirls of white.

The motion of the sled stopped. Daniel shouted something to her, but it was lost in the wind. She shook her head and he stopped, putting his mouth near her ear.

"The storm is picking up. I can't see the way."

Indeed, Isabel was surprised he could see anything at all. Tiny flakes whirled around them in a sudden swish and for a moment, she could see nothing. Her vision was filled with white. But then it passed and he stood before her again, covered in snow. Again he bent down to her.

"This is too dangerous. We aren't that far from the cabin and already I don't know where the road is. I need to retrace our steps before the wind obliterates them."

He didn't give her time to protest. Struggling, he turned the sled and headed toward the row of pines once more. This time, however, the space between them was not the soft, quiet place Isabel had enjoyed only moments before. The wind now hollered down the narrow aisle, threatening to steal their breaths. Bitter cold seeped in through the blankets, now completely covered in snow.

The howl of a wolf filled her with dread. She remembered that howl. It had to be the same wolf. She tried not to let her panic rise again, shifting down into the sled as her heart raced.

Daniel whistled into the wind, knowing it didn't travel far enough for Sasha to hear. But his pet's cry was enough to center him and he turned toward it. A moment later, the gray wolf stood before him.

"Sasha, my dear, you are a sight for sore eyes. Take us home."

The wolf nuzzled Daniel's hand a moment, then turned and trotted off. Keeping the wolf in view, Daniel tugged at the sled and trudged through the deepening drifts.

Isabel blinked several times. Had she truly seen what she thought she'd seen? Did this mountain man really just talk to a wolf? The very same wolf that had tried to eat her? She closed her eyes against the wind and buried herself in the snow-covered blankets.

Only the sudden stop of the sled let her know they had arrived back at the cabin. She was cold, tired, and weak. Daniel's arms lifted her and she wrapped her arms around his neck as he carried her into the cabin once more and set her in the big armchair near the stove to warm up.

The winter storm raged about the cabin in earnest now. Wind rattled the windows, and Isabel didn't know if the howling she heard outside was the wind or the wolf.

The gentle snow had turned nasty and Daniel knew the truth of their predicament. It was too late to get the woman home. Telling her she needed to piss in the pail had been bad enough. But still, she had taken the news like a trooper and simply dealt with it.

But how would she take the news that she was snowed in? And did he have enough supplies to get two of them through the winter?

He was saved the unpleasant task of breaking the news to her. By the time he divested himself of his winter gear and returned to her side, Isabel had curled her mermaid legs into the large chair and was fast asleep.

Chapter Three

❧

She had that dream again...

She stood upon the cliffside, shrouded in seafoam green, her eyes searching the sea beyond, desperate to find...what? What was she looking for? The breeze blew her hair from her face and again she heard the voice — deep, rich tones calling to her.

"I'm here, Isabella. Come to me. Come to me now."

She stepped off the cliff.

And jumped awake. The voice echoed in her ears and she sat up in the bed, staring around the cabin to find her mountain man, sure he must've spoken to her.

He sat with his back toward her, hunched over the table, writing something. A kerosene lantern lit the area where he worked, otherwise the room was dark. He did not appear to notice she was awake until she spoke. Only then did he set down his pen and turn to her.

"So how long did I sleep this time?"

He smiled and Isabel grinned back. She liked the way his dimples showed above his beard when he smiled at her. A vague wisp of her dream mingled with the fleeting thought of Daniel's bearded mouth surrounding hers in a kiss. The sudden warmth that sprang between her legs surprised her and she cleared her throat and shifted her position to hide her unexpected reaction.

Daniel checked his watch in the lamplight, apparently not noticing her blush. "You weren't out so long this time. Only eight hours. It's almost midnight."

She sighed and ran a hand through her hair. It was filthy. Her stomach growled. What she needed was food and a bath. She still wore the sweatshirt, but she noted the pants were gone. Damn the man, his consideration for her was certainly playing fast and loose with her nudity.

"Thank you for putting me to bed. At some point here, I need to get my sleep cycle back to normal."

He put down his pen and picked up the kerosene lantern, coming over to the bed to see her better. His hand brushed against her forehead for any signs of a returning fever, but the coolness of her smooth skin reassured him. A part of him felt some pity toward her, even if she was a fool for walking alone in the woods that night. What a stupid thing to do. Although he liked the iron bar of independence he'd glimpsed earlier. It showed there was a practical side to her. Still, he fussed with the covers for a moment, putting off the inevitable. He didn't really want to tell her what she deserved to know.

Her stomach growled again as he set the lantern on the desk. After she ate. She'd take the news much better after she ate.

"The soup from earlier is still on the stove. I added some meat to it. Think you could handle it?"

Isabel nodded. "I'd like to eat at the table, though."

She certainly had spunk. "Sounds good to me. Need some help?" He stood and offered her a hand, but Isabel shook her head.

"I'd rather have those pants...big as they are."

He grinned as she swung her shapely legs over the side of the bed, watching her discreetly pull at the hem of the sweatshirt to cover herself, sitting demurely with her feet resting comfortably on the floor. Daniel wondered what it would be like to slide his hand up under that shirt and discover the warmth hidden there. He remembered the tits now lost in the bulky shirt, how they bounced as she thrashed in her fever and wondered again how they would feel in his hand. The lantern-light gleamed on her face, her eyes narrowing with anger as she understood where his thoughts were headed. He turned away self-consciously to fumble with the lid of a pot on the stove.

"The sweats are on the bottom of the bed."

Daniel's voice was gruffer than he intended it to be. Damn it! This was not the time to let his hormones get the best of him. It was going to be a hard enough conversation he had to have with her, he didn't need to bring in the fact that he'd buried himself up here for more reasons than he'd told his father.

Isabel had seen that gleam in men's eyes before. Eyes that looked only at her shape and not at her other attributes and she'd had enough of it. As Daniel's eyes had met hers and registered her anger, however, she'd seen something rare—he'd pulled back as if ashamed of himself.

Isabel frowned, trying to figure him out. Why *did* he live up here all by himself? Was he hiding from something? Or someone? Suddenly she realized just how much she didn't know about this man. A man who had seen her naked and who had just looked at her with undisguised lust in his eyes. He might be ashamed of it, but the lust was there. So far he hadn't touched her. At least, she didn't think he had. Doubts ran through her and she reached for the sweats, pulling them on in symbolic protection. She had to hold them up with one hand when she stood and they flopped over her toes, but at least she was covered.

Although she was steadier on her feet this time, she still teetered and grabbed for the desk chair for support as she crossed to the table. The bench on her side was still pushed underneath the trestle table and she didn't know if she had the strength to pull it out, so she took the extra steps around the far end to sit on the side near the fire. It put her closer to him and brought home to her just how weak she was. If Daniel wanted to do something to her, there was precious little she could do to stop him.

Daniel saw her cower when he put the bowl on the table in front of her. Damn and damn again. The last thing he wanted was for her to be afraid of him. Although the fire was wonderfully warm on his back, he moved to the opposite side of the table, pulling out the bench and dropping down on it as Isabel picked up her spoon and eyed him warily.

"Here, you need some light." Reaching behind him, Daniel scooped up the kerosene lantern and set it on the table between them. Isabel smiled weakly and moved it to one side, the better to see into his eyes without being blinded by the light of the wick.

A blast of wind shook the cabin, reminding Isabel of the storm that had prevented her leaving earlier. It seemed a safe topic and she latched onto it. "So how long do you think the storm will last?"

"I don't know a lot about mountain lore yet, but this looks to be a nasty one."

"What do you mean, you don't know mountain lore? What does that have to do with anything?"

"My grandfather used to say you could predict the weather by watching the animals. I'm sure someone who's lived up here all his life could do that, but I haven't been here long enough."

"How long have you been here?"

"About six months. Long enough to put a new roof on and rehang the doors, replace broken windows and clean and repair the chimney."

"But not long enough to build an outhouse." Isabel grinned.

"I'm afraid that's been rather low on my priority list. All a man needs is a tree, most times. And a small pit at others."

She held up her hand and pointed to her soup. "I'm eating, thank you."

He grinned, and Isabel noted the perfect teeth in his smile. The soft light glimmered on his beard, bringing out all the red highlights. Full, sensuous lips peeked at her and she dropped her eyes. Under other circumstances, she would love to follow the thoughts that flickered through her imagination. But the reality was, she was far from any help and she had no idea how far to trust this giant of a man. Even if she had her usual fit strength, she doubted she could stop him from doing whatever he wanted.

"So you think the storm will let up soon? Will we be able to get down tomorrow?"

The moment was here. Pursing his lips, he let out a long sigh. "No. We won't be able to get down tomorrow."

She frowned. There was something in his tone that sent a prickle of apprehension along her neck. "Day after tomorrow?"

He bowed his head, then forced himself to meet her eyes. "No. Not the day after tomorrow either."

Anger and fear warred inside her. "Then when?"

He licked his lips. Here it came. "Next spring."

"*What*?" She slammed the spoon onto the table and a spike of pain ran up her arm. Wincing, she ignored it.

Daniel held his hands up, attempting to keep the storm clouds gathering in front of him from erupting. "The storm has snowed us in. On top of what we already had from the weekend, it's dropped three more feet and you can hear the wind still going. I don't know how long the storm will last and it doesn't matter. We can't get down off the mountain until spring."

Isabel's mouth hung open and her eyes flashed with a mixture of anger and fear as emotions warred inside her mind. "You can't keep me here against my will, that's kidnapping. What do you think my boss will think if I don't show up for work until April? Or Beth? She's my best friend and must be worried sick about me. And Eddie. He'll tell them he left me on the mountain. Modern machinery can cut through this snow in no time. In a day or two they'll have the road plowed and then we can just hike over to it."

Her words tumbled out like a river swollen with rain cascades over the rocks to find the quiet eddies at the bottom. But there was no quiet in her soul when her breath ran out.

Daniel held his hands up in surrender. "Whoa. Isabel, first off, I'm not keeping you here, the storm is."

"Semantics." She pushed her half-finished bowl of soup from her as if it contained poison.

Daniel leaned across the table and tried to get through to her. "I can't help you with your boss or your friend. Or whoever Eddie is. But this is an old abandoned road. Nobody plows it anymore. That's why I risked taking you out when I knew you really weren't strong enough." He pushed the soup back toward her. "I haven't drugged it, don't worry. I'm not so desperate for a woman that I'd take the first bedraggled cat that got herself lost in my woods. I wanted to get *you* down and myself back before the storm struck. Obviously my timing was off and now we have to share the cabin."

He hadn't meant to be so cruel. But her words had stung, even though he'd thought himself prepared for them. His dreams of a silent winter with no one and nothing but himself and his thoughts for company drifted into despair.

Isabel's mouth opened and closed several times as she apparently struggled to find arguments to refute him. In the lamplight, he saw her eyes gleaming with unshed tears as she struggled to accept her situation.

"I have no clothes. Nothing. Not even a toothbrush." Her lower lip trembled and she bit her lips together. "I can't stay here, Daniel. I have a job and responsibilities. Eddie will tell them where he left me. Then they'll plow out the old road and come looking for me."

He saw her struggle and admired her courage, even if he didn't really want her as a houseguest. Putting himself in her shoes, he knew he'd be ticked off, too. Letting a deep breath out slowly through pursed lips, he leaned back, folding his arms across his wide chest as he studied the woman he couldn't get rid of.

Her long black hair hung in lank clumps on either side of her face, accentuating the hollows under her dark eyes. Her lips, where she had chewed them in her shock, were reddened and swollen. He watched her dash a hand across her eyes and wipe away any trace of tears. Apparently she was not one to cry easily. That was good. At least he wouldn't have a bawling baby on his hands. No, the iron bar he'd glimpsed in her before stood her in good stead now as she took stock of her position. And once she had a bath, he suspected she might wash up pretty nicely.

"Who's Eddie? That's twice you've mentioned him."

"The date who left me at the top of the road by the old mine."

"Left you?" He tried to fathom why anyone would leave a woman all alone on an abandoned road.

"Let's just say he wanted more than I was willing to dish out." Dipping her spoon into the soup, she idly chased a few pieces of meat around the bowl. Eddie's groping fingers were what had gotten her into this mess.

Anger flashed in Daniel's eyes. "Is that where you got your bruises...and your cut?"

For a moment, Isabel was confused. Then understanding dawned and she shook her head. "No, he didn't go that far. Just groping in the car." She shuddered, remembering the sly fingers reaching for her dress.

"So you ditched him rather than him ditching you?"

Isabel couldn't stop the wry grin. "You're getting to know me quite well."

"Was it raining when he left you?"

Daniel's voice still sounded ominous and Isabel looked up. But he had leaned too far away from the lamplight and she couldn't read his eyes. "No, it was a beautiful Indian summer night. It didn't start to rain until about ten minutes after he left."

"And the slime didn't come back and offer to take you home."

She shook her head and grinned. "And on top of that, he took my purse. Oh, I don't think he knew he had it," she held up a hand to stop his exclamation of shock. "But I'm sure he's found it by now and has probably tried to return it to me. Through his friend, who is my best friend's brother-in-law. I don't think he's man enough to bring it to me face-to-face."

"So by now, people know you're missing and they know you were with Eddie. You think he'll tell them where you dumped him and they'll come looking for you?"

Isabel remembered Eddie's parting word—"Bitch"—and wished she could be as positive as she sounded. Nodding fiercely, she spooned soup into her mouth to prevent her voice from giving her away.

"Well, let's hope you're right. In the meantime, we'll have some living arrangements to hammer out come morning. Right now, I'm beat. I didn't take an eight-hour nap." He pushed himself from the table and saw to the fire in the stove, banking it for the night. Isabel finished the soup without another word, debating about offering the bed to him. Daniel took away her choice when he pulled the blanket off the back of the chair, covering himself as his large frame stretched out to encompass both the chair and the stool.

"Goodnight, Isabel."

"Goodnight, Daniel."

Isabel downed the last drop of soup and made her way around the end of the table. Too proud to use the pail again, she decided that, too, could wait until morning. Used to sleeping in the nude, she glanced over at Daniel's form in the chair and blew out the lantern before taking the last few steps to the bed and removing her borrowed sweats. If all the clothes Daniel had were in that one wardrobe, he wouldn't be able to lend her very much in the way of clothing anyway. And the flannel sheets were soft enough against her skin. Better to save the sweatshirt for daytime wearing.

Crawling into the large bed and feeling healthier than she had in days, Isabel lay awake for a while listening to the sound of the wind rattling the windows. In spite of the long sleep she'd already had, she drifted off to dreams of Eddie groping her, the word "bitch" sounding in her head over and over.

The sea crashed against the rocks at the bottom of the cliff, sending sprays of water to drench her seafoam green dress. The wind whipped the thin layers of chiffon, plastering them to her body as her eyes searched the storm. Part of her mind registered the rocks below — they hadn't been there before. Jagged rock edges sliced through the waves to cut the surf into shards of glass that shot upward to fall onto her, drenching her with water.

But it wasn't water. She looked down at her dress again. Blood from thousands of gashes poured from her arms. Pain shot through her and she screamed.

Her first scream woke him. He was out of his chair and almost to the bed when the second one ripped through the night. With no light, he had to feel his way to the bed and that slowed him down. Groping for the flashlight he kept for emergencies, he turned it on and saw her fighting with the blanket. Quickly putting the light on the desk so its beam filled the area, he tried to gentle her with his hands and words.

"Isabel, Isabel." Daniel held the woman's bare shoulders as she thrashed on the bed. Whatever dream she was having, she would pull those stitches if she didn't stop. "Isabel, wake up. It's a dream."

As suddenly as her thrashing had started, it stopped. Isabel's eyes flew open, wild and unfocused, blinking into the night as the dream faded. Her eyes sought his and her mind grabbed for his presence as a place of safety.

"Daniel? Oh my God." She shuddered as the last remnants of her dream faded back into the dream world where they belonged.

"Here, sit up and let me get you a drink of water." Putting his arms around her, he helped her to sit before taking the flashlight and moving to the other end of the room, hunting around for something.

Isabel pulled the sheet and blanket up to cover herself, taking several breaths to calm her heart as she remembered the long green dress and the cliff. She had been there before in her dreams. Only this time there was no voice, just the storm and the blood. Isabel wasn't the fanciful type who believed in dreams as a means of communication, but it was clear she was bothered by the storm and her inability to go home. Outside, the wind still howled against the cabin, making branches scrape along the new roof.

But why the glass and the blood? And the pain? She shivered and moved to pull the covers up over her. Except her arm hurt. A stabbing pain slashed through her arm as she pulled on the blanket and she cried out in surprise.

"It's all right, Isabel. You're safe now."

She shook her head. "My arm." Swallowing hard, she tried to command the sharp pain that shot through her arm again.

Daniel shone the light over to her arm where it lay limply on the blanket. Blood dripped down her arm and the bandage was stained with red.

"Okay, that's not good." Daniel handed her the flashlight. "Shine this over here and let me get some real light in here."

Numbly Isabel watched him light the kerosene lantern on the table and build up the fire in the stove again. She tried to keep the light steady for him as he pumped water into the teapot and set it on the flat iron stovetop, but her hand kept shaking. Finally deciding he had enough light to work by, she dropped the light in favor of concentrating on her breathing and fighting the panic.

It seemed an hour, but only a few moments were needed for Daniel to get ready. He pushed one of the buckets of water to the table with his foot while reaching for fresh bandaging from the cupboard. Had Isabel been in any shape to notice, she would have seen a ballet of economical movement as he prepared to tend to her arm again.

"If you can, I'd like you to come sit by the stove. You'll be warmer and the light is better."

Isabel nodded and accepted Daniel's hand to steady herself as she stood. A glance down confirmed the worst—her knee was bleeding as well, although not as much.

She sat on the bench Daniel pulled from the table, her nudity the least of her concerns, although she shivered in the room's chill. Cursing himself, Daniel grabbed the bloody blanket and tucked it around her waist.

"Put your arm up on the table. I need to light some candles and get us some more light."

Isabel nodded and used her left hand to guide her right elbow slowly upward to rest on the table. Her blood had soaked the bandage right through and then run down along her arm. As Daniel lit several candles, she saw in the increased light that the blood did not flow freely, but rather seeped. She decided to take that as a good sign.

Now Daniel set out his tools on a clean towel—a pair of surgical scissors, tweezers, sewing thread, several needles. Using the scissors, he cut away the bandage rather than take the time to unwrap it. Isabel forced herself to remain still and not flinch when he pulled the cloth from the wound.

"Just as I thought. You pulled out four of my five stitches." Gently he dabbed at the wound with a damp cloth. The water was still cold and she flinched in spite of her resolve, then giggled in a nervous response.

"Sorry," she apologized and tried to look serious. "I didn't mean to do it."

"I know you didn't. What were you dreaming that made you move around so much?"

She stifled an intake of breath as his cloth hit a more sensitive part of the wound. "It's mostly gone, but I remember something about being caught in flying glass."

"And of course, you had to dodge it."

"Of course." He got up to check the water. Almost boiling. He picked up several items from the table and dropped them into the pot before turning over a small egg timer.

She was holding up remarkably well. Now that the initial shock was over, Daniel watched her pull herself together, taking deep breaths to calm herself. Each time she did, her breasts rose, their hard little nipples enticing him to watch.

With an effort, he pulled his attention back to her arm. "It looks worse than it is. Still, I need to put those stitches back in."

"Wasn't it close to when they should come out anyway? I mean, you said you put them in four days ago. That would be five now."

Daniel pointed to her arm. "Look here, where the middle two pulled out. I think we could get away with not putting any at the edges. The cut wasn't as deep there and has held together fairly well. You're going to end up with more of a scar, though, because you pulled those out too early."

He moved a candle a bit closer. "Look here, though. Can you see?"

She could. The middle of the inch-long cut still oozed blood even though he had just cleaned it. The edges puckered where black strings hung limply, no longer tied, but broken and useless.

Gritting her teeth, she swallowed hard. "Do what you have to do."

"It'll be another few minutes. The stuff is in the water to sterilize it."

"Stuff?" She raised an eyebrow at him.

"Yes, my dear Isabel. I sterilize my instruments of torture before I use them on my victims." He affected a Bela Lugosi laugh and wiggled his eyebrows at her.

She laughed at his antics, then watched him take a pair of tongs and fish out several implements, setting them on a towel.

"I need them to cool before I pick them up. Or you'll be treating me for burns before I can treat you for cuts."

"So where did you pick up your doctoring skills?"

Daniel shrugged as he pulled the desk chair over so he could get a better look at her arm. "Around. I really did have loads of stitches when I was a kid. Always falling out of trees or slipping on the ice. You know, typical boy stuff."

"But just getting stitches doesn't mean you know how to tie them."

"Actually, it does. Last time I got them, I was twenty-five." He pointed to a spot on his chin hidden by the red-gold beard. "Five of them right here. Doc was great and it barely left a scar. Not that you could see it anyway." His grin suddenly made him look like a little boy and Isabel laughed.

"I asked the doc how to tie a stitch. Told him maybe I could save myself some trips in to see him. He laughed and showed me how. Told me it might come in handy if I ever took up fly-fishing. But I had to promise to come to him and not operate on myself."

"Well, it's a handy skill to have."

Keeping his eye on her as if he didn't quite trust her not to hit him, he picked up the tweezers. "Ready?"

She nodded and closed her eyes briefly to steel herself. Opening them, she nodded and set her jaw.

Gently Daniel used the tweezers to pick up one of the broken stitches and pull it out. When he wiped the thread off onto the towel, she looked at him in surprise.

"That didn't hurt at all!"

He grinned. "Take it from one who's been this route a lot. It hurts a lot more going in than coming out."

Fascinated, Isabel watched him remove the next two stitches, but she could see the last one would be tricky. The fifth stitch held, but it appeared the stitch beside it had gotten tangled in it. Daniel's hand was steady as he gently grabbed the thread with the tweezers and pulled. It was stuck fast, however, and Isabel winced as the short string tugged on the remaining stitch.

Shifting tactics, Daniel tried several other approaches before giving up. "I'm just going to have to take out that last stitch. Maybe it's healed enough like the bottom two."

Swallowing and holding herself still, she simply nodded her understanding. There was no permission to give or not give. The loose string could not stay there and risk infecting the wound. And he had said they hurt worse going in. Isabel fervently hoped he was right.

She barely felt the small snip of the scissors cutting the string. With a deft pull, Daniel cleaned the slice in her arm of all remaining traces of the original stitching. She breathed a sigh of relief and leaned back into the chair.

"You can rest a bit, then I'll have to put in the other two stitches again." He dabbed the damp cloth around the cut again to clear out the blood that welled from the holes of her stitches and from the center of the wound.

He could use a break as well. Isabel had been unconscious when he'd stitched her before. That had made it easy. But now? To put a needle through her skin when she was fully awake? Daniel understood this a different story altogether.

Taking a few moments to rinse the cloth and prepare the new bandages, he watched her in the candlelight. Sitting still as a statue and breathing slowly in and out, she was the picture of calm. Only the dark hollows under her eyes and the tightness at the side of her mouth gave away the pain she felt. He suspected not all her anguish came from physical wounds. He saw her shift the blanket with her uninjured hand, wincing as the cloth caught on the bandage on her knee. That scrape could wait until he'd gotten the stitches in. For the first time since he'd arrived on the mountain, he wished he had brought up a bottle of spirits. Strong spirits.

Inspiration struck him and he pulled a wooden spoon from the crock by the sink. Coming back to the table, he made himself comfortable on the bench and handed her the spoon.

"What am I supposed to do with this? Bite down on it?"

Daniel laughed. "I didn't think of that. But I can get you something to bite down on if you think it'll help."

"You're the one who's been through this before."

"And I had anesthesia every time. No, I figured if you held onto it with your right hand, it might help you to focus your energies so that you didn't flinch when I put the needle in."

Isabel nodded, hefting the spoon in her hand. Then a mischievous thought occurred to her. "Aren't you afraid I'll hit you with it when my muscle spasms?"

Daniel snorted. "You won't hit me. 'Cause if you do, then my needle will automatically plunge deep into your arm in self-defense."

"Sadist." A grin let him know she was teasing.

"Well, I'm just hoping you have a bit of the masochist in you, since this is going to hurt."

Isabel flexed the fingers of her right hand on the spoon, the nails of her left digging into the wooden seat of the bench where she steadied herself. Taking a deep breath and closing her eyes, she held it a moment while she calmed her thoughts and centered her mind. Only when she had let out the breath she held did she open her eyes and nod for him to begin.

Daniel picked up the threaded needle, and she watched him take a similar centering breath to focus his energies. Her skin gleamed golden in the candlelight, marred only by a single red line that cut along her upper arm. Pinching the sides of the wound together, Daniel pushed the sharp needle through her skin.

Isabel had pricked her fingers often enough when sitting through embroidery classes her mother insisted she take as a young girl. Even an act as simple as sewing on a button meant at least one prick with the damn needle. So Isabel thought she was prepared for the sudden shock of metal piercing her skin.

She wasn't. It hurt far more on the thin skin of her upper arm than it ever had on the pads of her fingers. Gripping the spoon, she watched the needle, reddened with her blood, slide through the skin on the other side of the wound and pull the string through.

Daniel tied the knot, pulling the edges of the cut together, totally focused on doing the job. He didn't miss her sudden intake of breath, nor the small whimper that escaped from the back of her throat. But she didn't move and he clipped the string. One down, one to go.

"All right?"

Isabel nodded, barely daring to breathe. "Just get it over with."

Without another word, Daniel took aim a second time. This time when the needle entered, Isabel's face screwed up tight and he knew she barely held control of her tears. But he could not rush. Not if he wanted the job done right. Carefully he pulled the needle through the opposite side of the small wound and watched as the sides drew together before he tied off the thread.

"Done."

Isabel's breath came out in a rush and she slumped against the table, her head falling back as her body slowly accepted and adapted to the pain. After several moments, it ebbed, letting her function once more.

"That wasn't so bad, was it?" Daniel smiled at her in reassurance. Isabel sighed and shook her head.

"No, it wasn't as bad as I was afraid it would be."

Daniel eyed the now-closed wound. "A little antiseptic cream on top with another bandage, I think, and we'll be finished."

At Isabel's nod, Daniel dressed the small wound, wishing he'd thought to stock some large adhesive bandages along with the miles of gauze he had bought. He taped the end and sat back. "Now, how about that knee?"

"It doesn't hurt at all." Isabel didn't really want to deal with it. Getting stitches hurt less than she'd thought, but she really felt she'd had enough for one session.

Daniel paused in the act of reaching for the blanket and looked at her. Fatigue bowed her shoulders and dulled the shine in her eyes. He reminded himself the poor woman had been through a lot in the past few days. The iron will she had shown him on more than one occasion was now bending under the strain of all she was carrying. He shook his head.

"I'm sorry, Isabel, but it really does need to be looked at."

She sighed, biting back the tears that threatened to overwhelm her. Nodding permission, she brought her leg out from under the blanket so he could examine her knee.

Even in the dim light, he could see the large spot of blood on the bandage. The tape he'd used to fasten the end of the gauze hung only by a thread, so unwrapping it should be easy. And it was, until he got to the stain of dried blood that had caked the gauze into a solid mass. Tugging experimentally, a gasp from Isabel made him stop.

"It's stuck to my knee. You can't just pull it off." Her face crinkled as a tear escaped her control. "Please don't pull it off, Daniel. I don't think I can handle that." Another tear slid down her cheek and she gasped, biting her lips and trying to maintain control.

Daniel pulled her into his arms, bringing the blanket up to cover her as the tears fell in earnest now. For the second time in a week, her emotions got the better of her. Sobs racked her as his kindness caused the last of her defenses to give way and she cried for the pain in her arm and cried for the pain in her knee. She cried for being lost and being dirty and for having a bad date. She cried for the job she was going to lose because she was stuck on a mountain, and she cried because it was snowing. She cried for a dream she didn't understand and barely could remember. And when the sobs finally subsided to sniffles, she cried in embarrassment for having lost control.

For his part, Daniel just let her get it all out. Apparently she had been holding a lot more inside than he'd thought. His shirt was soaked with her tears and he smiled over her head. No woman had ever broken down like this in front of him and he found it strangely comforting. Her hair slipped down into her face and he brushed it back over her shoulder, contentment filling his soul in a way he'd never felt. He didn't know what words to say, so he just held her.

And when the tears hiccupped into small whimpers, he reached for the box of tissues and took out several to hand to her. Her slender fingers accepted them and she wiped her eyes and blew her nose. But she made no move away from the big shoulders that she had soaked with her frustrations.

Daniel tucked the blanket more firmly around her, leaving open only the arm she used to wipe away her tears.

He felt her small frame heave with a huge breath and he looked down as she blew it out in a long exhale.

"Better?"

Isabel pulled away and nodded, but didn't trust herself to look him in the eye. She didn't want to see his look of self-congratulatory self-righteousness because he was the strong man and she the weak woman who cried just because she'd gotten a few stitches. The threads of the small control she had just pulled back together threatened to unravel again in defeat. She *was* weak. She couldn't even manage to walk across the room without needing something to hold on to. Her arm hurt, her knee hurt and her soul hurt.

Men generally either ran away from her independent and confident air, or they were only interested in the voluptuous figure she possessed. And now this man, the one who would be forced to bear her presence for the entire winter, had witnessed her total breakdown. She hung her head as silent tears slid down her cheeks.

Apparently she wasn't better. Daniel saw a glimmering tear fall to the blanket and stared at it a moment, unsure where to go now. "Isabel…" He put a finger under her chin and pulled her face up. "Did I hurt you with the needle? I tried not to make it hurt too much."

Isabel shook her head and smiled sadly. "No, Daniel. I suppose the bandage being stuck to my knee was just the final straw. I'm sorry. I usually don't go to pieces like this."

She still wouldn't look him in the eye. He sat back on his heels, his eyes narrowed as he watched her in the candlelight. "It's all right. I'm surprised you didn't go to pieces earlier. I would have. Actually, I did. That's why I came out here to live. To get my act together."

"You did?" Isabel sniffed again and looked at the huge man in wonder.

"Everyone falls apart once in a while. I'm honored you felt comfortable enough with me to have your breakdown on my shoulder." He stood and held out his hand to help her rise. "Come on. The knee can wait until morning. You've had enough excitement for one night."

Blood still streaked the sheets, so Daniel stripped them off the bed and dropped them in a heap in front of the wardrobe. Opening the closet door, he pulled out another set and made the bed in record time. Isabel helped tuck in one corner and smooth the sheet and blankets, tugging a beautiful old quilt into order on top of everything.

But then a wolf howled outside in the storm and Isabel started. It sounded close to the house. But Daniel only threw a glance at the back door as he eased Isabel under the covers.

"Tomorrow is laundry day and bath day for both of us. Go to sleep now and have pleasanter dreams."

Exhausted, Isabel crawled under the covers, wiggling as she found a comfortable position that didn't put pressure on her sore arm or throbbing knee. Her last sight was of Daniel leaning over the last kerosene lantern, his hand cupped beside the glass chimney before a quick breath brought darkness to the cabin.

Chapter Four

ဆ

The light in the cabin was still dim when she awoke the next morning, feeling better than she had in a week. With a sigh and a stretch, she stared up at the wooden ceiling, remembering Daniel's kindnesses of the night before. Testing her knee, she bent, then straightened it again under the covers. Bending wasn't a problem, but the bandage pulled when she tried to extend her leg. She was just going to have to suck it up and deal with it this morning.

Lying on her back put pressure on her bladder and the reality of her situation dumped the stress on her again. How could he honestly expect her to stay in this tiny cabin all winter long? She had a job and responsibilities.

Resolute and sure that she could talk him into taking her down the mountain as soon as the snow stopped, she threw back the covers and slowly sat up. The fact that she could do so with a minimum of discomfort was not lost on her. Only her knee hurt this morning where the bandage was stuck to the dried blood. She really couldn't say the stitches in her arm hurt, even if they did pull a little.

A reminder from her bladder forced her to her feet. Forgoing the sweats in her sudden need to use the pail, she stood on the cold floor and decided he needed more than just the one small rug if she was going to have to walk around barefoot all winter.

The overstuffed chair was empty, the blanket he'd used thrown carelessly over the back and Isabel decided she couldn't wait for Daniel to show her the way to his outdoor pit. The pail she'd used yesterday still stood by the door, emptied and ready for her to use again. Since standing didn't make her dizzy as it had yesterday, she tried a few steps. Grinning, she made it to the bucket and squatted over it, letting her pee ring against the metal side. If she moved a little, she could vary the tone.

But that set her to giggling. "Look at me…hovering over a bucket, naked, and playing music with my pee. Oh, Isabel, girl, you've come down a bit in the world."

The front door opened and the cold gave her goose bumps. "Don't you ever knock?" she asked the mountain man in mock irritation as she attempted to cover herself with her hands.

"Nope." He grinned and dumped an armload of snowy logs beside the stove, making a point to keep his face turned away from her. "My house, remember?"

The door hadn't shut completely with his kick. Daniel stepped over to close it, but before he could, a blur of white streaked into the room, shaking wet snow all over the cabin. Isabel shrieked, partly from the surprise and partly from the shock of cold, wet snow on her naked skin. But then she looked at the beast and drew back against the wall in fear. A white wolf stood in the center of the cabin.

"Sasha, you have no manners." Daniel knelt next to the animal, putting his arm around the beast's neck, which promptly licked his face. "Sasha!" Laughing, he pushed the wolf's snout away.

"You have a wolf for a pet?" Isabel didn't move from the wall.

"I found her when she was still a cub. Never found the mother. Guess she was abandoned." He grabbed a towel off the back of the desk chair and used it to rub Sasha's fur. The scent of wet wolf filled the room and Isabel shook her head.

"I didn't think you could tame wild animals."

"Sasha doesn't really know that. She isn't aware there's a difference between a wolf and a dog. Usually she sleeps somewhere outside. But she came in last night after you fell asleep. I think she didn't like the storm."

Daniel tossed the soaked towel onto the mound he had piled up for laundry and Isabel noticed her rag of a dress among the other clothes. Taking a deep breath, she tried to calm her racing heart as she accepted the fact that Daniel kept a pet wolf. "So how old is she?"

"I'm guessing she was five or six weeks old when I found her, and that was just a few days after I moved up here last spring. So best guess? Seven or eight months."

"She seems pretty big for that. 'Course, I really don't know how fast wolves grow."

She was just making small talk, she realized, in an effort to not radiate her nervousness. Dogs she could handle...barely. Cats were more her style. Wolves weren't even on the list.

When Daniel stood, Sasha turned her attention to Isabel, trotting over to make her acquaintance. Swallowing the sudden lump of fear that balled itself in her throat, Isabel held out a cautious hand, fingers tight together so the wolf would not mistake a digit for food. The wolf sniffed her fingers and stepped closer, her tail wagging in friendliness. But when Sasha tried to put her nose near Isabel's sex, Isabel pushed herself up against the wall and threw a look that bordered on panic toward Daniel.

"Sasha! Get over here and leave the poor woman alone." Daniel snapped his fingers and the wolf obediently turned and trotted over to her master.

"Sorry." Isabel cleared her throat as she regained her composure. "It's bad enough when a dog sticks his nose there and I'm fully dressed." Then she saw the look on Daniel's face and blushed, even as she pursed her lips in irritation.

Sasha had brought Daniel's attention back to a part of her anatomy he was trying not to notice. The dark patch of hair covered her mound, but that only made it more enticing. What did it cover? Were her nether lips as full and luscious as her upper ones? He envied the wolf's audacity and wished he could get away with putting his nose there.

But the way Isabel cleared her throat and turned away was a clear indication he didn't have a chance. He shook his head. Probably for the best. He doubted she was the type who would like his brand of sex anyway. Too independent. Although…breaking that independence could be one hell of a challenge. He mentally shook his head. No. To do such a thing without her consent was abuse and he had already seen the brutal consequences of that.

Any woman who gave control to him would do so because she wanted to. He envisioned Isabel on her knees, naked, her hands clasped behind her head, begging him to take her.

The whistle on the teakettle pulled him back to the present.

Isabel sighed as she gathered the sweats he had loaned her to add to the laundry pile. As irritating as his glance had been, she could not deny the dampness of the arousal that spread between her legs. And she wore nothing to hide it from him. A glance over her shoulder confirmed he was not looking in her direction, so she used the inside of the sweatshirt to wipe away the evidence and grabbed a blanket to cover her body and her embarrassment. Facing him again, she put on a forced smile and pointed out to the pots of water as she tossed the sweats into the laundry pile.

"How much longer 'til the water is ready?"

Daniel grinned. "For tea? Or the bath?"

"Both."

Daniel looked over at her, now wrapped in the old pale blue blanket that had been on his bed since he was a kid. She had pulled it up around her shoulders so that from her neck to her feet, not one inch of skin showed. Under the blankets, he couldn't see the way those wonderful heavy breasts rose and fell as she breathed when she was nervous. Because of the blanket, he didn't have to concentrate on not letting his eyes wander to that beautiful dark patch of hair hiding secrets he wanted to explore.

Forcing himself to think of cold things, like snow and ice, he managed to shrink the erection that threatened to give him away. He had come to this cabin partly to escape the memories of an incredibly bad relationship. Having a beautiful woman to spend the winter with had definite possibilities, all of them with disaster written all over them.

"The water on the stove is hot. Two full ten-quart pots. Should be enough to warm the bathwater. Once we're both clean, we'll wash the clothes and see about something more for you to wear." He glanced at the wolf, padding around the room, looking for a place to settle. "Sasha, do us both a favor...go lie down by the stove. You're tracking water all over the room."

"So is it still snowing out?"

Daniel kept his attention on Sasha, who was now circling a spot next to the stove. Finally deciding which was the best way to lie down, the white ball of fur settled and rested her snout on her paws, watching the room. Daniel had the distinct impression the wolf was keeping her eye on him. *Not to worry, girl*, he thought to himself. Now that Isabel was covered, he could concentrate on the conversation and not on his libido. A wry smile crinkled up one side of his face at the irony of Sasha protecting Isabel and not him.

"What are you grinning at?" Honestly, the man had the oddest sense of humor, Isabel decided. She made herself comfortable on one of the benches, one hand clutching the blanket together at the neck and the other sneaking through the opening at the front to grab the two sides and keep them together at her knees. "If it's stopped snowing, can you take me home tomorrow?"

Daniel's grin turned into a puzzled frown. "I told you yesterday, I can't take you home until spring."

"Why not? I know it's ten miles to the city, but it's only, what...four miles to the nearest town? Three miles to the nearest farm?" Isabel shrugged. "I know I'm not strong enough to hike that yet, but I will be soon. And once I've had that bath..." With her chin she gestured in the direction of the stove to hurry him along getting it ready.

Daniel shook his head. She truly did not understand. Taking a deep breath he tried to explain it to her.

"Isabel, yes, it's only three miles to the nearest farm. Over the past summer, the Bernsens have become, well, mentors to me. They're an older couple who have lived there for over forty years. In fact, Mr. Bernsen was born on that farm and has been there all his life. They're the ones who told me what to put in for the winter. The supplies and all. The road that runs by the cabin is a seasonal road. And it's a half-mile walk just to get to that road. No one comes up here after September thirtieth." He eyed her. "No one in their right mind anyway. The Bernsens are just a mile along the road from the town side and often get snowed in for three months of the winter. We're farther along, and they told me it's hard to get out until the streams are running in the spring. That's in April."

"Why? It's just snow, Daniel. On a clear day and a dry road, I could walk from here to the Bernsens in about an hour. With the snow, I know it would take longer, but even if it took all day and you had to stay overnight somewhere, I could still go home and not pester you all winter."

"If you were at full strength and had good boots and warm clothes, and if the storm had dropped one or two or even three feet of snow, we might—*might*—be able to make it in one day." He paused and leaned forward, his eyes boring the seriousness of the situation into her. Anger at her obstinance edged his voice. "But you don't have all your strength back and you don't have any boots, and the storm dropped *six feet* of snow under the trees. That means drifts of over ten and twelve feet in some of the open places. Isabel, we cannot get off the mountain until spring."

She bit her lip as tears formed and threatened to fall for the second time in less than twenty-four hours. Looking down at the covers, she twisted her fingers together as she finally understood. Taking several deep breaths and swallowing down her tears, she attempted a smile. "Well, then, I suppose if you don't want a smelly housemate all winter, you'd best get that bath ready."

Daniel smiled, his rust-colored beard framing the curve of his lips as he reached out to cover her hand that nervously picked at the blanket. Not a callus on them, as compared to his rough hands. "It'll be all right, Isabel. You're safe and warm and Sasha and I will protect you. In the spring, I'll go down the mountain with you and help explain everything." He squeezed her hand, tempted to bring it to his mouth and gallantly kiss her fears away.

Isabel returned the squeeze. Daniel was right. Things could be so much worse right now. Patience was never one of her virtues, but the situation was as it was. Time she just accepted it.

"All right, Daniel. I will try not to get in the way too much."

Daniel stood and headed over to the trapdoor. Pushing the rug aside, he pulled it open and headed down to the cellar to get the big washtub. Isabel shook her head and muttered to herself. "So there is more to this place than the one room. Wonder what else is around here that I haven't seen yet?"

Holding the lantern high, Daniel rooted around to find the large metal tub he'd uncovered when cleaning out over the summer. Up until recently, he had still been taking his laundry to the laundromat in town. The snow changed that and he'd have to do it the old-fashioned way now. A large pile of junk against one wall of the cellar reminded him he still had a lot of cleaning to do. "Later," he murmured under his breath as he pulled the bathtub out of a cobwebbed corner. Cleaning up the rest of the basement was a job he'd left for the winter. But with Isabel upstairs, that job would have to wait.

"I should warn you," Isabel called as he reappeared, pushing the large tub up the stairs. "I know nothing about surviving in the wilderness."

He laughed and the deep tones filled the room. "Let's get you clean, then we'll worry about survival training." With a final push, he got the long, narrow tub into the room and then picked it up and set it in front of the stove.

The aged aluminum tub was five feet long and large enough for her to submerge her entire body. And yet, Daniel lifted it as if it were a paperweight, setting it in place as neatly and gently as he might set down a dozen eggs. Was it really that light? Or was he really that strong? Isabel eyed the tub. It looked heavy to her, but then again, she was used to a preformed tub that was cemented to the wall. Carting a bathtub around wasn't something she had a lot of experience with.

Daniel disappeared downstairs again, coming back up with the lantern and a clean, if old, bucket. He needed to fill the pail from the pump several times, then dump the water into the metal tub before taking one of the pots of hot water off the stove and adding it in. Swirling the water with his hand and making a show of testing it with his elbow, he grinned and proclaimed it ready.

"It ain't exactly the Ritz, but the water's clean. I'll even give you first dibs on the bathwater."

Isabel smiled, suddenly shy at the thought of taking a bath naked before this bear of a man. Up to now, her nudity had prickled her consciousness — she knew she should be much more concerned about it than she had been. But circumstances being what they were, there really wasn't much of an alternative. And Daniel had been such a gentleman about it all, really. She'd caught his appreciative glances at her figure, but he had leered only twice and never drooled or done anything stupid, like try and grope her.

But revealing herself on purpose and taking a bath in that huge tub in front of him was different. And even though he stood beside her now, holding out his hand to help her, she hesitated.

Daniel saw the hesitation and frowned, considering. He noticed how she pulled the blanket tighter almost imperceptibly to cover a bit more of her body and understood. "Just let me hand you into the tub so you don't trip over yourself and then you can take your bath in peace. I won't watch."

Narrowing her eyes, Isabel pulled away the blanket, revealing her nudity. With a deep breath she put her hand in his, accepting his assistance.

Daniel gently took her hand and helped her to her feet. Just three weeks ago he'd hunted a deer that had had that same stricken look in its eyes when he'd finally gotten it in his sights. At the last moment, he had sighed and lowered his rifle, deciding vegetables would be better anyway. If Mr. Bernsen hadn't brought up that cured venison, Daniel would have little meat other than rabbit and goose for the winter.

Now he led another skittish animal. Isabel might have a rod of steel at her core, but her sudden shyness told him there was much more to her than he'd thought. He watched as she placed one long, shapely leg over the rim of the tub and tested the water. Finding it to her liking, she leaned heavily on his arm as she lifted her other leg over the aluminum side and stood on her own. Quickly he handed her a washcloth and bar of soap with instructions. "The quicker you're done washing yourself and your hair, the quicker I can get in before the water gets too cold."

Isabel looked at him in surprise, then down at the water that came mid-calf, her dreams of soaking in hot water up to her chin dissipating in the cold, hard reality of taking a bath in the middle of the woods. Of course they would share the water. A vague mamory of her grandmother telling her stories of washing with her brothers and sisters in one washtub stirred deep in the recesses of her mind. Washing in front of him suddenly became more practical than sexy. Kneeling on her good knee, she dampened the cloth, wrapped the bar inside and attacked the dirt that covered her from head to toe. Even if this wasn't the luxurious soak she had hoped for, out of modesty she kept her back to him as he took the emptied pot over to the sink and filled it with water.

Daniel pointedly did not glance in her direction as he put more water on the stove to warm. Probably he should have gone first for sanitary reasons. The end of the bloodied cloth around her knee floated in the water as she crouched down, letting the warm water soak it off. He watched out of the corner of his eye as she managed to get it off, then look around for somewhere to put it. Keeping his back to her, Daniel held out his hand to take it from her.

"Not looking, hmmm?" Sarcasm dripped from Isabel's voice, but she didn't sound angry as she dropped the sodden mass into his hand. Served him right. Daniel made a face and deposited the bandage into a trash bag he kept near the sink.

"How's it look?" He resisted the urge to look.

"Better. I don't think it'll need a new bandage at all. Mostly it's just a big brush burn."

"Wash your hair. I'll decide if it needs a new bandage once you're out of the tub."

"Oh, you will, will you?" Isabel dunked her head into the shallow water, then came up, groping for the shampoo.

Daniel stifled a chuckle. She'd learn that taking a bath like this was more difficult than it looked. There was definitely an order to washing in a tub like this and the woman had no idea what it was. He offered a little advice. "Only use a little shampoo. Too much will be hard to rinse out."

"Getting a little bossy, aren't you?"

The look she sent in his direction had a definite edge of anger to it. Clearly she didn't like the situation and instead of being grateful for the advice, she had decided to let her temper flare. Well, he could take care of that. She might as well learn right now—there was only one boss in this cabin and she wasn't it.

Daniel picked up the pail she had been peeing in, a wicked grin flashing across his face. He wasn't so mean as to use it, but he wasn't above teaching her a lesson either. Moving the pail out of sight, he pulled out another one just like it that he kept under the sink. With a few deft pumps, he filled the clean pail with cold water, stopping at the stove to add only a little warm water from the teapot. Isabel still knelt in the washtub, making a futile attempt to get the shampoo out of her hair. Not giving her even a second's warning, Daniel promptly dumped the entire contents of the pail over her head.

"What the— Daniel!" She screeched as the mostly cold water hit her head, cascading down her back and drenching her in shampoo suds. "What the hell are you doing?"

"Rinsing your hair for you. Wait, and I'll do it again."

She stood, her hair dripping in front of her face and anger turning her cheeks pink. "Oh, no, you won't. That was uncalled for and you know it." She watched as he filled the bucket again, her eyes darting to the empty spot beside the door. "Oh, no. Not that bucket. Daniel, what are you doing?"

Silently he added water from the teapot, then looked full at her. Difficult as it was to ignore the water dripping from her bosom, he kept his eyes on hers. With one gesture, he pointed to the tub, expecting her to kneel and take what was coming to her.

His meaning was clear. If she wanted the shampoo rinsed out of her hair, she had only one option. Soap still dripped from her hair, but for several heartbeats, Isabel stood her ground, her nose searching for the evidence that he had just dumped a pail of her own pee over her head. But the scent wasn't there. He had only used water. A cold draft raised goose bumps on her skin and still Daniel waited with the bucket in his hands. Gritting her teeth and baring her lips, she gave in, kneeling on her good knee, and bending over so he could pour the water over her head.

But this time, Daniel didn't pour the entire contents over her in one big deluge. Instead, he poured at a slow and steady rate, lifting her hair with one hand and letting the warm water rinse away all the dirt and grime along with the soap. And when her hair was clean, he poured a third bucket of water along her back, letting the warmth caress her muscles and ease away her stress.

Isabel tried to stay angry at him, but the deliciously warm water enveloped her and eased her concerns. Give her indoor plumbing and electricity and she got along just fine. Take away life's amenities and she floundered. But now, with Daniel's hands running the water along her back, she found her thoughts heading in a most disturbing direction.

For the next several months, she would be confined to this cabin with only this mountain man for company. While his clothes fit the stereotype, Isabel decided his manner certainly did not. Nothing shy or retiring about him. Or gentle. He was used to giving commands and being obeyed. Maybe he had a military background? She tried to imagine him as a drill sergeant, but the image wasn't quite right. A few books lined the shelves above the beat-up old desk beside the bed, except Isabel hadn't had a chance yet to scan the titles for more clues to his personality. Then his fingers slid over the skin on her back, and book titles were far from her concern.

Gripping the metal sides of the tub, Isabel took deep breaths to steady her heart, which had begun to beat very quickly as soon as his fingers had lifted her hair to rinse it. There was nothing sexual about the act, yet the jolt that splintered through her was centered squarely in her pussy. And when he poured the water along her back, chasing away the soap suds with his hand, it was all she could do to stifle the purr that rose in her throat.

Daniel dropped the metal bucket and the clang startled Isabel. When had her eyes closed? Damn. She couldn't lose control like that again. It was bad enough that she was walking around naked, she didn't need the man getting the wrong ideas. He already had enough of those thoughts, in her opinion.

Turning his back to her, Daniel handed her a towel to wrap her hair in. Standing, Isabel created a turban to keep it out of her way until she was ready to deal with it. Silently she accepted a second towel for her body, again taking his hand as he helped her out of the tub to stand in front of the warm stove. Carefully wrapping the towel, she tucked the end in just above her breasts and relaxed. The bath was done and her nudity was covered.

With a sigh, Daniel looked at the soapy water waiting for him. He stripped off his blue work shirt, tossing it into the pile of clothes to be washed and was in the process of unbuckling his belt when Isabel noticed what he was doing.

"What the— Oh…right." Isabel's cheeks colored as she realized Daniel was only stripping to take his bath. She really needed to get her thoughts under control. She shook her head as he grinned and dropped his drawers. Until now, she hadn't considered herself a prude. But this whole experience was calling into question every bit of moral behavior she thought she'd answered.

A glimmer of mischief sparkled in her eyes as she turned away from the sight that caused her blood to course madly. He would need to be rinsed off, too. Isabel took the bucket to the sink and lifted the pump handle. Using her left hand made things awkward, but she managed to get the pail half full. Going back to the stove to get the teapot, she stole a look at her rescuer.

Daniel's back was to her, giving a fine view of the tight muscles of his ass as he bent over to dampen the washcloth. Isabel's stolen look lingered lower, on thighs as big around as her waist. Sinewy muscles stretched as he dipped the cloth in the water, squeezing it with one powerful hand as he rose. And when he stood, she sighed over the breadth of his shoulders and the impressive muscles that rippled under his bronzed skin.

Her breath quickened to see him gracefully reach around to wash what he could of his back and she even took a step forward to help him before stopping herself and dropping her eyes. She wasn't supposed to be watching. Biting her lip, her gaze drew upward again in fascination.

Daniel's ass gleamed white where no sun had touched his skin, darkening into a tan on his legs below. A sharp line crossed his waist and Isabel had a vision of him standing in the summer sunlight, arms raised, poised with his axe to split the wood that now crackled in the stove.

A sudden pop from that wood made her jump. Gathering her wits, she turned away from the sight of the naked man and took the teapot from the stove, adding hot water to the cold and then refilling the small teapot from the pump. This time when she turned around, she studiously kept her eyes on the floor in front of her.

"If you'll hand me the pail, I'll rinse off."

Shutting her eyes against temptation, Isabel turned away before opening them again to see where she was going. Although she had intentions of returning his favor and dumping the water over his head, the pail was just too heavy for her to lift with one hand. She could have used her sore arm to guide the stream of water, but probably would end up just making a mess. Without looking at him, she held out the pail with an arm that trembled at the weight.

"I see we need to strengthen those muscles after such a long time in bed."

The humor in his voice covered Daniel's concern. This was a city girl, bred to a life of easy amenities. How could he expect her to stay here in this tiny cabin all winter long?

"I'm getting stronger. I haven't fallen over yet."

Isabel's retort showed that iron bar was back in place. Daniel was glad. He didn't quite know what to do with her when it wasn't. He knelt in the tub and rinsed his hair before standing and shaking his head.

Isabel desperately wanted to see his cock. A man that big ought to have a cock to match. Okay, so size wasn't supposed to matter. And in her limited experience, it hadn't. She'd had her share of lovers over the years, a fact she most definitely had not told her mother. As far as her mom was concerned, Isabel was an old maid and destined to stay one. While she was no longer a virgin, Isabel had recently begun to think she might never find love.

And here in this cabin, stuck with Daniel all winter long meant her hopes of meeting anyone over the holiday season were now gone. All the parties her friends would give, the sometimes awful, sometimes fun office party would be held without her. Although now she didn't have to worry about a date for New Year's Eve. She knew exactly who she would be spending it with, if she really couldn't get him to take her down the mountain sooner.

But right now, stealing surreptitious glances at his muscled back and smooth ass, she really, really wanted to see his cock. And why shouldn't she? Hadn't he seen all of her parts when she was ill? Okay, maybe she had been unconscious, but still, he'd had the opportunity to look. Biting her lip, she craned her head to try and see around those magnificent thighs.

Daniel felt her eyes on him as he stood up, water dripping from his hair into his eyes. Grinning, he shook his head again, sending water droplets to fall like a spring rain shower around the cabin. Her squeal told him he'd hit his target. Stretching, indulging himself in the feeling of being clean, he reached his hands outward and upward, rippling his muscles, his vanity getting the best of him. Even before coming to live on the mountain, he had kept in shape, riding stationary bikes and lifting weights in the neighborhood gym. Since spring, the months spent putting on a new roof, repairing windows and doors, hauling in supplies and cutting firewood had hardened those muscles into steel.

Isabel tried not to gape at the Hercules who rose before her. His hair clung to his neck, sending little rivulets of water cascading down the creases of his back to drip most intriguingly from his ass. A tight, firm, beautiful ass. So awestruck was she that, when he turned around, she did not turn away as she knew she should. Instead, she looked her fill at the god before her, seeing Daniel as if for the first time.

Even soaking wet, with his hair plastered around his face, he was beautiful. Like one of the ancient gods from Olympus come down to spend time on Earth. His high cheekbones, half-hidden behind a thick beard of red-gold, betrayed an aristocratic heritage that befit a higher being. Broad shoulders, bronzed from his time in the sun, showed only a smattering of freckles across their massive width. Fine hairs, water-plastered to his muscle-rippled chest, led her eyes down to his muscle-ridged abdomen. But they did not linger there. Her gaze wandered farther downward.

Nestled in a tuft of hair the same beautiful russet shade as his beard, Daniel's cock lay at rest. Longer than her hand, his length did not startle her as much as his circumference. His cock was almost as thick as her wrist. Large and long it lay there as if waiting for her to stir it.

Daniel stood still and let her look. It was only fair. And practical. The two of them would be living together for the next several months in a cabin with only one room. They might as well get used to seeing each other. And the way she stood, almost not breathing, holding the towel around her as her eyes drank in his appearance, certainly appealed to his male ego. He felt his cock begin to harden, and turned away, grabbing a towel from the chair and wrapping himself in its protection before stepping out of the tub.

Isabel blushed when she saw the slight movement of his cock before he turned away. She certainly hadn't meant to cause such a reaction in him. They had many months of enforced togetherness. Sex would only complicate matters. She sighed and turned away as well, giving him the privacy he deserved while he dried off and dressed.

A randy feeling spread through her pussy again and she sighed, tightening her muscles and doing her Kegel exercises in an attempt to make her sudden desire go away. She must be feeling better. Her back to Daniel, she grimaced. How was she to make it all the way to spring without an orgasm?

One of the reasons she had never married was that she'd never found a partner with a sexual appetite to match her own. Isabel came once a day at her own hand. Sometimes twice. Sex was important to her. She liked to come and knew she was multi-orgasmic. Except she hadn't had much luck with her partners. In the beginning, each lover she had taken had been willing to have sex often. But as time went on, the sex became less and less until her beau would confess he couldn't keep up. Just once Isabel wanted the feeling of being truly sated.

And now, with Daniel around, how was she ever going to find the privacy to take care of business? When she had the energy, that was. A sudden weak feeling took her in the knees and she groped for the bed to sit down.

"Are you all right?" Daniel was immediately at her side.

Isabel sighed and smiled as she sank onto the bed. "I can't believe something as simple as a bath can wipe me out so easily."

"Another reason you're not going down the mountain any time soon."

An I-told-you-so tone in his voice made Daniel sound self-righteous. Isabel felt she should take offense. Unfortunately, he was right.

"Here, let me check those stitches."

She obediently held out her arm for him, a flush coloring her cheeks as his large hands gently unwrapped the sodden gauze from her arm. This close, she could feel the warmth of his freshly washed skin and smell the scent of the soap still clinging to him. His head bent close to examine his handiwork and Isabel felt her heart skip a beat.

The towel around her breasts had loosened and Daniel tried not to notice. He blinked and refocused his eyes on the neat stitches he had placed in her arm last night. But he could still see her breath quicken as her face turned toward his.

Her parted lips invited his kiss. So close, all he had to do was lean an inch farther and their breaths would mingle, joining just a moment before their lips touched. He felt her breath, saw her eyes close and knew she wanted to kiss him as much as he wanted to claim those beautiful, heart-shaped lips and caress them with tenderness.

Instead, he pulled back and put on a brusque, matter-of-fact tone. "Looking good. If you don't have any more nightmares, you should be just fine."

Isabel sat back up with a start. How had she managed to lean so far over? Had he noticed her momentary lapse? That's what she got for daydreaming about coming. It was going to be a long five months.

"Good. I'm glad to hear it. And no more nightmares, if I have anything to say about it."

Daniel chanced a glance back at her as he headed over to begin the laundry. The towel was firmly back in place and no trace of the wanton remained in her manner. He shook his head and wondered if he had simply transferred his own sexual desires onto her. So far, he seemed to be the only one who couldn't stop thinking about sex.

Two mounds of dirty laundry were just the thing to halt the direction of his thoughts. A stir from beneath his towel made him realize just how far his own fantasies had gone.

Isabel stood. "Which pile first?"

"I can do this. You lie down and rest."

"I'm not going to let you do all the work, Daniel. I'm fine. I'll never build up my stamina by just sitting on my duff all day. Come on," she kicked the pile closest to her, "is there a special order here? Do we need fresh water?"

She eyed the water in the tub. The suds from their baths had faded and she fancied she could see a light layer of dirt on the bottom.

"I have another pot of water already hot. We can put these really soiled ones in the tub and reuse the bathwater to give them a good soaking and first wash." Daniel held up her filthy dress as an example. "Although I'm not making any promises."

Isabel sighed and made a face. "That wasn't a cheap dress, either. I don't think it'll ever be the same."

Laughing, Daniel dropped it into the water. Bending again, he retrieved the sweatshirt he had loaned her that she had bled all over last night. Isabel eyed the bloodstains. "Another truly disgusting piece of laundry."

He added a few more pieces, then went over to the wall and brought back an oar.

"Going boating?" Isabel moved to one of the benches and watched with curiosity.

"My fancy agitator. Knowing I was going to spend the winter up here, I looked up how laundry was done in the old days and they had a paddle they used to stir the clothes. I picked this up at a garage sale this past summer and figured it would do. Here, hold it for a sec."

Isabel stood and held the oar while Daniel poured hot water into the tub. Measuring out a small amount of powdered detergent, he added that as well. Isabel pushed at the clothes with the oar, using her good arm, soaking them and starting to make bubbles.

Daniel watched her carefully. He didn't want her to overdo too soon. But he also didn't want to spend his winter coddling her, either. "Want to agitate? Or get more water ready?"

"I'll agitate until my arm gets tired, I think."

Isabel pushed the clothes with more force, making them swish against the sides of the tub. It was an easy enough job. Besides which, it gave her a chance to watch him pad around barefoot and naked but for the towel around his waist. She enjoyed the view and turned over what she knew about her roommate. There was a great deal of mystery to him, she decided.

"Hey!" A thought suddenly occurred to her. "How could you go to garage sales if you have no car?"

Daniel grinned. "You should be a detective." He plopped a full pot onto the stove and added more wood to the fire as he talked. "I never said I didn't own a car, though. I told you I didn't have one here."

"Where do you keep it?"

"Down at the Bernsens. They have room in their barn and Mr. Bernsen takes it out for a spin every once in a while so things don't lock up if I don't get down there."

"So just why are you up here, Daniel...um...Daniel..." Isabel stopped, her brow furrowing as she tried to remember if he had told her his last name.

"Fox. That's all right." He turned the subject away from her question. "I don't remember your last name either."

"Don't know that I mentioned it. My cautious nature at work, don'tcha know. One never knows who to trust." Despite a lingering reticence, she decided there was no point in keeping her name secret. "It's Ingandello. Isabel Ingandello."

"So that would make you Irish, right?" Daniel's teasing grin poked fun at her obvious heritage.

"Yeah, from the southern part of Ireland. Way southern part." Her answering grin continued the tease. "You know, the section of Ireland where we learn to watch out for Foxes because they eat little Irish children."

His grin turned devilish. "Good thing you're not a little Irish child then, isn't it."

"Does that mean you're not going to eat me?"

The words were no sooner out of her mouth when the double entendre smacked her between the eyes. With her cheeks flaming pink, she stammered and tried to backpedal. "I mean, it's a good thing— I mean, that I'm—" Words failed her. To cover her embarrassment, she stirred the clothes with a vengeance.

Daniel watched her squirm for a moment before rescuing her. Sort of. He didn't want to let her off the hook too easily. It was much too much fun watching her blush. "Don't worry, I won't eat you unless you beg me to."

Isabel's cheeks grew even hotter. "Maybe you'll be the one doing the begging!"

Daniel's rich, barrel-chested laugh filled the cabin. He put his hand over hers and stilled her frenetic agitation of the clothes. Only the tub between them prevented him from moving closer to her.

"Believe me, Isabel. It won't be me who begs."

In alarm she looked up. His eyes, still laughing, glinted with steel and she knew he wasn't joking around. Her hands grew hot under his and she tried to pull the oar away. But he held her fast, his stronger hand clasping her fingers firmly against the oar.

Something snapped inside him and he didn't let go. "Might as well get this out in the open, Isabel. You are a very attractive woman, and I do not intend to spend an entire winter trying not to look at your body. It's much too beautiful to ignore. Nor do I expect you to spend the time trying to ignore me. I like to walk around my own cabin naked at times, just as I suspect you like walking around naked when you're alone. I'm not going to continually hide the fact that, on occasion, you give me a hard-on. Was I tempted when you were naked and tied down? More than I liked. But I'm not an animal with urges I can't control. I'm not going to force you to do anything you don't want me to do.

"You are a beautiful woman, Isabel Ingandello. But understand this—if you want sex with me, you'll need to ask for it. In no way am I going to force you or entice you or in any other way take advantage of you. I know full well the legal ramifications if I do. And I'm not going there.

"So don't go getting on your high horse because of a little teasing. You don't like sexual innuendo? Then keep your mind out of the gutter when you look at me."

With an oath, Isabel angrily tossed the oar against the side of the tub. Water soaked them both.

"My mind's not in the gutter, you…you…conceited sex fiend. I don't want sex with you, and I don't intend to spend the winter walking around your cabin naked. Your mind is the one in the gutter all the time. I see the way you look at me. You want me and I know it. Well, you can't have me. I'm not available."

She wished desperately that she could make a decent exit, but the only place to go was outdoors or down into the cellar. Instead, she contented herself with a righteous pull on her towel, making sure it was firmly tucked in and not about to fall off.

"Oh, you've made that more than clear, believe me." Daniel grabbed the oar and fished out Isabel's dress, grabbing it to wring the water out of it. "Apparently you like to tease, wearing skimpy little dresses like this and leading men on, then slamming the door in their faces."

"I am not a tease. I wore the dress because I hoped that, for once, I might meet a man I wouldn't mind going to bed with. Someone who liked me for who I am rather than for my boobs."

"And obviously the way to do that is to wear something sexy." Daniel held the scrap of material between his hands. Even dripping wet, the short length of the dress gave lie to her argument.

"What's wrong with dressing sexy? Why shouldn't I want to look good?" She was losing her train of thought. What was her point? How had they gotten into an argument? Why did his comments confuse her?

Daniel pressed his advantage. "You're a tease, Isabel. You say one thing and mean another. You send mixed signals all the time. Heck, you've been doing it since you woke up. I don't know whether to fuck you or push you into a snowbank!"

Isabel's eyes flared at his use of the vulgar word. She stuck her chin out and sneered at him. "You wouldn't dare."

Daniel flung the dress over the back of the chair and advanced on her.

"Don't you dare." Her voice shrieked as he grabbed her hands and pulled her up to him. "Daniel!" Heat from his body warmed her as his arms slid around her waist, pulling her tightly against his chest. Isabel's hands, released from his grip, had nowhere to go but onto his naked, muscled shoulders. Months of manual labor had chiseled strength into every fiber and her knees weakened. She smelled the scent of soap still clinging to his broad chest and felt his smooth skin under her fingertips. An answering heat grew between her legs.

But she would not give in to her body's sudden flush of desire. Struggling to control herself, she locked her knees.

Daniel reached up to smooth the wet, dark hair back from her face. But before he could touch her, he saw the change in her eyes as the iron rod that governed her emotions slammed back into place. She pushed against him and his course of action changed. Abruptly, he scooped her up into his arms and headed for the back door.

"Daniel, no! Don't you dare! Daniel!" Isabel frantically kicked her feet and fought against the brick wall of his chest, but Daniel ignored her. He didn't even look at her as he opened the door and stepped out into the cold.

No snow fell from the sky. They stood in a small area the wind had carved around this side of the cabin. Two steps farther the snow piled to a depth of several feet. Daniel raised Isabel's thrashing body, prepared to toss her gently into the deep pile of soft snow, a grin on his face.

Only her towel came loose. Her breasts, jiggling with her struggles, took on a beautiful luminescence in the gray winter light. He paused and gave her an option.

"Admit that you're a tease and I won't throw you in."

She countered. "You're the tease, you bully. Just because you're bigger than me—" Her sentence ended in a squawk as he raised her an inch higher. "All right, all right! I'm a tease! There, I said it. Now take me inside."

"Ask me nicely."

"What?"

"Say please."

She shivered in the cold and gave in. "Please."

"Please what?"

Sighing with exasperation, she bit the words out. "Please take me inside. I'm cold."

He brought her down, close into his body and hugged her tightly. "Of course I'll take you inside."

Daniel carried her in, kicking the door shut and setting her gently into the overstuffed chair. He covered her with a blanket, tucked it in around her and waited to see what kind of a tongue-lashing she would give him.

But he didn't get one. To his surprise, he saw tears in her eyes and wondered if he had pushed her too far. Brushing her wet hair away from her face, he leaned in, patience and questions in his eyes.

Isabel swallowed hard and fought to bring her raging emotions under control. "I *am* a tease," she whispered. "I guess I've always been one." Her fingers played with a loose string on the blanket, idly twisting it back and forth. "It's a defense, I know. I want men to be attracted to me. I want to find love and romance and all, but then, when they get too close, I push them away."

"Why?"

She slammed her hands down on her lap. "Because otherwise my heart gets tramped all over and it just hurts too much." She tried to look Daniel in the face, but couldn't bring herself to do it.

"So you tease and when men get too close, you dump them before they dump you."

"Yes." The admission was no more than a whisper.

"Except you can't dump me."

Isabel looked at Daniel with confusion. "What?"

"I said, you can't dump me. We're stuck together and you have nowhere to run. How are you going to handle that?

Tease and push me away over and over for the next five or six months?"

Isabel didn't know what to say. She shook her head, but she had no answer for him.

"As I said before, Isabel. I won't take you to bed unless you beg me to. You need to learn to listen to your heart."

A small flame of anger flickered in her soul. "You think I'm going to fall in love with you? Just because we're stuck together?"

He grinned. "No, but I won't put up with teasing. If you want sex, I'm more than happy to oblige." He shrugged. "Provided you beg enough." Reaching out, he took her chin in his hand, forcing her to look at him. "But understand this. No more teasing. You want to look at me when I take a bath, then look. No more coyness, no feigned shyness. No games. Understood?"

She nodded, her stomach suddenly flipping over with an arousal she did not understand. "Understood."

"Good. Now, let's finish this laundry."

Chapter Five

೫

They finished the laundry without incident, although their relationship remained strained for the rest of the week. Isabel used a wall calendar Daniel had hung off the side of one of the shelves over the desk to mark off the days. November had dawned two days ago and winter was settling in. It was time she did the same.

Her scratches had mostly healed and the way her knee itched assured her it was on the mend. Every day Daniel checked her stitches and said the same thing, "Another day or two, I think." Then she would yank the gray, oversized sweatshirt she had declared as hers over her head and the day would begin.

As she regained her strength, she realized she would need more clothing than the sweatshirt, however, if she intended to help out with Daniel's chores. Not doing so didn't even cross her mind. Now that she was finally staying awake longer than she was sleeping, her hands were getting itchy to get to work doing something. Anything.

Besides which, her legs were often cold and she was tired of her ass showing every time she leaned over. She knew Daniel watched every time she did so, and part of her hated it. Another part of her found it very satisfying. But keeping in mind his injunction about her teasing, she tried to stoop down like a lady whenever possible, giving him only a few peeks at her ass.

So pants were the first order of business, she decided. Curled into the oversized chair, Isabel set about downsizing the matching sweatpants that went with her shirt, feeling better than she had since the night she'd left Eddie in a huff. Except the thread she had found was cheap and kept breaking every time she pulled too hard. Which was often.

"Damn it!" She growled at the short broken piece of thread and started pulling out the last few stitches, again, so she had enough length to tie off the troublesome thread. From the hearth, Sasha lifted her head and looked over at her.

"Don't worry, Sasha-wolf. I'm not really mad, just frustrated." Sighing, Isabel measured off a fresh length of thread to start again.

A blast of cold air hit her and she pulled the blanket tighter around her legs. Daniel's voice boomed into the room as Sasha rose and trotted out the door.

"Hi, honey, I'm home!"

He dropped an armload of wood into the large, rectangular bin he had built yesterday. One of the many projects on his list to keep him busy during the daylight hours.

"I still don't understand why you go out and cut that wood every day when you have an entire pile of it under that lean-to back there."

"I told you." Daniel pulled off his coat and gloves as he patiently tried to explain again. "That wood is all green. I cut down two trees this summer and that's the wood from 'em. The wood I'm cutting now is all dead stuff I dragged here from the woods over the summer. It was already dead and therefore will burn better."

"Seems to me fresh wood would take longer to burn than dry wood. And then you wouldn't have to use so much."

"Yes, but then it would smoke up the house."

Isabel shook her head. "I like gas furnaces where all you have to do is turn up the thermostat." She jabbed the needle through the layers of fabric and gently pulled the thread through. The thread did not break and she bit her lower lip as she started the next stitch.

Daniel paused to watch the scene of domestic bliss. When she'd first suggested "taking down" a pair of his pants, his dirty mind had gone right back to their argument the day they'd done the laundry. Keeping his face neutral, he'd listened to her explanation, then handed over the sweats.

"Couldn't have the kind that tie around the waist, could you?" Isabel had asked him with a shake of the head as she'd accepted them. "An elastic waistband is more work."

Apparently a lot more work. Another "damn" from the chair clued him in. The sewing job was not going well.

"If you used this thread on my arm, it's no wonder the stitches broke. This stuff is awful!"

Daniel came over to take a look, then did a double take. He picked up the spool of thread and turned it end over end. "Where did you get this?"

"From the basket downstairs. You know, you really should dust down there one of these snowed-in days."

"What basket?"

Isabel looked up at him as if he'd gone mad. "The one down in the cellar. At the bottom of the stairs. Right in front of the pile of junk you need to clean out? I was going to bring the basket upstairs, but it was too dusty and the thread was right on top, so I just brought up what I needed."

"I don't have a sewing basket downstairs. The thread I used on your arm came from this kit here." He went over to the desk and opened the bottom drawer. Pulling out a small plastic container, he snapped it open and showed her the array of threads, needles, extra buttons and other sewing paraphernalia he had put together as part of his survival kit.

"Well, you could have told me that was there!" Isabel slammed her hands down in exasperation. "Here I'm swearing at this cheap thread when you have good thread right there."

"Sorry. I thought you knew it was there. It's where I got everything the night I resewed your arm. Speaking of which, it's about time to take those stitches out permanently, you know."

"I know. You can do it later, if you want. Hand me that dark green? I can finish up with that."

Daniel handed her the small spool of thread, then picked up the other one again. "This is really old. Look, it's a wooden spool underneath. Not plastic."

"I noticed that. But there are still some companies that use wood. I think."

"Downstairs, you said? I'll be right back."

Isabel ignored him as he lit the kerosene lantern and lifted the trapdoor. Using her needle, she tied off what few stitches she had managed to get out of this piece of thread, pricking her finger in the process.

Daniel reemerged, carrying the small wicker basket. Covered with dust, the design on the cloth top was impossible to make out. The wicker catch that held it shut had broken long ago, so Daniel held it on the bottom instead of carrying it by the dusty handle.

"This basket?"

"That's the one. I went down there looking for a sewing kit and found that one. The thread is right on top, so I just picked out a spool of something dark and brought it back upstairs. It was too cold to stay down there for long in nothing but a sweatshirt." Her needle, now threaded with new thread, dipped into the folds of fabric and pulled through easily. Smiling, she settled down to finish her make-over.

Daniel set the basket on the table and dampened a rag to wipe the dust from the outside. "Hey, the top looks like a picture of the cabin!"

"Let me see." Isabel set aside her sewing and came over to the table to inspect the basket. Without the cloud of dust, she could see the fine stitching that had gone into the creation of the embroidered picture. It did, indeed, look like the very cabin she stood in.

"Well, since men rarely were known for their needlework, I'd say this was created by a woman. Your grandmother, maybe?"

"No, Grandma never really liked the place. Mostly it was just my grandfather and me. Are these initials? Or grass?" He pointed to small stitches in the corner of the basket's top.

"I. F." Isabel squinted and could just make them out. Time and dust had faded the thread, making it difficult to distinguish from the fabric. "Do those initials mean anything to you?"

Daniel nodded, considering. "Isabella Fox. My great-grandmother."

"Your great-grandmother's name was Isabella? Why didn't you tell me? It's not exactly a common name, you know."

Daniel shrugged. "Guess I just never really thought about it. But this box must've been hers. Grandpa always told me this cabin was meant to be part of a larger house. But that something had happened and his parents had moved to the city instead. They kept this only as a hunting cabin after that."

"Apparently your great-grandmother left this behind. And that's why the thread kept snapping. It wasn't cheap, it was old."

Daniel lifted the lid of the basket to reveal what Isabel had seen—an entire tray of multicolored thread, their colors still bright, even if the thread was no good after all this time. Lifting the wooden tray, Daniel set it aside so they could examine the rest of the contents.

Isabel stepped back a bit and watched Daniel's face as he sorted through the various sewing items in his great-grandmother's basket. Cards of snaps and hooks-and-eyes, a scrap of fabric with several threaded needles stuck through it, a small plastic case of straight pins. Daniel handled each item with care, as if his large fingers might somehow break the precious objects he found. His absorption of every detail made Isabel realize the connection he felt to the cabin was far more than just the attachment one feels to a favorite haunt. Daniel had roots here, history. This place was as much a part of him as he was a part of it.

At the very bottom of the basket, Daniel found an envelope. Carefully pulling what looked like a piece of cardboard out of the yellowed envelope, he turned it over, but one look at it and his face changed. He sat down hard on the nearest bench and Isabel hurried around the end of the table to see what he had found.

The images of two people stared back at her. The old-fashioned clothes dated the photo as being from the early part of the twentieth century. The formal pose of the man, who stood stiffly with one hand on his waistcoat and the other on the shoulder of the seated woman, looked very familiar. Squinting and doing a double take, Isabel grinned.

"That has to be your great-grandfather. You're the spittin' image of him!"

"But look at the woman, Isabel."

"Isn't it your great-grandmother?" She looked at Daniel in confusion.

"We have no pictures of her. She died when my grandfather was young. So yes, it could be. But look again." Daniel held it out to her, barely breathing as she took it from his fingers.

Isabel turned the picture to get the light from the front window. The woman's long-sleeved dress, frilled and poufed to show off her slender figure drew one's eye to her. A wide-brimmed hat perched carefully on her Gibson Girl hairstyle matched the frills of the dress.

And then Isabel did a double take.

The woman wearing the hat was the spittin' image of herself.

* * * * *

The basket, its contents still spilled over the table, sat ignored as Isabel and Daniel grappled with the images in the photo. Coming to no conclusions, Daniel had finally propped it on one of the shelves above the desk, leaving the couple to stare out at the cabin. Isabel worked on her sewing under their watchful eyes.

Daniel sat on the bench turning the envelope over and over in his hands as if he would find the answer written there if he flipped it over fast enough.

"You're sure that woman is no relation to you."

Isabel slammed her hands down in frustration. "Daniel, we've been over this. My one grandmother came to this country from Italy in the 1920s, leaving her parents behind her. My other grandmother was born in the city, but her parents came from Massachusetts just before she was born. There's just no way you and I can be related."

Daniel sighed and ran his fingers through his hair. He flipped the envelope onto the table and stood. "I need to go cut more wood."

Isabel opened her mouth to protest. The wood box was filled to the brim. But then she saw the haunted look on Daniel's face and understood he just needed to do *something*. Nodding, she continued with her sewing, trying to ignore the picture.

It was a bit unnerving. To see her own face peering back from a photo taken almost a hundred years ago. The gentleman in the picture was as well-dressed as the woman, but that didn't necessarily mean anything. What little she knew of the culture back then didn't go very far, but she thought that such photos were usually of some special event. Perhaps a wedding picture?

She finished the first seam and set the pants aside for a moment, getting up to take another look at the photo. The sepia tones had not diminished over the years, probably from being kept in the bottom of the sewing basket and out of the sun. But why keep the picture there…almost as if hidden? On a hunch, Isabel checked the left hands of the couple.

A thick ring with a large stone gleamed on Daniel's great-grandfather's finger where it rested on the woman's shoulder. Could be a wedding band, Isabel decided. Or a family heirloom. Or just a ring. The woman's hands were folded on her lap, the right hand over the left. Very little of her fingers showed. It was impossible to tell if she wore a similar ring.

"Damn. No way to tell."

She put the picture back on the shelf. Without being able to see the woman's other hand all she could tell was that the man in the photo might be married. But was he married to the woman? And if not, why would the photo be in his wife's sewing kit?

Isabel picked up the pants. Tucking her cold feet up under her again, she made an effort to put the picture and all the questions it raised out of her mind.

* * * * *

"Ouch!"

"Don't be such a baby. You can't tell me that really hurt." Daniel pulled the next thread out gently, not really sure if he had hurt Isabel or not.

"Well, okay, maybe it doesn't hurt. But it feels weird." Isabel watched Daniel snip the thread that held her skin together and grab it with the tweezers to slowly remove it. "Even though it didn't hurt the other time, I still expected it to hurt this time."

"Oh, well, since you expected it, then it was all right to say it." Daniel grinned at her as he removed the last stitch. He had had enough stitches removed as a kid to know this was the easy part. "All done."

Isabel looked at her arm. Small red dots where the stitches had been surrounded a thin red line. "You did a good job. If I have a scar at all, it won't be a big one."

"You'll probably have a scar. I'm not that good."

Daniel cleaned up while Isabel started dinner. To put away the tweezers, he had to go past the desk and found himself staring at the picture again. Slamming the desk drawer shut harder than he intended, he turned away and put on his coat.

"Going out to do chores."

Isabel watched him go and sighed.

* * * * *

The light faded fast as the afternoon dwindled to evening. They no longer discussed the photo, but it remained between them the rest of the day. Clearly it had upset Daniel, although Isabel wasn't sure why. He seemed sure the woman was not his great-grandmother, even though he had admitted the family did not own a picture of her. Isabel's attempts to get him to explain had been met with shrugs and distant silences.

She finished the last stitch and tied off the thread with a flourish. Smiling, she slipped on the now-smaller sweatpants. Perfect! With her sleeves rolled up and the pants trimmed down, Isabel now officially had one outfit of clothes to her name. The dress she had consigned to Daniel as a rag. Even laundering it had not improved its appearance. Long after they had swished it around in the hot water trying to get all the dirt out, they had discovered the tiny tag inside that read "Dry clean only".

Daniel had disappeared down into the cellar shortly after a very quiet dinner. Taking up the flashlight, since lighting the kerosene lanterns still made her nervous, she headed down the stairs to show off her sewing skills.

Daniel had been going through the pile of junk, but hadn't gotten very far. Isabel saw a few items pulled aside, but in the dim light wasn't sure if those were "keepers" or "get-rid-ofs" as her mother called them. She heard a crash and an expletive from the gloom at the other end of the basement and shone her light in that direction.

"Bring that light over here, will you? I think I'm stuck."

Isabel tiptoed around some sharp-looking implements and made her way to his voice. But he wasn't there. "Daniel? Where are you?"

"Here." His voice came from behind a screen of fallen gardening tools. A spade with a long wooden handle, several poles for tying up plants, a hoe, and a precariously perched pitchfork had slid from where he had put them and wedged together, blocking his way out of the corner.

She cocked a hand on her hip. "Hmmm…seems to me I could just leave you here and have the cabin to myself for the winter."

Daniel reached through the tangle of stuff to grab the spade and move it out of the way, but the pitchfork leaned in toward him as soon as he tried to shift the other implement. The opening wasn't large enough for him to slip two hands through to hold up the one while moving the other in the giant puzzle.

"I can still throw you out in the snow."

Isabel liked the way his voice growled when he wasn't really angry with her. Made her think of a big grizzly who was really a teddy bear inside.

"You'd have to get out of there first. Here, give that to me." She took the spade, moving it out of the way before he impaled himself on the unstable pitchfork.

She cleared the area and Daniel emerged, his chestnut hair filled with cobwebs. Isabel reached up and pulled one from his beard, hoping there were no spiders in it.

"What were you doing back there, anyway?" She shone the light into the recess.

"Looking for anything that might give me more clues about my great-grandparents."

"Look, Daniel, I like a good mystery as much as the next person, but why are you obsessing over this? So I look like your great-grandmother. A little creepy, I grant you. But not unheard of."

In the cold of the basement, Isabel suddenly shivered. For a moment, she heard her own grandmother's voice in her head. *Someone has walked over your grave, cara bella. That's what that means.* Isabel loved her Italian grandmother, but rarely listened to her old sayings. Standing here in the damp basement of an old cabin, far from home and all she knew, however, the words echoed eerily in her mind.

"You're cold, Isabel. You shouldn't be down here." Daniel reached for the kerosene lantern and gestured to the stairs. Isabel didn't argue.

"You didn't even mention my new outfit," she teased as they headed for the warmth of the cabin. Daniel shut the trapdoor and pulled the rug over the seams to keep the cold downstairs and watched Isabel pirouette in her oversized sweatsuit.

"I do believe it will be the latest fashion, come this spring. Wait 'til the magazines get hold of the new sexy." He set the kerosene lantern on the table so he could get a better view.

Laughing, Isabel struck a seductive pose—hips slanted provocatively, eyes dropping down to look at him through long lashes with a demureness he knew she did not really have. While her teasing had been considerably less over the week, Daniel understood it was ingrained in her nature. Her lower lip came out in a small pout and he could not resist the urge to run his thumb over its softness. Stepping close to her, he murmured, "Best put that away before some little birdie comes along and poops all over it."

He tried to watch impassively when Isabel's breath caught and she tipped her head into his hand, setting a kiss in his palm. But the warmth of her breath on his skin ignited heat in his loins that was just too pleasant to ignore. What was there about a woman in a sweatshirt three sizes too big for her? Especially when it had been his sweatshirt. The pants, even though cut down, still were too wide in the legs and he longed to pull them off her and reveal the slender legs he'd grown accustomed to seeing. His hand cupped her cheek even as his thumb slid over her parted lips. In spite of himself, he bent down to claim the kiss she offered.

He paused as he drew near, expecting her to pull away as she had every other time he had come so close to her. Their breaths mingled as he waited, touching, tentative, expectant. And when she did not move, he leaned forward ever so slightly, his lips closing over hers to taste her for the first time.

Daniel felt her give way, but did not push his advantage. He was determined—he would not take her until she begged him. The more he thought about this woman on her knees before him, the more the idea seduced him. He had yet to find the woman of his dreams. One who was strong and independent, yet willing to submit to him sexually, on his terms. Was she that woman? In spite of the warmth that now coursed through him, there was no point in pushing Isabel, no matter how much heat she caused in him or how many fantasies he had about her. With months of enforced togetherness ahead, he didn't want to think what would happen with her if she turned out to be like all the others. The thought made him pull back.

The kiss ended, but Isabel didn't want to give up the tingles that filled her. Her head swam with the warm, gentle touch of Daniel's mouth. In the old-fashioned light of the lantern in a cabin far from civilization, she held out her hand to him. "Come to bed, Daniel. It's getting late."

Daniel gazed steadily at her, as if in warning. "If I come to bed, Isabel, it will be to sleep. I will not touch you again unless you ask me to."

For the space of several heartbeats Isabel was tempted to do just that. His lips awakened the sexual need she found harder and harder to control. Only his insistence on her begging stopped her. Instead of answering from her clit, her independent streak reared up. With a toss of her head, she dropped her hand and defiantly raised her chin. "Then come to sleep. That chair can't be all that comfortable."

"It isn't. Shall we?" With his hand, Daniel indicated the bed and Isabel marched over to it with a bravery she did not feel. Grabbing the bottom hem of the sweatshirt, she started to pull it over her head and then stopped. It was one thing to sleep naked when she had the bed to herself. It was another thing entirely when his body would be so close to hers. Her stomach gave an annoying, aroused flip at the thought.

"Something wrong?" Carrying the lantern, Daniel stood near her. Too near, he decided. If he wasn't careful, he might not be able to live up to his word. His cock, still hard, threatened to give him away.

"Blow out the lantern and then I'll undress."

Daniel grinned. "It's not as if I haven't seen you naked before, Isabel."

"I know." She frowned. "But do it anyway."

He allowed her this modicum of control. Probably it was best for both of them anyway. Bending over the lantern, he blew a puff of air and the room went black. No moon shone tonight, which was just as well, he decided. No sight to tempt him.

He heard the springs of the bed give way as Isabel climbed in and over to the far wall. Stripping off his own clothes, he let them fall in a heap then slid under the covers. He could not see her, but he knew exactly where she was. Stretching, he accidentally on purpose brushed his foot against the softness of her calf, not surprised when she jerked her leg away. In the darkness, he grinned and turned his back to her.

"Goodnight, Isabel."

"Goodnight, Daniel."

For many long minutes Isabel just lay there, solid and unmoving, scared of touching him accidentally in the night and giving him the wrong idea. But even as she considered it, she wasn't sure the idea was wrong. She was horny. Except having sex with him would complicate an already mixed-up situation. And yet, he was sexy and gentle and ruggedly handsome. But he was also the only man she was likely to see for several months.

Her brain and heart doing battle, Isabel finally fell asleep.

The bitter cold wind blew the long, dark hair from her face and reddened her cheeks. Her hat, clutched tightly in frozen hands, tossed itself against her dress as the wind whipped it about. She stood on the same cliff, the same waves billowing beneath her to crash on the jagged rocks below.

Isabel closed her eyes, willing the dream away with the small conscious part of her brain she could control. But the wind only snapped her dress against her legs as the rain fell in cold drops against her skin.

She bent her head into the wind, opening her eyes to the storm. The seafoam green of her dress darkened as the rain mottled the soft lace trims and satin bows that waltzed around the hem of her skirt. A gust of wind blew the hat from her hands and Isabel reached for it, hearing the voice calling her as she teetered on the edge of the cliff.

"Isabella, come to me. You are mine and I claim you."

Daniel slept like the dead. After over a week of sleeping in the chair, his body relaxed into the comfortable bedding. He felt Isabel turn over a few times in the night, but didn't wake enough to really care about it, even when her leg brushed against his in the darkness. He craved a long, uninterrupted sleep, and got one until light crept in through the curtains.

But finally he bowed to the inevitable, his bladder telling him he could lie in peace no longer. And Isabel's restlessness was starting to drive him insane. Tempted as he was to throw one leg over her and pin her still so he could get a little more sleep, he decided it was best if he rose. Donning a clean pair of sweats, he did little more than nod in her direction before heading out the back door to take care of his needs.

Isabel quickly used the pail beside the back door. This method was definitely getting old. But it did beat the alternative. She peeked out the back window, but could only see the top of Daniel's head several dozens of feet away from the house. Indoor plumbing was everything civilized, she decided as she stretched the kinks out of her back. Daniel was obviously used to sleeping alone and hadn't left her much room. That, coupled with the fact that she jumped a mile every time their bodies touched, had made her sleep restless.

In their effort to remain casual about the fact that they had shared a bed, both were quiet as they went about the morning chores and prepared breakfast. As they ate their pancakes, Isabel attempted to ease the awkwardness.

"I had that dream again last night."

Daniel's only answer was a raised eyebrow. Taking that as a good sign, she continued. "You know the weird part, though? I was wearing the dress in the photograph."

Daniel frowned across the table. "The one my great-grandmother was wearing?" He thought about it a moment, then dismissed it. "Not surprising. You saw the dress in the picture, and then when you had the dream, it came back as a fragment of memory. Happens all the time."

"No, that's not what I meant. The dress I wear in the dream was the same dress I've always worn in the dream. It's floor-length and billowy with long sleeves that the wind blows against my arms. And I'm wearing a corset. I can feel it under my dress."

"Like I said, you saw the dress in the picture and only think you've always worn it." He refused to think there could be any other explanation. After all, what other could there be?

Isabel shook her head. She couldn't explain it. But when she'd looked at the picture yesterday and had been so taken with the woman's face, the dress had only dimly registered. Not until she stood on the cliff face last night did she realize why it had seemed vaguely familiar. She not only had seen it before, but knew the color and the feel of the light muslin fabric.

"And last night I fell off the cliff. I think."

"Lots of people have falling dreams."

She shook her head impatiently and speared the last of her pancakes. "No, this is different. I didn't actually fall. Well, I don't think I did. My hat blew out of my hands in the storm. And I reached for it and then the voice was there again."

She stopped in shock and her fork dropped to her plate from fingers suddenly gone nerveless. Looking at Daniel in horror, she tried to remember how to breathe. "Your voice. The voice in my dream all this time. It's your voice calling me."

Skepticism twisted Daniel's face. "Of course, it's my voice. Mine is the only one you've heard since you started having the dreams. Who else's voice would you hear? Mine is the most recent in your memory."

Fumbling with the fork, she mechanically ate the last bite of her breakfast, her mind grappling with Daniel's explanation. Of course, he was right. What other explanation could there be? She shrugged and cleared the table. "I suppose you're right. I'm just transferring recent events into a dream that doesn't make any sense at all."

"Exactly." Daniel pushed away from the table and gazed out at the snow-filled landscape. The storm had ended and yet drifts still piled up as high as the cabin roof under the trees. It had taken him two days just to shovel out a path to his latrine.

There was wood enough for the next two days, he could forgo that chore today. Not that he minded it. Splitting wood was good exercise. He thought of all the hours spent in the gym, working out and running on treadmills. He was in better shape now. Fresh air and a good axe was all a man needed.

Clouds were moving in from the west, their light-colored edges turning a decidedly nasty gray back toward the horizon. Shrugging his coat on, he bent to lace up his boots before grabbing the rifle from the corner.

Isabel's gasp had him turning around even as she spat out the words. "You have a gun!"

Daniel looked at her as if she had lost her mind. "Yes, I have a gun. It's a rifle and it's been sitting in that corner ever since I moved out here. In fact, I also have a shotgun that I've used several times since you showed up. You have a problem with that?"

She looked again. Another long gun stood in the corner in a small rack she hadn't paid any attention to. "You used it? On what?"

"Rabbits, mostly. One lazy duck. What did you think you've been eating?"

Isabel's mouth hung open and she made an effort to close it. She considered the meals she'd eaten since her fever had broken. Meat had played a part in several of them, but she hadn't considered how he'd happened to have it. And the chicken they'd had the other night... "That chicken was duck!" she exclaimed.

"I haven't made a big secret of it. Guess I thought you knew I was out hunting."

She shook her head. "I didn't. I just thought you spiced the chicken...differently." A lopsided grin twisted her face. "Guess I'm just too used to going to the supermarket and buying meat from the case. Nicely packaged and ready to just plop on the grill. Or in the stew." She turned slightly green. "The stew. That was rabbit in the stew, wasn't it?"

He nodded, grinning to see her turn suddenly queasy. He liked shocking her sensibilities. Took some of the high, city wind out of her sails. "Sure was, ma'am. Can't say as ye seemed to mind it."

His false country accent should have irritated her, but her mind was too preoccupied to care. While she had never plucked a chicken, her parents both had told her stories of doing so when they were younger and still living on the farm.

"I didn't see you scald the duck to get rid of the pinfeathers."

"You were sleeping. Isabel, this can't be a problem for you. I have to hunt or we don't eat meat for the winter. The supplies I put in before the snow are enough for one person, not two. And even if it was just me, I would still hunt every once in a while for fresh meat, rather than canned." He looked at her, still standing like the proverbial deer in the headlights and a small anger blossomed inside him. "If this is a problem for you, too bad. I hunt. And I'm not apologizing for it."

Isabel shook her head. "I'm not asking you to apologize. You've fed me and stitched me back together. You've given me something to wear..." Her fingers tugged at the cut-down sweatpants. "I'm sorry, Daniel. I guess you just took me by surprise, that's all. I really never noticed the gun...er, rifle...in the corner until just now."

Another thought occurred to her. "You don't keep it loaded, do you?"

He relaxed. "No, I don't. I'm not stupid, Isabel."

She grinned. "Just making sure." Sighing and putting her chin up, she shooed him out the door. "Well, get something good for dinner. Now git!"

* * * * *

Daniel followed the deer tracks through the snow. Leave it to the animals to find the easiest passages, he thought as the tracks detoured around another huge snowdrift. The deer seemed to be heading toward the small stream situated a short distance from the cabin. In fact, it was the same stream he'd gotten the water from to prime the pump the day he'd been so preoccupied with Isabel's arrival that he'd let the pump run dry.

Silently moving through the cold air, Daniel set each booted foot carefully so he didn't make noise in the snow as his tracks obliterated those of the deer. Coming around the side of the bank, he spotted her drinking from the stream not too far ahead. He raised his rifle to get her in his sights. When she raised her head, she would be their dinner.

But a young fawn not quite tall enough to be full-grown yet broke from under the bushes beside the stream and came up to nuzzle its mother. One thing his grandfather had drilled into him—no taking mothers from their young. Even if the fawn was almost full-grown and old enough to survive on its own. Stifling an expletive, Daniel lowered his rifle.

His movement startled the fawn and he watched the two of them bound over the stream and turn toward the top of the mountain. Well, so much for venison stew. Glumly, he turned to retrace his steps.

A hawk screeched overhead and Daniel looked up, catching sight of it winging toward the east. Sighing, he wished his grandfather was there to tell him if that meant anything. The old man seemed to know so much about the mountain and the inhabitants that dwelt there. Said he'd learned it all from his father.

Crooking the rifle in his arm, Daniel started back to the cabin. The image from the faded photograph of his great-grandfather sure did look a lot like himself. He didn't realize the Fox genes were so dominant in him. And Isabel could pass for the woman in the picture. It was almost as if the two of them had gone to one of those fairs where you could dress up in old clothes and get your picture taken. Except he'd never met Isabel before the night in the woods. He was sure of that.

Deep into his own thoughts, Daniel jumped when a pheasant flew up in front of him. Quickly he brought the rifle to bear, but too late. His shot went wide and the bird flew away unharmed.

"Well, we're not going to be eating meat any time soon if I keep shooting like that." He shook his head and put his mind on the task at hand.

* * * * *

Isabel heard the shot and hoped he would be home soon. She really needed to find herself a hobby or she was going to go stir crazy this winter. While she'd never considered herself an accomplished seamstress, she found herself eyeing the sewing kit and wondering if there wasn't some shirt of Daniel's that needed mending or a pair of pants that needed a patch or something. Anything to keep her hands busy.

Because the cabin wasn't very big, it didn't take her long to tidy up after breakfast. And Daniel hadn't come back after that shot, so he must've missed whatever game he was going for. Bored, Isabel gathered her courage and lit the kerosene lantern. A small flame sprang up from the wick and she grinned at her accomplishment. Setting the glass chimney in place, she pushed the rug aside for the trapdoor.

She hung the lantern on a convenient hook beside the stairs in the basement so she could survey the clutter. One side of the fieldstone walls had been neatly lined with shelves and the wooden slats bowed under double layers of canned goods of every description. Vegetables, fruits, bottled juice— it looked as if he'd cleaned out an entire grocery store. And he was worried about running out of food?

Still, he had said it might be as long as six months. That figure was hard to fathom and she wasn't sure she believed it. The January thaw should certainly melt enough snow so she could get home. Even so, that was another two months away.

With grim determination, she started sorting through the junk in the pile. Most of it seemed to be nothing more than odd scraps of things. An old box spring, an axe handle with no head, a dull knife blade with no handle.

Separating the useful from the hopeless, she made several piles. The axe handle could be burned, she thought, and the knife blade simply needed a new handle and a good sharpening to be as good as new. The box spring, as far as she could see, had no earthly purpose left.

While tugging at one end of a long, thin board, she heard the back door slam. "I'm down here," she called to Daniel, then giggled at the absurdity. Where else would she be?

"Be down in a minute."

His voice, oddly comforting floated down to her and she smiled, rubbing her hands over her breasts and hips as if remembering their uses. There were much worse men she could have been stuck with.

She got a good grip on the board and tugged again, but it wouldn't come loose. Something seemed to be holding it down on the other end. But she couldn't get back there to see with the pile in the way. Abandoning it for now, she set about moving the slew of junk she could reach.

Daniel's tread on the stair was a welcome diversion. She turned and saw him sit down about halfway down and grin at her.

"So are you planning to laugh at me or help me?" Stretching, she felt a familiar warmth tingle in her pussy. Damn, but she needed to come soon.

She was quite a sight in her baggy sweatshirt with the sleeves rolled up to her elbows and the hem covering her pretty derriere. Even though she now wore pants, he enjoyed the memory of that cute tush. From somewhere she had pilfered a pair of his socks, which were getting filthy on the dirt floor of the cellar. And that wasn't the only thing showing dirt. A cute smudge marred one of her perfect cheeks, making her look like she was auditioning for linebacker. He chuckled at the thought.

"I'd be happy to help you, except I have a buck to clean. Don't suppose you'd rather help me than clean out this musty old basement?"

Isabel shuddered. "That's all right. I like to think of my meat as if it comes in Styrofoam trays and wrapped in plastic. If I see it staring at me with those big brown, dead eyes, there's no way I could eat any of it."

"Then I'll get to work and leave you to yours."

The answer hadn't surprised him. She might have a will of iron for some things like her own independence, but he knew her stomach would turn at the job he was about to do.

Not that he had done that well the first time his grandfather gutted an animal. He seemed to remember his grandmother comforting him and scolding his grandfather for showing him such things. His grandfather's answer echoed in his ears. *He'll be fine, Mama. Just needs to get the first one out of his system.*

Determined to prove his grandfather right, Daniel had stayed and helped all the way through the following year. He still hadn't been able to eat any of the meat, though. That had taken a few years.

He still didn't much care for the job, but it was one that had to be done if they were to survive. He headed outside to finish cleaning the deer.

* * * * *

Isabel heard the door shut upstairs and brushed her hands off on her sweats. The thought of Daniel going out and providing for the two of them, then coming in, smelling of fresh air and sunshine, was too much. She had ignored her own needs far too long. For the first time since she had been stranded on the mountain, she was healthy and alone.

Sighing, Isabel leaned against a wooden support, closing her eyes and letting out a deep breath. Clearing her mind of all thoughts, she focused on the blossoming heat between her legs. Her nipples tingled and she brought one hand up to caress them through the fabric of her heavy sweatshirt. A small smile played on her lips as relaxation spread throughout her entire being. Relaxation that was soon supplanted by a pleasant tension.

Her hand slid down along her stomach, enjoying the flatness of her belly and the curve of her hips as she sought the source of her heat. Bending her knees slightly, she opened the access to her throbbing clit and hot pussy lips.

Her scent wafted up in the darkness and she breathed in deeply as she ran her fingers lightly over the fabric that separated her dirty hands from her needy pussy. Bowing her head into the feeling of contentment, she lazily circled her covered clit with her fingers, pinching it through the thin sweatpants as she imagined Daniel's fingers seeking her clit and finding her sweet spot. A gasp broke the silence of the basement and she rubbed her clit with purpose, her breathing quickening as her mind obliterated everything but the wonderful tension building inside her body and the image of Daniel as she had seen him naked in the tub, only now his rough hands moved with purpose over her skin…

Sunlight beamed through the window to illuminate every line of his powerful chest, the small hairs glimmering with dampness. She remembered his words. "I will not have sex with you unless you beg." The thought maddened her, yet she gasped at the image that sprang to mind — standing naked beside the tub, his fingers straddling her clit as she begged him, "Please, Daniel…please let me come!"

Pushing her fingers along her pussy, she bit her lower lip as she hovered on the edge of sanity. Daniel wrapped his fingers in her hair and pulled her head back to stare into her eyes. "Come for me, Isabel. Let me feel you dance in my hands."

With a small cry, she fell, her body racking against the powerful waves that pounded through her. It had been a long time and her built-up need had poured out. The world consisted only of his voice inside her head and the pulses that tingled all the way out to her fingers and made her knees weak.

Isabel slowly returned to earth, gasping for breath. Leaning her head back against the wooden post, she pulled a deep breath of cleansing air into her lungs, grinned as she held it a moment, then with a sudden release, let it go back into the darkness. Shaking her head and still grinning like a fool, she stood and opened her eyes to the world once more.

Daniel stood on the lower step, watching her with interest.

Chapter Six

~80~

"Need the tub." Daniel made no move from the bottom step of the cellar stairs, choosing instead to continue leaning against the post at the base, his arms crossed over his wide chest. With an insolent jut of his beard, he indicated the large metal tub beside her. Isabel recognized it as the one they'd used for bathing and laundry.

Fury and shame mingled to silence her. Turning her back on him, she choked out the words. "Take it, then." Her cheeks flaming red, she pulled blindly at several of the items in the pile, picking them up and setting them down again in embarrassed fury.

Daniel watched her move things around and waited for the storm to break over his head for witnessing her total abandonment to ecstasy. The last time Daniel had watched a woman come, the worn videotape had been spliced together in all the best parts. Seeing a woman pleasuring herself was much more fun when witnessed in person.

But Isabel continued to ignore him and he had work to do. Grabbing the handle of the tub, he slid it along the floor and pulled it up the stairs.

Isabel heard the tub being dragged across the floor upstairs and paused in her mindless sorting. She listened as the back door opened, heard him pull the tub through, and waited for the door to shut. Creeping up the stairs, she poked her head above floor level and checked. Daniel wasn't there.

Sitting on the stairs, she felt the tickle in her nose that heralded tears and made no effort to block them. She tried to feel anger at being spied upon, and succeeded only in feeling embarrassment. A tear trickled down her dirty cheek, leaving a streak that was soon joined by others. She missed her tiny, practical apartment. She missed her friends who were really just coworkers she hung around with. She even missed her parents' suffocating doting and her mother's constant harping on her lack of a husband.

The crying stilled into sniffles as she realized there was one thing she did not miss…her job. Armed with a college degree in business and accounting, Isabel's high grades had assured that she could have whatever job she wanted. She had chosen wisely, accepting a place in one of the city's leading accounting firms. She had gone to work every day, taken her place among the legion of accountants employed by the firm, collected her weekly paycheck and gone home to her apartment.

She frowned and rubbed her nose with her sleeve as she came to the realization that she didn't really even like that apartment. It was functional. Nothing fancy. Fairly plain and nondescript. Just like her life.

Bitter tears held back too long made her nose tickle again. Listening a moment for Daniel, she heard him whistling outside and knew he wouldn't disturb her a second time. Giving in to the truth that her life was fast going absolutely nowhere, she let the sobs come, racking her shoulders as she accepted what she didn't want to face—no one wanted her, and most probably no one even missed her.

Why hadn't someone come looking for her? Even as she accepted Daniel's word about being snowed in for another five or six months, a part of her expected the police to shovel a path to his door looking for her. Where else would they think she was? Even Daniel had said the road *could* be plowed, it just wasn't.

But in the weeks since that Friday night, not even a helicopter had flown overhead. She had not been missed. Sighing, she put her head in her hands and sat there, the energy to move completely drained from her by the tears that still silently flowed down her cheeks.

* * * * *

Daniel tried to push Isabel from his mind and concentrate on butchering the deer before him. But the image of her tanned skin, flushed with passion, would not leave his thoughts. He remembered her head thrown back against the pillar, that little hollow where her collarbone kissed the soft skin of her neck to expose the delicate pulse beating wildly in her fervor. He imagined himself kissing that throbbing vein as his cock slid home.

He remembered the way he had been forced to tie her to the bed, lest she hurt herself in her fever and felt his heated blood rush to his cock, making it press hard against the fabric of his jeans. The sight of those ample breasts, jiggling as she struggled when she woke up, furious at having been caught in a web not of her choosing...and then to see her pleasuring herself in the basement...

The knife sliced wrong and Daniel swore, pulling his hand back quickly. His broad shoulders tensed, then relaxed as he realized he hadn't cut himself. Just come close. "Focus, Fox. You need to forget about the gorgeous woman in your basement who needs fucking and focus on the deer that needs cutting."

Working methodically, Daniel shook his head as he grieved the loss of his peaceful, uninterrupted solitude. This retreat from the real world was something he'd looked forward to for almost a year. He'd spent the spring and summer and into the fall preparing the cabin and himself, for the time he would spend alone. Life in the city had become unbearable and he had retreated, monk-like, to the mountain to heal.

Instead, he had a fool of a woman, and one hell of a sexy one at that, sleeping in his bed and masturbating in the cellar. Last night he had slept hardly at all, always conscious of her presence beside him. She was so small curled up next to the wall that he was afraid he'd roll over on her in the middle of the night and squash her. And after what he'd witnessed today, tonight was going to be agonizing.

Shaking his head, he refocused on the task at hand. Gripping the knife, he set to work, forcing thoughts of Isabel aside, substituting thoughts of all the ways one could prepare venison instead.

* * * * *

After the incident in the cellar, the two reached an uneasy truce. Grateful that Daniel didn't bring up having caught her in the act, Isabel vowed never to masturbate again. Of course, the more she tried to forget the needs that simmered inside her, the more insistent they became. Still, she held to her vow, curbing her natural flirtatiousness in an effort to find peace.

Daniel noted that Isabel seemed a bit more withdrawn. If she was embarrassed by having been caught with her fingers on her pussy, all the better. Although she was more subdued, her quietness helped him achieve a little of the solitude he had come here for.

The venison lasted for several weeks. Isabel ate hardly any of it. After helping to salt some and make jerky out of what they couldn't immediately use, she had no stomach for eating meat of any sort. Even after Daniel told her the deer had been an old buck who could barely walk and who would have frozen to death in another month or two, she didn't know whether to believe him or not. It was better to go vegetarian for a while, she decided.

Her strength returned and she started to find little things she could do around the cabin to help out. She filled her days with ordinary activities that, in the absence of electricity, became a challenge. Washing and drying the few dishes they used each meal became one of her chores, as did dusting and sweeping the floor each day.

The days were easy to fill. It was the nights that were agony. Each night she would undress only after he blew out the lantern. The springs would creak as he climbed into bed beside her, the warmth of his body welcome in the cold cabin. She longed to snuggle closer, but didn't dare. Each time they accidentally touched in bed, the two parted as if they'd touched a live wire. Which, Isabel decided, wasn't so far from the truth. Life was complicated enough without adding a winter fling into the mix. And Daniel was right. She was a tease. Pulling toward the wall under the covers, she confronted a truth she admitted only in the silence of her own soul.

I will not give up my hard-won independence to any man, no matter how gorgeous he is. Just because my mother was raised in the Fifties when men were supposed to make the money, just because she gave up her job in order to stay home and raise me and never let me forget it. I learned your lesson well, Mom, even if it was one you didn't intend to teach me. No man will take away my independence.

Setting her jaw in the darkness of the night, she shrank away from Daniel, the memory of his kiss burning her lips even as her mind pushed him away.

* * * * *

"Don't think this place has sparkled this much since my grandmother was alive," Daniel told her late one sunny afternoon. Taking advantage of the clear skies, he'd spent the entire day outside adding a lean-to to the house for storage while Isabel apparently spent the time cleaning the inside of the cabin.

Isabel surveyed the room. The curtains at the door were freshly laundered, the counterpane on the bed straight and neat. No papers were out of place on the desk and the table sported an old mayonnaise jar filled with bittersweet twigs Daniel had collected for her, their bright orange berries complementing the worn pine of the cabin's walls.

"Well, I have to say, I never in my life thought I'd find doing housework fulfilling. 'Women's work'." She snorted. "My apartment isn't this clean, I can tell you that!"

"You say 'women's work' as if it's something low. Like it's not valued."

Her lopsided grin gave her eyes a mischievous glint. "It isn't, and I know it. Women have spent the last several decades trying to get out of the house. And here I am, stuck in one. And you know something?"

She paused, watching Daniel unlace his boots and drop them by the back door. The smell of fresh air had come in with him and she inhaled deeply, a contentment filling her that she never felt when in the city. Grinning, she gave another swipe over the already dust-free desk.

"I'm enjoying housework. No, really." She held up her hand to stave off the sarcastic remark she could see forming. "Really. I don't quite know that I could take this year 'round, but the past month has not been as unbearable as I thought it would be."

"Gee, thanks."

Isabel glanced at him, but realized he understood her comment was not an insult. She continued. "It's been almost relaxing to have nothing more important to worry about than whether the dishes were clean."

Daniel's eyes grew serious. "Now you begin to understand why I'm here."

If Isabel hoped for more of an explanation, she was disappointed. Before she could ask him for details, he disappeared into the cellar.

* * * * *

Since Daniel had several pairs of sweatpants, she spent some time taking down another set for herself. Getting used to taking a bath only once a week hadn't been so hard when she decided she could take sponge baths every morning and wash her hair out in the sink every other day.

Daniel rather enjoyed watching her comb out her long, dark hair after each washing. Fresh from the towel, her locks fell in loose curls that she painstakingly straightened with each pull of the comb, although he didn't understand why she wanted it straight. He rather liked the way the curls twisted and bounced around her face. He watched her now, bent over before the stove, a towel around her middle, her hair hanging in a thick curtain, hiding her face. Her comb glided through the tresses with ease, snagged, and a moment later, slid through again. He had never known long hair took such care, but he was very glad Isabel was willing to go through such an ordeal just so he would have those dark locks to admire.

The sexual tension between them ebbed and flowed. Aware that she was a sexual being who also had needs somehow made her easier to avoid in that arena. Knowing that she was a big girl who could take care of her own sexual needs gave him permission to jack off when he felt the pressure rising.

Watching her now, natural grace flowing through the simple task, warmth spread through him that wasn't entirely physical. Grateful for the cooling water, Daniel soaped as he took his turn in the metal tub.

Isabel stood, flinging back her hair, unaware that Daniel had gotten into the tub. The ends of her hair slapped against his shoulder and he hollered in counterfeit pain.

"Yuck! Cold, wet lashes…" His booming voice trailed off as he shivered in mock horror.

She laughed. "You'd rather have hot, dry lashes?"

"As long as you're not having hot flashes, I think we're okay."

"Not for a while yet. A good twenty years away, if my mother's calculations are right."

Daniel fished for the soap that had slipped out of his fingers. He was curious. Isabel rarely talked of her parents. Every once in a while she'd tell a story of her grandmother, who seemed as important to her as his grandfather was to him. But only in passing did she ever mention her own parents. "What calculations has your mother made?"

"Every month she calls me long distance, to let me know my biological clock is ticking down the minutes until I can no longer give her grandchildren." Isabel gestured to him to turn around and dropped her towel when he did so. With the stove going full blast and all the hot water they heated on these days, the cabin was almost stifling. With regret, she pulled on the clean pair of pants and a second large sweatshirt. "I'm an only child, you see. So if I don't give her grandchildren, no one will."

Daniel nodded, contenting himself with only a surreptitious glance as she slid the towel off and the pants on. "Understood completely. One-note conversations with parents is a part of what drove me up here."

"About kids?"

"About responsibilities." He dunked his head under the water, trying to drown out his father's lecture. A lecture he'd heard so many times he could practically recite it by heart.

"Ahhh… This is the one I get. Tell me if yours goes the same way." Isabel struck a pose, her hands on her hips and her feet planted firmly on the floorboards. Her brow knit into a fierce frown and her voice, beginning low, ascended as she worked herself into a mock frenzy.

"Now listen here, young lady. You're not getting any younger and all the men are passing you by. Your standards are too high. You have a responsibility to this family, you know. You're the last Ingandello and even though the name will not continue, the bloodline should not falter with you and your selfishness."

Daniel grinned at her imitation. From where he sat in the now-cool water, he wagged his finger back at her as he gave the speech that had become so familiar to him.

"You have a responsibility to the family name, Daniel. How can you throw away your future and the future of your sons? Leaving the firm now, just when you are about to be made a partner smacks of irresponsibility and self-centeredness that I'd hoped you had outgrown."

With a rueful grin, Isabel shook her head. "What a pair we are." She snorted. "You know, I've never told anybody that. About my mother's pressures." She ducked her head to hide the pain.

"Turn around so I can get out of the tub." Daniel made a turning motion with his hand and waited until Isabel complied before standing and grabbing a towel to wrap around his waist. "I think it's easier to talk about up here because we're so far removed from it all. Like it's another lifetime." Grabbing one of the pots, he ambled over to the sink to fill it again for the laundry.

"Is that why you came up here? To get away from your father?" Watching him pad around the cabin in nothing but a towel often fed her fantasies for the rest of the week. She contented herself with watching the play of sunlight over the strong planes of his back. A small stream of water dripped from his hair straight down his spine to the towel and Isabel resisted the playful urge to tug off the towel and watch the drops of water continue their descent.

The vow she made to never have another orgasm as long as she was stuck here had lasted only a week. She had come at her own hand several times since Daniel had caught her, each time carefully checking to make sure he was not around. Her own shyness kept her quiet when she came, and often she wished for the sanctity of her own apartment in the noisy city where she could come at top volume and no one noticed. At least, she didn't think they did.

Daniel turned to grin at her and Isabel blushed to be caught looking at the man's towel-covered ass. She turned away and pretended to straighten the covers on the bed.

"I thought after the laundry was hanging to dry, we might tackle some more of that junk pile downstairs." Isabel spoke quickly to cover her embarrassment.

Daniel nodded as he dressed. "Sounds good, although I wish you'd thought of that *before* I took a bath. It's really dirty down there."

Isabel grinned. "Sorry. Just thought of it." Her grin turned wicked. "We could always just take another bath when we're done." Mentally she slapped her hand for wanting to get him naked again so soon. Just because she enjoyed watching the way the water dripped along those incredible crevices made by the muscles of his back…

Daniel grabbed a handful of soiled clothes and threw them into the tepid bathwater. "Not fair. You're taking away all my excuses to ignore that pile of junk."

"Oh, you want to go through that pile and you know it. Lots of treasures down there." Isabel got out the oar and pushed the clothes under the water, stirring them around while Daniel poured the hot water in.

"Only you would call them treasures."

"What? Wouldn't you? C'mon, Daniel...I already found a terrific picture of your great-grandparents. How can you not call that a treasure?"

Effortlessly, Daniel swung the large empty pot over to the sink and filled it as his voice hardened. "We don't know if that's my great-grandmother or not."

Isabel rolled her eyes. "It doesn't matter. It's still a treasure."

She stood with her arm on her hip, the oar at rest in the tub. Her lips were pursed in determination and Daniel laughed at her stubborn side.

"I give. They're treasures. Hey, look." With his jaw he gestured out the window. "It's starting to snow again."

Isabel glanced out the window, aware Daniel was changing the subject. Small flakes drifted down, making lazy landings on what she was beginning to understand were permanent snowdrifts. Sighing, she shook her head. "By the calendar, we should be having Thanksgiving dinner tomorrow."

"I'm planning to go hunting tomorrow morning. If I get a turkey, we'll have a real Pilgrim Thanksgiving."

Isabel grinned. "I've been thinking about trying to make bread in that stove of yours. I read through the cookbook you brought up here and there's a recipe for making cornbread in an iron pot. Don't suppose you might have what we need?" She measured out the soap and poured it in, swishing the clothes around to make suds.

"I put in flour and sugar and stuff like that. It's in the cellar in airtight plastic bags. We can root around down there and see what we can find. And I do seem to remember an iron pot that I threw into the junk pile." Daniel strung the clothesline and got the clothespins out of the cupboard.

"You threw it into the junk pile?" Isabel stared at him. "Why?"

Daniel shrugged and grinned that lopsided grin that just poked through his beard and mustache. Isabel liked to see that look—a combination of grown man tease and little boy mischievousness. "Guess I never thought about making cornbread in it."

She shook her head and snorted, going back to stirring the laundry. "Never thought about using it for heating water? Or making stew?"

"You have no idea how heavy an iron pot is, Isabel. The skillet is hard enough for you to carry with your sore arm."

"Okay, but I have another arm, you know. The skillet is harder for me to manage with my left arm, but carrying a pot should be easy."

Their easy banter continued as they finished the laundry and hung it along a rope Daniel strung from hooks on either side of the room. The resulting curtain of clothing divided the space into two distinct sections and Isabel enjoyed the homey feel the cabin got when it was "decorated". She watched Daniel hang up her sweatpants and wondered when he had become her friend. When she'd first woke up and he had nursed her back to health, she hadn't really seen him as anything more than the person who'd helped her out. But now, as she watched the way he wrung out the clothes in his strong hands, she felt a fondness stirring in her.

"Done." Daniel turned and watched her dredge the pail into the tub, pulling up water to dump in the sink. Even his old, baggy sweatshirt, the sleeves rolled up to her elbows, didn't hide her fluid motions as she bent, filled, turned, stepped and poured, pivoting to repeat the motion. He shook his head a little as he watched. When had she stopped being a nuisance? He tried to imagine the winter without her and found he didn't like the picture at all.

In short order, the tub was empty enough for Daniel to pull it out the back door and pour the rest of the water outside, away from the walkway. He took a moment to piss in the snow before heading back into the warmth of the cabin. By the time he got back, Isabel was already at work in the basement, looking for that iron pot. She hummed a snatch of a song as she worked and Daniel stopped to listen at the top of the stairs. He recognized the tune. As he started down the stairs, he picked up the melody.

"Oh, Shenandoah, I'm bound to leave you.

Away, I'm bound away

'Cross the wide Missouri."

Isabel stopped humming to listen to his beautiful baritone. She let him finish, then motioned for him to sing the next verse. As he did so, she joined in with a traditional alto harmony.

"Oh, Shenandoah, I love your daughter.

Away, you rollin' river.

Oh, Shenandoah, I love your daughter.

Away, I'm bound away

'Cross the wide Missouri."

He smiled in surprise as she joined in, her voice complementing his, raising the spectre of singers from long ago. And when they finished the verse, they both stood in the lamplight, grinning at one another.

"I didn't know you sang." Isabel looked at him with appreciation.

"I didn't know you do harmony." He came away from the stairs to join her at the junk pile.

"I've sung in choirs since I was in sixth grade. Was moved to the alto section in seventh because the director needed more altos. Once I discovered how much fun harmony was, I never looked back." She turned and surveyed the pile.

Daniel chuckled. "I started out as a soprano, but then my voice changed. I was lucky. It slid all in one summer and when it stopped, I was a baritone. My director wasn't too pleased to lose a boy soprano, but was happy I wasn't another tenor."

Bending down, he tried to pull up a board that seemed to be in the way, but it was stuck fast at the far end where it disappeared under the junk.

"I tried that one already. Something's weighing it down. We'll need to move a bunch of stuff to get to it."

Daniel nodded and the two of them began sorting through the tangle at the edge of the pile.

"Is this all stuff you found and just dumped here?"

"No." Daniel shook his head as she held up an old metal fan, the wide openings of the grate testament to the fact that it was made long before government regulations. "Most of it was already here in a heap. I added stuff that I found upstairs, then added more when I cleared away the far walls so I could load in supplies for the winter."

"So this is a true treasure hunt."

"How so?"

"Neither one of us has any idea what we may find here." She handed him the fan. "Though why that's here when there isn't any electricity, I have no idea."

"Needs a new cord." He eyed the brittle electrical cord. The old insulation was gone in several places. "I'll set it aside for now and see if I can get what I need in the spring to get it in working shape."

"Why? You don't have electricity."

"At the moment, I don't have electricity. All a part of the plan, don't ya know." He gave her a wink.

"Like the outhouse."

She liked making him laugh. His chuckle at her jibe made her feel less like a nuisance and more like a friend.

By late afternoon, the pile was noticeably smaller, although Isabel observed there seemed to be four piles now — the original one, still teeming with odd shapes, a large pile to be hauled out in the spring and taken to the junkyard, one medium-sized pile of items to be mended, and the smallest pile of things that could be of use to them right now. Among them was the rusted iron pot.

"Well, I think we made progress, today." Daniel surveyed the original pile, and still the largest.

"We did." Isabel laughed. "But next time, let's work first and bathe in the evening. I'm filthy!"

"Mmm...baths by candlelight. Sounds much too romantic."

Isabel's stomach fluttered at the thought. "It does sound romantic, doesn't it?"

He threw a sidelong glance at Isabel's back. Was that a note of wistfulness? "I think we're both too tired to go through all the work for a bath tonight. A sponge bath will have to do. But, I need to go hunting tomorrow if we're having turkey for Thanksgiving dinner. And I'm sure I'll need a bath again tomorrow night after cleaning the bird."

A slow smile spread through Isabel, understanding his hint. "I'm sure you will," she replied, not trusting herself to turn around and let him see how much she liked the idea.

Daniel stood behind her. She could feel the warmth of his body and held her breath. He bent down and whispered in her ear.

"Then tomorrow night we will bathe together in the candlelight."

And he was gone. She heard his steps on the stairs and resisted the urge to call him back and throw herself at his feet. Damn, but she needed to come. Automatically, her hand went to her pussy, the fabric of the sweatpants damp from her arousal.

With an oath, she pulled her hand away and grabbed onto the shelf in front of her. "No, dammit. I am not going to come. Not now. Not with him upstairs." She would wait until he left tomorrow to go hunting. Then she would be alone and could scream out her need into the emptiness of the cabin.

* * * * *

Isabel tried not to hurry him out the door the next day. Sleeping next to him had been almost unbearable. She had tossed and turned so much, trying to ignore the need building to painful levels that Daniel had reached over and put his hand on her ass to quiet her. Even though his hand was above the covers, Isabel fancied she could feel the heat pouring into her from his touch.

She'd lain still after that, finally falling into an exhausted and unsatisfying sleep sometime in the early morning hours. And now Daniel was fussing around doing little things, totally oblivious to the fact that she wanted him gone.

But finally, with his rifle tucked under his arm and a last wave of his hand, he was out the door. Isabel watched his back until he disappeared around a snowbank. The sun just peeked over the horizon, turning the snow a brilliant white in the crisp air. From her position on the doorstep, she glanced up and stared for several moments at a sky clearer than she had ever seen. Not a cloud marred the perfect smoothness, not a hint of smog or exhaust cast a film over the blue.

Taking a deep breath of air so cold and fresh it bit deep into her lungs, she blew it out in a puff of white. Standing on her toes, she looked down the path that led from the back door into the trees for any sign of Daniel and found none. "Now to it, girl. One good, huge, stupendous orgasm is what you need."

She flung herself onto the bed and shoved a pillow down between her legs. This was her favorite way to have an orgasm and one she had not yet been able to achieve since coming here. But Daniel should be gone for quite some time and she was determined to make this an orgasm that would last her a while.

Maneuvering the pillow into position, she turned over to lie on her stomach. The pillow would give her the friction she needed, so she propped herself up on her hands and let her imagination roam…

Massive male hands stroked her naked body. He stood behind her, the warmth of his skin against her back. She simply stood, her arms to her sides, letting his hands investigate her breasts, her stomach, her thighs as she gave up her independent streak to his explorations.

He was a tease, and did not touch her pussy, not even to brush his fingertips over her pubic hair. Not yet. This fantasy was going to last a while. Isabel whimpered in the silence of the cabin as she imagined his hands urging her to part her legs, to reveal her private treasure.

Isabel moaned again as her mind continued the fantasy. Her lover pulled her hands back now, holding them together in one of his rough hands as he used the fingers of his other to explore the sensitive skin inside her thighs with lazy circles that drove her mad.

Isabel moved on the bed, her eyes closed and her breathing fast as she rubbed her clit on the pillow. The thought of being so vulnerable, so controlled was a fantasy she often had. Her passions were strong and, so far, she hadn't found any man capable of handling them. She scared men off with her intensity. An intensity that grew now as the man in her fantasy changed tactics.

"You are mine, Isabel. You have always been mine. Say it."

Daniel's voice! In her head, his voice became the voice of her lover claiming her body and soul for his own. A piece of her wall of control broke away and she whispered, "Yes, I have always been yours." The words ignited the fire inside her and she rubbed fiercely as her body responded.

"You are mine, Isabel. And I can prove it. You will come on my command." Her lover's fingers plunged between her legs to press against her pussy, one finger sliding in deep as he took her with his hands. She wanted to come, but he had not given permission and her moans and cries echoed her frustration and need.

"Please let me come," she whispered with desperation.

"Are you ready?" He pulled her tight against his chest, letting go of her hands so he could wrap his arm around her, grabbing a breast in one massive hand.

Isabel felt as if she would faint. Unsteadily she stood upon a cliff, clothed in seafoam green, the wind blowing fiercely against her face. She waited, her entire body alive, tense, as time stopped.

"Come to me, Isabel. Come for me now."
With a cry from the depths of her very soul, she fell off the cliff.

* * * * *

Daniel found her an hour later, asleep on the bed. Her arms lay stretched above her head in an attitude of surrender. Grinning as he noticed the pillow between her legs, he wondered how much longer it would be before she would prefer him to the pillow.

"And there's nothing like falling asleep after a good fuck," he muttered to himself, feeling his cock grow at the sight of the woman on his bed, her legs and arms thrown open in careless abandon. But he had a bird to pluck. He would make time for himself later.

Scalding the bird and taking it outside to pluck took less and less time each time he did it. There was something very satisfying about catching your own dinner, he decided.

He came in from the cold a second time and saw her stir on the bed. To see her there gave him a satisfaction of a different sort. And yet, the feelings were not all that far apart.

Somehow, Isabel made the place feel less like a hideaway and more like a home.

* * * * *

The scent of roasting turkey filled Isabel's senses and she smiled without opening her eyes. Waking up to the smells of Thanksgiving dinner had to be the absolute best way to wake up. Still smiling, she started to roll over, but the pillow between her legs brought her to full consciousness. This wasn't home and she wasn't a little girl. Stretching, she got up onto her knees and pulled the pillow forward. Only then did she see Daniel's form in the overstuffed chair, his back to her and a cup of coffee warming his hands.

A guilty look of worry crossed her face. Had he seen the pillow? Did he know what she had done? A glance at him in the late afternoon light gave her courage. What did it matter if he had? She was a grown woman and was allowed. With nonchalance she did not feel, she smoothed the covers and sauntered over to where he sat.

"Smells wonderful. How much longer?"

"Soon as the potatoes are done." Daniel indicated a pot of boiling water on top of the woodstove. White foam licked the edges of the pot. He pointedly did not look at her. "Have a nice nap?"

Her bravado went only so far. Not looking him in the eye, she answered, "Just fine, thank you."

"Good."

Daniel stood and stretched. For the first time in his life, he wasn't watching the ball game today and found he missed it. "Funny how a little thing like a football game can make you homesick."

"What?" Isabel paused as she got the plates for the table. Even though grateful for his change of subject, she had no idea what he was talking about.

"The football game. And the parade? We're missing them."

Her stomach lurched and she set the plates on the table. Talking of home brought back memories. She thought of her family sitting down to Thanksgiving dinner without her. Were they worried about her? She imagined them praying over the meal and praying for her. And she had no way to tell them she was safe and well and riding out the winter in a cabin on some forsaken mountain.

"I haven't watched the parade in years. But suddenly I miss it. A lot." Her voice cracked.

Daniel shook his head. "I shouldn't have mentioned it. This is my first Thanksgiving without my family, however dysfunctional they might be. Guess I let it get to me more than I realized."

"This is a time for family. And neither one of us are with our families now. Me, out of stupidity. You, out of..." She paused. She didn't know why he wasn't with his family.

"Why *did* you come up here, Daniel?" When he didn't answer, she prompted him further. For some reason, knowing was suddenly important to her. "I know you said you had an argument with your father, but there's more than that, isn't there?"

After a moment, Daniel nodded. He turned on his heel and pulled serving dishes off the shelf above the sink as he struggled with his demons. At last, he turned back to her and gestured to the overstuffed chair he had just vacated.

"I've been sitting there, thinking of all the Thanksgivings I've known, remembering my mother's turkey and the special dressing she made. I didn't find out until I was in my teens there were giblets in the dressing, or I think I never would have tried it. But by then I'd been eating it for years and loved it."

He paced over to the table. Words bubbled up inside him and forced themselves out. Perhaps it was the poignancy of the day, perhaps it was loneliness. Perhaps it was the simple fact that she was there and not judging him. Whatever the reason, he knew he needed to stop hedging and answer her question. For his sake, if not for hers.

"My mom died when I was eighteen. I was the youngest of four and the only one still home with Dad. He shut me out. Was too much of a man's man to cry in front of his son...or show his grief in any way other than by anger. And I was too young to understand that his anger wasn't directed at me.

"Within months, I left for college, finding excuses to stay with friends over some of the minor holidays. But Thanksgiving, Christmas and Easter were always at home. With family. My older brothers and my sister never really did know me very well, so we didn't really keep in touch much other than the holidays."

He shrugged and Isabel realized he had closed his heart to the hurt that distance from his family caused him. She remained standing at the end of the table, afraid that if she moved, he would remember she was there and stop talking.

"But in spite of my anger at my dad, I still went into law. He was a respected lawyer and hoped one of his children would follow in his footsteps. None of the others did, so I felt it was my responsibility. And I liked it. At first."

His eyes darkened as he recounted his past. "I got a job as a public defender. Went in with noble ideals and all that. Protecting the common man. Giving the downtrodden the benefit of law." He snorted. "Bullshit."

Isabel started at the harshness of his tone. He wasn't looking at her, but at a spot in his memory. After a moment, he looked at her and his eyes were hard.

"I got off one criminal after another, Isabel. That's the reality of what I did. I knew they were guilty and I defended them anyway. I was a damn good lawyer and I argued for reduced sentences when I couldn't get them off entirely. Which was rare. And for that, my father was proud of me."

He shook his head and swore again, pushing himself away from the sink to pace the room. Isabel thought of an angry lion she had seen at the zoo once, how he had paced his cage, roaring every so often at nothing in particular. Daniel had that same look now as he strode back and forth across the narrow cabin.

"After five years, I couldn't take it anymore and applied for a position in his law firm. He, after all his time there, was still a junior partner. But he was sure I would pass him before too long. And that made him proud. I would achieve what he could not. Except I couldn't."

Daniel stopped pacing and stood with his back to her. Isabel held her breath.

"I was assigned a case defending a man who allegedly had beaten his wife. Halfway through the case, I realized the client was guilty. He had gotten drunk one night and beaten the woman senseless. Her twelve-year-old son had found her on the kitchen floor the next morning. At first, the guy told the cops it had been a break-in and that his wife was just making up the story because he had filed for divorce. But then his story started to unravel until it was obvious he was lying.

"I went to my boss and told him. You know his answer? That if that was the case, we shouldn't go to trial. We should make a plea bargain with the judge." Daniel's jaw tightened. "Guilty as sin and still I went to the judge and got him a slap on the hand. Weekends in jail for the next year, counseling and alcohol rehab. His wife's lawyer demanded a restraining order and we agreed."

Daniel turned and looked at Isabel with haunted eyes. "And then the guy left the courthouse, drove to his wife's place and stabbed her twenty times. She bled to death on the very same kitchen floor he had beaten her on before."

Isabel wanted to tell him it wasn't his fault, that he didn't know the guy was dangerous, that he couldn't predict the future. But she didn't. The blame wasn't his alone, but some of the responsibility for that woman's death did lie squarely on his shoulders.

"I quit the firm the next day. My father and I argued about it and I left to come here. The land and the cabin are mine. My grandfather left it all to me in his will. And I had a lot of money saved up." He held his hands up in defeat. "I ran away. That's why I'm here."

Another reason nagged at him, but he had revealed enough for the morning. He didn't need to share the fact that Anna had left him when she'd found out. Or the words she had thrown at him when they'd parted.

"Thank you, Daniel. I appreciate you telling me."

She still did not move from the table, digesting all that he had told her and trying to figure out how she felt about it. Anger at him for letting a violent man back on the streets? Pity because he'd been stuck in a tough spot? Disapproval because he'd run away?

The negative feelings softened, however, as she looked at him, standing forlorn in the center of the cabin. Who was she to judge him? He carried baggage that would break other men. He'd shown wisdom in leaving, not cowardice. Until he came to grips with what he had done, he was no use to his law firm or his father.

She nodded at him, a small smile trying to make its way to her lips. Her stomach tightened and she wanted to go over and hug him, tell him it would be all right, only she was sure he would see it as patronizing.

The potatoes boiled over and saved her. She hurried to the stove and pulled the pot off the fire. But it was heavy and she didn't have a good grip on it. The pot started to tip and Isabel squealed.

"Here, let me." Daniel stepped forward and scooped the pot out of her hands, taking it to the sink to drain the water.

Isabel stepped back, happy to let him take over the task. She watched the easy way he poured the boiled potatoes, skins still intact, into a bowl for serving and remembered her mother's peeled and mashed potatoes. Loneliness washed over her and pushed her inhibitions aside. Maybe Daniel needed a hug and maybe he didn't, but she sure did.

Stepping behind him, she rested her head on his shoulder, wrapped her arms around his strength and rested her hands over his.

The comfort and love surrounded him and Daniel turned, gathering her into his arms. The top of her head just brushed against his beard and he kissed the dark silkiness of her hair. For several long minutes they simply stood, embracing, neither one strong enough to face the holiday alone. Daniel knew if Isabel hadn't been there, he would have simply marked the day off the calendar and run away from it as he had run away from his thoughts all spring and summer, exhausting himself with manual labor. But in her acceptance was a measure of safety. In her presence, he could face his demons and deal with them.

Isabel soaked up the comfort Daniel gave. Had she been back in the city, she would have visited with her parents today and again heard her mother's lecture. She would stay only a few hours before she needed to run from the house, again feeling like a failure because she wasn't married like all her friends. But in Daniel's arms, she didn't care what her mother thought, or that every one of her childhood friends had found a husband. Daniel's arms were supportive and understanding.

"Thank you, Daniel."

Her quiet voice broke the silence. Daniel pulled back to look at her. "Thanks for what?"

"For a lot of things, actually." She didn't let go. Hugging him was far too comforting. "For stitching me up and giving me clothes and a place to spend the winter. For telling me about the case. For being a friend."

He brushed a stray wisp of hair from her face. "Is that all I am? A friend?"

Isabel swallowed hard. "I won't deny I have…deeper feelings." How many nights had she pretended just that?

Today was a day for honesty, however, and she could not deny the fact that she was falling in love with him. "But how do I know if these feelings are true or not? I have no idea if I'm falling in love with you because I'm lonely and you're here and you're nice to me, or if what I'm feeling is the start of something wonderful, like in all the romance books." *Something I might have to run away from*, she added silently. She paused, her brow furrowed in her frustration. "Ever hear of the Stockholm Syndrome?"

"Sure," Daniel replied, as she made a small movement to pull away. He kept his hands around her waist, forcing her to stay. "But that deals with kidnappers and hostages."

"Semantics. I know I'm not a hostage to you, but I am to the weather. And since falling in love with a snowflake is a little difficult…" She grinned without mirth. Inside, her heart beat so hard against her rib cage, she marveled it didn't break through.

"It goes both ways, you know. The kidnapper often falls in love with the hostage." He tilted her chin up, wanting to see the emotions playing in those beautiful, dark eyes.

"I can't. Daniel, I can't be hurt again." She closed her eyes and buried her face in his chest. She could not bear to fall in love again with a man who cast her aside when someone else came along and caught his fancy. No more one-sided love affairs. She had promised herself. And no giving up her freedom.

Pain filled her voice and Daniel hugged her close as he considered. "Isabel," he finally ventured, pushing her again so he could see her face and read her eyes. "I took you in out of duty and kept you here out of necessity. You were a nuisance I neither wanted nor enjoyed." His voice softened. "But seeing you voluntarily pitch in and help out with the chores, and the way you've taken old clothes of mine and made them your own? Feeling you beside me every night, watching you fight not to look at me when I'm taking a bath, talking to you now…well, somewhere along the way, you stopped being a nuisance and started being a friend." His heart skipped as he admitted the truth to her. "All right, more than a friend."

Sighing, he dropped his arms and let her go. "We have several long months ahead of us yet, and I don't want to run away anymore."

Isabel's voice was barely a whisper. "What does that mean?"

"It means I'm falling in love with you, my dear, beautiful, damaged woman. And I don't know what the future holds. I can't promise to stay by your side after the snow melts because I don't know what I'll do then. Will I go back to the city and pick up my law practice? Or will I stay here and become a hermit for the rest of my life? I can't think past the first thaw and, be honest, neither can you."

She shook her head. "You're right. The only time that's real to me is right now. I have no idea what I'll be facing when we go back. Probably no job and no apartment."

He gathered her into his arms again. "Then let's not think beyond the first thaw. The world out there doesn't exist. Only here. Only now."

"No strings afterward?" She held her breath.

"No strings afterward. Once we go back to the city, we go our separate ways." He couldn't resist the temptation to smooth back her hair and brush his fingers over the worry lines in her forehead. Immediately, the lines disappeared as she smiled and tilted her head up at him.

"Yes."

The word was no more than a whisper in the cabin, but it filled Daniel's heart. Softly, his lips touched hers, gently brushing along their fullness.

Isabel had never known such a tender kiss. Standing on tiptoes, she leaned into him, letting the kiss deepen as she let her heart go. For a moment, for an eternity, it didn't matter. Only here. Only now.

And then Isabel's stomach growled and they stepped away, laughing.

"Well, they say the way to a man's heart is through his stomach." Daniel grinned at her. "Think it'll work if the man makes dinner for the woman?"

"I'm willing to give it a shot."

He bussed her on the lips again, just because she looked cute standing there, rubbing her belly. "Then sit, my lady, and let me serve you tonight."

The afternoon had moved into twilight as they spoke, so Isabel lit the lantern as Daniel took the turkey out of the oven.

The easy camaraderie they had established before now developed another layer. A wall had been breached between them and small touches became monumental. Several times at dinner, Daniel took Isabel's hand, caressing it with his thumb as if he held something precious. Later, Isabel found herself making excuses to touch his arm or his back as they cleaned up.

And when they crawled into bed together that night, for the first time, Isabel did not keep her back to him, but lay facing him in her nudity.

"Come here," Daniel lay on his side and held his arms open, inviting her. Isabel accepted, meeting him in the middle of the bed and finally allowing herself to snuggle into his warmth.

Daniel's cock, hard and ready, poked her in the leg and Isabel's stomach fluttered. Was she ready for this? Unsure, she swallowed hard and buried her head in his shoulder.

The heat from her body warmed him. How often had he fantasized about having her right where she was now? Pushing her hair so it fell off her shoulder and onto her back, he reached down and pulled her chin up so her face was level with his.

For a brief second, Isabel resisted. Her heart beating wildly, she looked up at him in the darkness of the cabin, wishing she could see his face.

"Isabel," he said softly, his lips almost brushing against hers. "Remember what I said. I will not take you until you beg me. Only when you are ready will we have sex."

"But your...you..." She couldn't bring herself to say the word.

"I have a hard-on. Yes." Daniel smiled. "And it is quite pleasant, believe me." He kissed her then, gently. "But I do not need to come every time my cock rises."

A spasm in her pussy caught her unawares. She kissed him even as she knew she couldn't do anything but share his bed yet. No matter how eager her pussy was, her mind and heart just weren't ready.

"Then I think I'd rather wait, if you don't mind. There are too many demons chasing me tonight."

"Then we wait." He kissed her lightly and hid his relief. They both had demons shadowing them. Playfully, he nudged her shoulder. "Now roll over and get some sleep."

Smiling in the darkness, she did so, snuggling her back against his as he did the same.

"Thank you, Daniel. I had a very good Thanksgiving."

"So did I. Thank you, Isabel."

Feeling more comfortable in the bed than she had since she had arrived, Isabel fell asleep, lulled by the gentle movement of Daniel's back against hers as they breathed in tandem. In her mind, the words repeated themselves over and over like a mantra as she drifted off to sleep. "Only here. Only now."

Chapter Seven

෨

Somehow Isabel expected the holiday season to pass more slowly when there was no last-minute shopping, no department store Santas, no hustle and bustle filling up the time. But the next three weeks passed in a blur of activity that kept her mind and hands busy. Daniel found a huge holly bush when out hunting and brought her several twigs and branches to use to decorate the cabin. She found a blue crayon in the junk pile and used it to color several sheets of loose-leaf paper. Cutting the sheets into strips, she looped the thin slices of now-colored paper together to make a festive paper chain that Daniel hung across the width of the cabin.

The junk pile turned out to be a great place to raid for materials and making decorations gave Isabel a mission. Using Daniel's hacksaw, she managed to cut several springs from the old box spring. A bit of ribbon from the old sewing kit woven through the spirals made very unique ornaments.

"They look like modernist Christmas trees," Daniel told her when she unveiled her creations.

Laughing, she cocked her head at them, considering. "They do, don't they? Speaking of which, when are you going to get a Christmas tree?"

Daniel frowned. "Wasn't going to."

"What? We need to have a tree, Daniel. It doesn't have to be big. There are only the two of us."

"Maybe I don't celebrate Christmas."

"Why not?" The words were out of her mouth before Isabel realized what he meant. "Oh. I guess I never thought of that."

"Not everyone in the world is Christian, you know."

"I know." She sighed as her mind turned over the thought that his faith might be different from hers. "But I'm Italian Catholic…and no one does Christmas with more vigor than the Italians!" She rolled her eyes, shaking her head at the sometimes stylistically challenged decorations she remembered seeing at her cousins' houses.

"So what are you?" She eyed the steel springs with their bright ribbons and wondered if what she had made was offensive. Fervently she hoped they weren't.

"Actually, I'm a lapsed Catholic. Haven't been to church since I was a boy." Daniel picked up an ornament and turned it over in his fingers. "I was just challenging your assumptions to keep in practice."

"Glad I could be of service." The dry tone in her voice was tempered by the twinkle in her eye. "So why not a tree? I mean, I could see if you were all by yourself out here, but you're not now. There are two of us. It could be just a little tree."

There was such hope in her voice Daniel knew he would find some poor sapling of an evergreen and chop it down to brighten the holiday. He sighed. "I haven't had a real tree in years. Not since Mom passed away." He set the ornament down and stretched, his elbows brushing against the blue Christmas chain. "But I guess we can have one this year."

"Oh, Daniel, thank you!" Isabel jumped up and threw her arms around him, practically knocking him off his feet. She hugged him tightly and Daniel realized how important this tradition was to her.

"'Course, we're going to need more ornaments than just a few of these spring-trees if we don't want a homely lookin' tree. And no, little girl, I'm not putting in a fireplace for Santa to come through."

Grinning, Isabel reached up and gave him a quick kiss on the cheek. "No fireplace. Got it. Won't even ask for it." The grin changed to a sly smile. "Long as I get my tree."

* * * * *

He brought it in the week before Christmas. Isabel stood in amazement as Daniel pulled a ten-foot tall evergreen in through the back door and leaned it against the wall of the cabin near the desk. The branches hung in perfect order, the widest ones on the bottom reaching over to brush the papers neatly stacked on the desktop. The tip of the tree, still several feet from the peak of the ceiling, towered over her head.

"Daniel, it's beautiful!"

"Thank you. It's an Austrian Pine," he volunteered as he divested his coat and boots, then warmed himself by the stove. "You can help me get the base into a bucket."

The idea was good in theory. Daniel's strong arms would lift the tree and all Isabel had to do was slide the steel pail under the trunk. Daniel could set the tree in place, then have her stand up and hold the tree upright while he secured it to the wall by means of strong twine looped around the trunk of the massive tree and tied off on two hooks he had screwed into the wall earlier.

That was the theory. In reality, Daniel swore as the sharp needles dug into the back of his hands when he reached in through the branches to grab the tree trunk. Isabel, underneath, was deluged by a fall of dead needles as the branches swayed over her head.

"A little higher," she shouted from beneath the tree. She just needed another half an inch and she could slide the bucket under the tree.

Daniel grunted above her, tightened his muscles and strained to lift the large tree even higher. From below he heard Isabel's voice call out. "Clear!"

Daniel tried to set it down carefully. He really did. But the trunk slipped from his fingers and the bark scraped against his palms. Daniel stepped back, yelping in pain, and more needles pricked his hands as he yanked them through the branches. The tree slammed into the pail, and Isabel, still facedown on the floor and trying to wiggle out from under the branches, was covered with another layer of pine needles.

With no one to hold it, the tree swayed first right, then left as it tried to find its balance. Daniel didn't notice, too busy pulling little slices of agony out of the backs of his hands where they had embedded themselves. Bouncing off the desk, the tree now tipped forward. Only Isabel's muffled shout from underneath alerted Daniel to the impending catastrophe. He looked up in time to see the top of the tree coming toward him and grabbed for it, hollering as more needles found the backs of his hands. He couldn't stop the momentum, however, and the tree gracefully slid to the floor with Isabel underneath.

"Isabel! Are you all right?" Concern flashed to panic when she didn't answer right away. Stitches for small cuts he could do. Setting broken bones was another matter all together. "Isabel!"

Ignoring the needles, he grabbed the tip of the tree and yanked it up, heaving a sigh of relief when she wiggled out from underneath. He righted the tree, leaning it against the angle formed by the wall and desk and turned to check on the woman he was sure he had hurt.

She came up spitting out a mouthful of dead pine needles. "I'm thinking you should've shaken the tree a bit more when you were outside, Daniel. It might look great on the outside, but the inside of this thing is all dead!" She giggled as she spit out another needle.

Daniel sagged against the heavy oak table, grateful for its strength as he got back his own. He shook his head. How could he have thought a little thing like a tree falling on her would have hurt her? How many times had he seen her indomitable spirit? She shook her head and dry needles went flying all over the cabin.

"Hey!" He put up his hands to protect himself and laughed. His hands burned where the needles had pricked him, but the sight of Isabel sitting on the floor, covered from head to foot in brittle, dead needles was a welcome sight after what he'd expected.

She grinned and brushed a few of the needles from her shoulders. "I'm not sure it's *that* funny."

He snorted and nodded his head. "You look like a porcupine!" The needles had embedded themselves in her sweatshirt and pants and stuck out at odd angles all over her. "Be careful brushing those off. They bite." He examined the backs of his hands. Small red dots covered his skin. "And itch."

Isabel stood, a cascade of dry needles falling to the floor from her clothes. "Let me see."

Dutifully, he held out his hands for her to examine, letting her play doctor this time. He hid his grin as he wondered if she'd make him take off all his clothes.

"Well, I don't know. Looks pretty serious here, Daniel. I think the only way to repair the damage is by skin grafts."

Her tone was so serious and her look so intent that it took a moment for him to realize she was kidding. He chuckled and picked a few pine needles out of her hair.

"Depends on where the skin comes from."

Isabel gave him a wicked grin and waggled her eyebrows at him and he couldn't help laughing again. "You are a naughty little girl. Santa's going to bring you coal."

She giggled and turned toward the tree, surveying it. She stood with her hands on her hips, giving a critical once-over. "It's tipped to the side."

"Time for you to get pricked, my dear."

She rounded on him, her eyes wide with mock horror as she deliberately misunderstood him. "What did you say?"

He grinned again. "Stick your hands through the branches and grab the trunk. You'll find out exactly what I mean." He watched her carefully thread her small hands through the openings between the branches and waited until she was almost there. Then coming up behind her and pitching his voice low and sexy, he added, "Unless you'd like to get pricked some other way."

She jumped and the needles got her. "Ouch. You did that on purpose."

"Yep." With a self-satisfied smile, he finished the task of securing the tree. He wrapped the rope tightly to be sure the entire affair would not come down again. Giving the twine a final tug, he stepped back. Isabel joined him and took a deep breath. With a whoosh, she let the air out and grinned. "Now it smells like Christmas!"

"Takes me back to when I was a kid. They say smell is the strongest memory-provoker." Daniel examined the tree. "Somehow it didn't seem this big in the forest."

Isabel laughed. "I've made enough ornaments for about half of it." She cocked her head to the side and eyed it critically again. "But it will need a star."

"No angel?"

She shook her head. "We used to alternate at our house. Angel one year, star the next. The star was always my favorite."

"Then a star it shall be. That will be my job."

Isabel directed Daniel to pull down the paper chain and the two of them wound it around the tree. He had to give her credit. He never would have thought to make ornaments out of half the stuff she had recycled.

"Is this what I think it is?" He held up a delicate glass tube painted with a small snowman on one side. Metal prongs stuck out of the top of the tube and she had tied a string around them to make a loop.

"Yep. Again, I have no idea why any electrical anything would be in the basement when this place never had electricity, but I found half of an old radio and pilfered the vacuum tubes from it. That's the only one I finished painting, though."

"Let me guess, the paint is my leftover primer from the shutters."

"It *is* leftover primer. Does the cabin have shutters?"

He frowned, then remembered she had never seen the outside of the cabin. She hadn't made it as far as the cabin when he found her running through the rain. Had it really been almost two months since he had carried her into the cabin? And she had been inside all this time because she had nothing to wear on her feet. "Yes, the cabin has shutters." He ducked behind the tree so his face wouldn't give away the idea he'd just had.

"Well, if you have any other colors hanging around, I'd use them. Aren't too many pictures you can make with only one color. Had to use a black marker I found in the desk to make the hat and nose and eyes. And the buttons."

"Sounds as if you've been making yourself quite at home here. Digging through this and that to find what you need." Daniel came out from behind the tree, crossing his arms over his massive chest and staring down at her in mock admonition.

She crossed her own in imitation, her eyes flashing with an answering mock indignation. "Well, you're always busy fixing something or cutting wood, or out hunting. You didn't really expect me to sit around and twiddle my thumbs, did you? Ask you for permission before I did anything?" Isabel's gaze took in the small cabin. Her voice dropped. "Besides, I sort of forgot it wasn't mine."

She spoke so quietly, he almost missed her last comment. Dropping his pose, he stepped toward her. Taking her hand in his, he gestured to the room. "It is yours, Isabel. For as long as you need it to be."

She looked up at him, her heart in her throat at the kindness in his voice. "Thank you, Daniel. I know how hard it was for you to have me here. And you've done so much to make this feel like home for me, that I guess I got carried away."

"You didn't get carried away. Before you came, this was just my grandfather's hunting cabin and all I was doing was fixing it up. It's you that's made it feel like a home." He stepped closer.

"My apartment isn't really my home, either. It's a place where I sleep and keep my stuff." She looked up at him. "Maybe it takes two to make a place into somewhere special."

"I'll buy that." His heart leapt at her words, a little confused even as he agreed. What was there about this little slip of a woman that brought out all his protective instincts? Why did he suddenly feel as if he would miss her when she left? Gently, he pulled her into his embrace.

"Only here. Only now," he whispered into her hair as he held her close, as much to remind himself as to remind her.

"Only here, only now," she repeated, turning her face up to him, wanting his touch.

He could not resist. His lips closed over hers, savoring the warmth of her kiss, the softness of her skin where his hands cupped her face. He kissed her again as his hands slid down her back, pulling her closer, as if he did not want to let her go. Ever.

And for the moment, he did not. Life without her would be empty. Until she'd shown up in that rainstorm, he hadn't realized just how many holes in his life her smile could fill. He loved the way she poked into every nook and cranny to make decorations for a tree in a house she had never expected to be in. He loved the way she looked in his cut-down clothes that still bagged in odd places no matter how hard she tried to get them to fit right. And he loved how she felt in his arms as she pressed against his chest, her fingers reaching up to twine through his hair.

For just a moment, Daniel forgot his vow to not make love to her until she begged. For just a moment, he didn't care if she pleaded with him or not. He wanted her. Her lips under his parted, inviting him deeper as he plundered her mouth, his tongue seeking hers, entwining and filling his soul with her taste.

Isabel's head swam. Her senses were assaulted by the touch of his hands on her back, caressing, pressing her to him in a tight embrace. Her hands reveled in the silky waves of his hair, and she held on to him as he raided her mouth with his tongue. She felt her heart beating wildly and knew with a sudden clarity that she wanted him. Passionately. Desperately. Immediately.

"Now, Daniel, please. Don't stop. I want you." she whispered when he released her mouth to explore her face with his kisses. She could not keep up with him. All she could do was hold him and pray that he not leave her behind.

His mind registered what she asked for and with an effort, he gathered the remnants of his control. "Beg me, Isabel." He planted small kisses on her cheeks, around her temple, crossing her forehead as he touched every part of her face, memorizing it with his lips. He didn't stop until he found her ear. "I won't take you unless you beg," he whispered.

Pride rushed up, coloring her cheeks and she struggled to push him away. "No, I'm not..." But then his tongue tasted the rim of her ear, running down along the outer circle before tugging and sucking the lobe into his mouth. The words died on her lips even as her pride fell aside. "Oh, Daniel," she breathed into his chest as he nibbled on her ear. "Please, I beg you. Make love to me. Please."

Her plea ended several pitches higher as his tongue darted into the inmost recesses of her ear. No one had ever tormented her with such pleasure. With a whimper in the back of her throat, her knees gave way. Daniel scooped her into his arms and carried her to the bed.

"I want to make love to you, Isabel." His dark eyes bore into hers as control settled deep inside his being. "At my pace. At my direction."

Isabel stared, mesmerized by the command in Daniel's eyes. Her thoughts whirled around in a fog of building passion. What did he mean at his direction?

And then his lips closed over hers and the voice disappeared into the haze of her arousal. She wrapped her arms more firmly around him and kissed him back with a fervor that surprised them both. All the pent-up emotions, the hurried orgasms, the sneaked looks at Daniel as he bathed, all the thoughts bottled up inside her for the past weeks rose up and overwhelmed her. Ferociously, she found his tongue, possessing it, pressing her answer into him with the force of her kiss.

If he could have, Daniel would have grinned at the passion locked up inside her. But while one part of his mind acknowledged her fervor, another was too busy reasserting his command. He let her have her way with him for several heartbeats, then slowly pushed her back, forcing her tongue to give way to his as he bent to lay her on the bed.

Isabel relinquished control. Always before lovemaking had been equal, both partners taking turns leading, following...letting their arousals take them where they would. But Daniel wanted more and Isabel understood that when his eyes caught hers again as his hands slid down and under her shirt in one fluid motion. She started to help him, lifting the hem, but stopped when he shook his head.

"Let me find you, Isabel. I don't want your shirt off just yet. Keep your hands to your sides and let me explore."

Heart pounding, she brought her hands down, arching her back so he could slide the sweatshirt up. He demanded her obedience, her independence. A whimper of frustration bubbled up in her throat and she swallowed it down as she waited for Daniel to remove her sweatshirt. But Daniel wasn't quite ready for that yet. His plan was much more nefarious.

Sitting on the bed beside her, Daniel trailed one hand across her belly under her shirt. His fingertips just grazed her navel, circling once before continuing. His eyes knew how well-endowed she was, but he wanted his hands to have the opportunity to find out for themselves. The backs of his fingers brushed against her breasts and Isabel gasped, pushing up to meet them even as her hands came off the coverlet to caress his arms.

"Hands at your sides."

Isabel swiftly obeyed Daniel's gentle, but firm reminder. She didn't fully understand this game, but in her desperation for his touch, she would comply. There was no way she could stop the slow arousal of her senses. When at last Daniel pushed up her shirt, she tried not to move too much no matter how hard her heart beat. But when he bent to kiss her navel, she couldn't help herself. She giggled and her hands came up to push his shoulders.

"What's the matter?" Daniel's face peered up at her, a slight frown on his brow. Giggling was definitely not the reaction he had been going for.

"Your beard. It tickles!" Isabel laughed and reached up to stroke his coppery beard, the wiry hairs smoothing under her fingers.

Daniel grinned and brushed his chin over her stomach, reasserting his sway over the passion he saw in her eyes. "Oh, it will tickle much more than that before I'm done, woman. Lie back down. Hands at your sides." Although his eyes remained merry, the firm tone of his voice demanded her obedience.

Isabel complied with a mischievous smile. Deliberately, Daniel brushed his beard over her skin, finding every inch that reacted to his feather touch. He watched as she tightened her stomach muscles, clenching her hands at her sides to keep from pushing him away. But she didn't touch him again. That took him by surprise. He had not really expected her to be able to obey his commands. So few women could. Or wanted to. Pushing his memories of another woman and another time into the past, he concentrated on the very sexy woman beneath him. He slid his hand up to cup her breast. A very deep sigh gave him permission to continue.

"Sit up for me, Isabel." And when she did so without hesitation, he concealed his wonderment. Was she truly as eager to submit as her actions implied? Or was she just plain horny?

Isabel almost helped him off with the shirt, then remembered his injunction to keep her hands at her sides. Grinning, she kept them in place, not even raising her arms to give him aid in getting the shirt over her head. He wanted her hands at her sides? Then she would keep them there until he told her differently, no matter how impossible it made his next movements. That would teach him.

Daniel saw the grin disappear into the recesses of her shirt as he finally got the darn thing over her head. So she wasn't quite as compliant as he thought. Good. He liked a challenge.

With a quick toss, the shirt was gone. Before him, the twin globes of her breasts invited his inspection even though he had seen them often. In fact, the memory of seeing them bounce during her fever was strong in his mind. Daniel watched as Isabel fidgeted a bit with her hands before finally putting them back at her sides.

Daniel lingered, prolonging the sweet torment. His cock, which had risen when she first begged him, now hardened into a mass of desire that threatened to engulf him. Concentrating on her breasts, rising and falling with each breath she took, Daniel wrestled his pent-up needs into order. Isabel had tempted him from the day she had arrived. He wanted their first time to be soft and smooth and seductive. If he didn't get hold of himself, he knew she would never speak to him again.

He examined her with his eyes for so long, Isabel squirmed. Her nipples, hard and erect, begged to be touched. Her face squished up with the effort required to not move and Daniel sensed her patience was ending. If he didn't move soon, she would. But he was now in control, and he intended to remain that way. Just as he judged she had reached the breaking point, he reached and cupped one of her breasts in his hand, enclosing it almost entirely in his large hand.

Isabel whimpered and thrust her breast into his palm as the warmth of his fingers on her skin sank through to her soul. Hadn't she fantasized about this moment every time she masturbated in the cellar? His grip tightened on her breast, the fingers slowly closing. Gasping, she bent in toward the pain that became pleasure. And still his fingers tightened.

"Do you like this, Isabel? Slow and sensual? Or rough and passionate? Or a little of both as I see fit?"

"Oh, Daniel, yes." His grip made it difficult to focus. All that mattered was contained in the palm of his hand.

"I can be cruel." His gripping fingers tightened briefly, then released her breast. "Or kind." Bending down, he licked the nipple, his beard and mustache lightly brushing against the tender skin of her breast.

"Both. Oh, Daniel, be both to me." No one had ever made love to her like this before and Isabel wanted more. He played with her mind even as he played with her body. Trying to focus on him through the fog that threatened to overwhelm her, the words ripped out of her soul. "Daniel...be cruel, be kind, be loving—just touch me." She leaned forward, begging with her eyes as well as her body. "Touch me. Please."

Daniel's control coiled into a tight whip that he would use to bring pleasure and pain to her body. He knew he could bring her to the brink of ecstasy over and over, never letting her fall off until he desired it. He knew how, in this state, she would do almost anything he wanted. Power flooded through him and his hard cock throbbed.

But power means responsibility and he let it course through him only a moment before corralling the forceful energy. He was several times her size and strength. While dominating her excited him, breaking her did not.

With a single pull, Daniel tugged his shirt over his head, throwing it into the same vicinity as hers. His ego threatened to swell as Isabel drank in the sculpted muscles of his chest and arms. Fine, light hairs rose from the static caused when he'd ripped his shirt over his head. Isabel put out her hand to rub her palm across their feathery softness and Daniel allowed it, enjoying her light touch.

But then her hand curved inward, and she dug her nails into his skin, skimming along his stomach toward his waist. A twinkle and a challenge in her eyes made him growl.

His eyes glittered at her unexpected change. "So you like it rough?" He grabbed her hand, pushing her down onto the bed as he knelt beside her. Taking both her hands, he raised them over her head, dwarfing them in his. He bent down to her breast, taking the nipple in his teeth, biting and sucking the pink nub until she squirmed.

Isabel struggled to move her hands, but he held her fast. The sudden vulnerability made her stomach flutter even as he attacked her nipple. She wiggled under him, not really wanting to get away.

"I like to tie my women down and make love to them for hours." Daniel's finger drifted over the reddened nipple. "But I don't think you'd last that long, would you? You're ready to come right now." He wouldn't admit to her that he doubted his control would last much longer either.

The fire in Isabel's eyes would have melted a normal man. But Daniel was made of sterner stuff and he simply looked at her with teasing patience even as his cock throbbed inside his jeans.

"Yes," she finally admitted as her writhing got her nowhere. "I want to come. Now." She wiggled on the bed again, her pussy flooding with her need. She hadn't known being restrained would excite her so much.

"Not yet."

Daniel released her and stood up. For a moment, Isabel's head swam as the haze drifted, then cleared. She snarled in frustration, but Daniel only threw his head back and laughed.

"Such a proper young woman you are, Isabel Ingandello. Yet, you want to rut like a slut in heat."

"Maybe I really am a slut," she shot back, rising to rest on the heels of her hands. "You don't know me any better than I know you. Maybe I'm a hooker!" Her eyes flashed brightly.

Daniel considered as he deliberately undid his belt, slowly pulling it through all the loops 'til it fell clear of his pants. "Perhaps." He nodded. "You might be a slut. Or a hooker." He snapped the belt in the air like a whip. "Or then again, you might be just as you've been all along…a horny broad who desperately wants to come." The belt whistled through the air to snap again.

The sound of the belt echoed in Isabel's soul and for a moment she quailed when a small voice nagged at the back of her mind. What *did* she really know of him besides what he had told her? Could she really trust him? And would he really use that belt on her? The thought of that leather slapping against her skin first made her cringe, then added fuel to her desire. Mesmerized, she watched him remove his pants and shorts, almost drooling as his magnificent cock, fully aroused and standing proudly from its nest of dark hair, came into view.

Dark with the throbbing of his blood, Daniel's glorious cock extended more than twice the width of her hand. Purple veins stood along the shaft, the ridges marching toward a perfectly smooth tip. Already a small drop of pre-cum glistened at the tip and Isabel licked her lips in anticipation.

He saw her tongue dart along her lips as she stared at his hard cock and desperately tried to hang on to the last vestiges of control he had. Snarling, he grabbed her pants, yanking them down and off in seconds. "I want you. Now."

Isabel spread her legs and arched her back, wanting his thrusts. "Then take me, Daniel. Hard. Please."

Again her voice cracked on the last word as her need threatened her sanity. Daniel saw the wetness between her pussy lips and knew she was ready for him. It was too much. He climbed between her legs and poised himself at the entrance to her pussy.

"Beg me, Isabel. Beg me again."

His raspy voice echoed in her soul and her nails dug into the coverlet as she screamed out her plea. "Yes, Daniel, please. Please let me feel your cock inside me!"

His control disappeared. Pushing against her, he felt her pussy give way and he entered. Slowly, relentlessly, he pushed himself inside her. He heard her cries as if they came from far away. Part of him knew he was hurting her, but he couldn't stop. Burying himself inside, he paused only a moment before pulling out all the way, only to thrust again.

Isabel thought she would rip into pieces. His merciless entry forced the cries from her throat and yet she did not want him to stop. She wanted him buried firmly. And when his cock touched her womb and stretched it, she arched her back and urged him deeper.

Each thrust became easier as her muscles stretched and welcomed him. Wrapping her legs around his back, she urged him to quicken his pace. "Faster, Daniel, hurry!"

Her voice cracked and he thrust deeper, harder. His control vanished and he became an animal, rutting for his own pleasure, repeatedly thrusting his cock deep inside her. Beneath him, her cries filled the cabin and he heard her distress. He didn't care. It had been too long and his body demanded release.

Exquisite agony filled her. She knew her cries were loud, and she didn't care. Let the world hear her. Relinquishing the last of her control, she felt their bodies merge as their souls became one.

Thoughts fled and only sensation remained. The world drifted into nothingness as the two of them rocked in a timeless dance. Isabel felt herself lifted up, as if she stood on the side of a great cliff. For a moment, another woman stood with her, a woman in a seafoam green dress. And then the waves crashed over her and all was forgotten but the cries of pleasure as she came over and over again.

Daniel felt her muscles contract around his cock. Her legs pressed against his back as she writhed beneath him, her entire body consumed by desire. Bending down, he claimed the last vestiges of her orgasm with his lips over hers, feeling her cries echo down his throat. The pressure inside him exploded and his voice echoed hers, his baritone roar of satisfaction growling a perfect counterpoint to her alto cries. His seed spurted into her, he felt invincible, strong, complete. The animal had control and Daniel relished the power that pulsed through him.

He could not stop until the animal was sated. How long had he thrust into her? How hard? He didn't know. All he knew was she had grown quiet beneath him as he collapsed onto her breasts.

Chapter Eight

ഇ

"I'm so sorry, Isabel. I didn't mean for that to happen."

Daniel lay beside her on the bed, his eyes closed and a frown on his face.

"Didn't mean for what to happen? You told me you wouldn't take me unless I begged. And I distinctly remember begging you. That was consensual, Daniel." How could he mistake it for anything else? Isabel still floated in the wonderful haze created by their lovemaking. If she played her cards right, she hoped the haze wouldn't go away for a very long time.

"No, I mean my loss of control there. At the end. I've never done that."

She grinned. "I rather liked it, myself."

"Isabel, I came inside you."

The anguish in his voice finally broke through to her.

"Oh."

She hadn't really considered it. Since coming here, she had already had her period once and had learned a rather messy lesson in what it meant to be literally "on the rag". Mentally, she counted the days. "Damn."

"Damn?" Daniel sat up and looked at her. "Then there's a possibility?"

She screwed up her face as she considered the timing again. "Yes, there's a possibility. Small, but possible."

"Damn." He sat beside her, his hands hanging between his bent knees and shaking his head. "I'm sorry, Isabel. I didn't expect to be sharing my bed this winter, so I don't have protection with me. I meant to pull out before I came."

Having a baby at this particular point in her life wasn't in her plans, but there was little either of them could do now. "I always figure what comes, comes. If you'll pardon the pun." She giggled.

Daniel didn't know quite how to take her attitude. He wanted to be relieved, yet still felt very responsible. "I don't know what to do now."

Isabel propped herself up on one arm and looked at him fondly. "Daniel, I understand your concern and I find it wonderful that you care. However, the chance is slim to nonexistent. In fact, I wouldn't have even thought of it if you hadn't brought it up. Believe me, that was way too intense to not do it again." Her hand caressed his naked thigh. "Soon."

"Isabel, you must've realized some things about me by now." He lay down facing her and took her roving hand in his to keep it still.

"That you're bossy when it comes to sex? I figured that out." She grinned. "And you, I'm sure, have figured out I tend to *like* it hot and quick and passionate."

His wonderful chuckle rumbled across the pillow. "Yeah, I figured that out. But you're not going to get it that way very often. The only reason I lost control this time was because, well, because it's been a while."

"Not because I'm a beautiful woman and you just lost yourself in my charms?"

His grin broadened. "Nope."

She laughed, swatting him playfully on the arm. "Wise guy." Rolling over onto her back, she considered. "So you like to tie women up until they plead for mercy."

"You don't seem upset by that." Daniel held his breath as he waited for her answer.

"Why should I be? Sounds kinky." She looked over at him. "And fun."

"Really?" Daniel looked at her in surprise. "Most women I've suggested it to have run screaming into the hills."

"Including the woman you were going to marry?" Her voice was soft and understanding.

"Including the woman I was going to marry." Then it registered. He had never told her about Anna. He looked at her in shock.

"It was just a guess. You said your father and the court case were only a part of why you were up here. I've had a lot of time to puzzle it out, but I figured a woman was in there somewhere as well." Isabel sighed. "Want to talk about her?"

Daniel shook his head in amazement. "No, not really. I just didn't realize I was so transparent."

She shrugged. "It seemed a logical conclusion to reach. And seeing how you jumped my bones..." The mischievous twinkle was back in her eyes.

"You figured I was a horny bastard who needed to assert control, even if he couldn't hold on to it. And that my sexist need to dominate got me in trouble with a woman, so I came up here to pout."

"Was I right?"

"More than you know." He fell back onto the bed, his arm across his eyes as if he could shut out the final shouting match with Anna.

It hadn't been pretty. His self-esteem had been near bottom because of the court case. Funny thing was, he'd almost canceled the date he'd had with Anna that night because he'd felt so...dirty. They'd only planned to have dinner, however, so he had made the decision to go over to her place.

They'd argued over dinner, then made up over dessert. He no longer remembered what the argument had been about. Something little, probably. But his passions were still running hot when they'd made their way into her bedroom.

Anna claimed to be a traditional girl who considered sex to be her conjugal duty, and Daniel had set out to change her mind, intending to show her the pleasures a man could bring a woman. But it hadn't quite worked out as he'd expected, Daniel thought now as he played over that last night together. He had made love to her on several occasions, each time asserting more and more control. He'd figured eventually Anna would give him exactly what he wanted in the bedroom and forget her more traditional notions.

Except he'd misjudged. That night, convinced she would understand him, he had confessed his kink to Anna — that he loved tying a woman down and making love to her for as long as he wanted. Once Anna had realized he was serious, she'd called him every name she could think of. Daniel had left the apartment and moved to the mountain within the week.

Isabel saw the pain furrowing his brow. He lay with his eyes closed and one arm thrown over his face as if to block out the memories. She allowed him some time, then decided he didn't need to brood any longer. Not when she'd just had so much fun. Her pussy twitched and she knew getting them started again would be her job.

Using the old stretch ploy, she raised her arms over her head, pushing her breasts into the air as she did so. The plain headboard gave her no place to grab onto, however, so she let her arms lie on the pillows. When Daniel didn't move from his spot, she turned over onto her side, facing him, one hand holding up her head.

"I can be more blatant if you need, Daniel, but I was hoping my submissive act might do the trick." Giving her best "come hither" smile, she allowed a little pout, and ran one foot along his muscled leg.

Daniel turned his head to gaze at the sexy woman beside him, putting thoughts and past regrets aside. *Only here. Only now.* The phrase ran through his mind as Anna drifted into his memory where she belonged. Hitching himself up on his hip, Daniel faced the waif he had taken in. Briefly he wondered if she would be like the last lost puppy he'd taken in…a wolf now almost full-grown who came and went at her own pleasure. Gently Daniel cupped Isabel's breast in his palm and rubbed his thumb absently over the hard nipple.

"This one's a little smaller than the other one, did you know that?"

"I did." Her eyes began to lose focus with the constant motion of his thumb over her sensitive nipple. "Does that bother you?"

Daniel shook his head. "Nope. Will make binding them an interesting project." He was determined not to make the same mistakes he'd made with Anna. This time he would not try to hide his sexual preferences. Might as well find out right now if Isabel really understood what he wanted.

"Binding them? You mean like in the old days when women flattened their chests with corsets?"

"That's one way of binding a woman's breasts." He squeezed her breast into his palm and watched her reaction, pleased when she closed her eyes and her lips parted as he sparked her arousal. "But there are other ways as well."

"I'm listening."

Daniel looked at her closed eyes and parted lips and knew his touch was arousing her. Maybe what she needed was a short demonstration of what he was talking about. Her reaction couldn't be any worse than Anna's had been. He rolled over and pulled out the drawer of the desk nearest the bed. He reached inside and pulled out a small bag of rubber bands he'd bought. Even with all the assorted sizes, he had actually not found many uses for them up here in the mountains. Now, however, he was glad he'd brought them along. Choosing several of the size he wanted, he gave silent thanks that he had gotten them.

"Sit up. Put your hands behind your back and close your eyes."

Stretching one of the rubber bands between the forefingers and thumbs of both hands, Daniel took careful aim. With her hands clasped behind her, her breasts stuck out, giving him a perfect target. He stretched a large band and encircled the larger of her breasts, letting the band snap around the base to tighten the breast into a beautiful, shiny globe.

The sudden constriction made Isabel gasp. She had seen him get out the rubber bands, but had no idea what he'd intended to do with them. With an effort, she did not open her eyes, not even when she felt his fingers encircle her other breast and snap the rubber band into place. His touch caused a wonderful range of tingles all the way out to her fingers and down to her toes, with an enticing stopover between her legs. She grinned. "May I peek?"

"Not yet."

But when he put a second band around each breast, she couldn't hold her curiosity and she peeked to see the result.

Her breasts, now rounded globes with smooth skin, poked upward in an almost jaunty fashion. The skin of the areola, sometimes a bit bumpy, now stretched glassy smooth. Daniel reached up and held one breast lightly in his hand and Isabel gasped at how different the sensation was with her breasts bound like this. Before, when he squeezed, the network of nerves that ran from her nipples to her pussy activated immediately. Now, she found other parts of her body affected as well as the sexual highway. From her quickened breathing to her loss of focus, she knew every nerve of her body all found their roots in the touch of his hand cupping her bound breast.

Raising her hands, she put them behind her head, pushing the globe of her breast deeper into his hand. But the sudden outward thrust caused the rubber band on her larger breast to give way. With a snap, it gathered up the other band and rolled down her breast. "Ouch!" She recoiled as the band snapped and her hand flew up to protect her nipple. Too late. Pausing only long enough to whip against her nipple, the band flew off toward Daniel's chest.

He laughed as he picked up the spent missile, stretching it between the fingers of one hand as he eyed her breast. "Looks like we need something a little sturdier." He cocked his head sideways. "Or a smaller rubber band might work better."

"I think I'm done with rubber bands at the moment." She eyed the ones that remained in place on her right breast, trying to figure out how to remove them without causing a similar reaction. Finally deciding that flinging them off was the best way, she arched hard. The band remained tight around her breast.

"I'd say the little buggers like being where they are." Grinning, Daniel watched her contortions as she tried to remove the bands he had strategically placed.

"I think I'd rather have them off now. Please." She liked the sensation well enough, but was a little chicken about the stinging.

"It's going to pinch no matter what." Could she take a little pain with the pleasure?

"That's okay. Just be gentle."

Isabel held her breath as his fingernails pulled gently on the rubber, making every effort to not pinch her skin. But in spite of his best efforts, the last rubber band rolled and snapped her nipple as it left.

Grimacing, she rubbed her nipple. Daniel wondered if perhaps he had asked too much of her. "Let me," he told her, bending down to draw the nipple into his mouth, circling it with his tongue and gently licking away the sting.

"Ohh, I like that," she murmured as her hands moved of their own accord, twining her fingers into the short, dark curls of his hair.

"So do I." His actions were not hurried this time, the urgent need of their first time giving way to a more relaxed exploration. "I'd still like you tied down, however."

His hands slid under her back, pulling her up toward him and Isabel wrapped her arms around his broad shoulders. The embers of their last lovemaking still glowed brightly and the interlude with the rubber bands served to fan them further.

"Then tie me down," she whispered in his ear.

Daniel looked at her, studying her face. Did she mean it?

With a lazy smile, Isabel returned his gaze. "Please?"

"And manners, too!" He grinned and couldn't resist those beautiful lips. He claimed a kiss, taking a small taste before crawling out of the bed. "Be right back."

He kept the clothesline they strung each week stored on the shelves beside the sink. Padding over to them, Daniel paused only to throw another log into the stove before returning, letting out the rope as he went. Quickly he found the center of the line and turned to Isabel.

"Will you let me bind you any way I please?" Might as well find out now. Then if she hated it, he had the rest of the winter to make up to her.

"What, spread-eagle isn't your first position of choice?" Even as she made fun, Isabel's stomach clenched at the sight of the rope. This was a game none of her lovers in the past had ever even suggested and she wasn't sure if she would like it or not. Although she had the occasional fantasy that involved her being unable to move, she knew full well that fantasy was often a far cry from reality. So far, Daniel had proven to be a skillful lover and she desperately wanted more. "You're not going to spread me on the bed and have your way with me?"

Daniel saw her slight hesitation and held out his hand to her. She put her smaller hand in his and he pulled her forward, helping her to stand beside the bed.

"Nope. I like to make things a little more interesting than the traditional maiden-in-distress pose." He draped the rope over her neck so that even lengths of it fell to either side of her. "Tell you what. You don't like something, or want me to stop immediately, call out 'red'. Just like the traffic light."

"All right, I suppose I can do that." She watched him finger the rope, pulling it a little and putting pressure on the back of her neck. It wasn't unpleasant, but made her realize who was in charge. Grinning, she held her chin high.

Taking one length of the rope, Daniel brought it down through the wonderfully tight cleavage of her breasts, looping around to bring it up along the other side. He let her breast bounce a moment, teasing her, then closed the loop and brought it around again, circling it in a light binding of rope.

"And if you only want to pause, just tell me 'yellow' and I'll know we need to talk about what I'm doing. Saying 'green', of course, gives me permission to continue."

Isabel found it hard to concentrate as he looped the rope a second time before tying it off. Still, she managed to squeak out a whispered, "Green," as Daniel paused to gauge her reactions.

Taking the other end of the rope and doing the same, Daniel noted how her breasts moved faster with her increased breathing. Her eyes followed every movement and he suspected if he touched her clit, she just might explode from the simple binding he had done. Hardly believing what he was seeing, he kept going.

For the first time in her life, Isabel took a slow, meandering saunter toward her orgasm instead of running toward it at full tilt. Daniel circled the ropes around to her back, tying them where she couldn't see. When he took her wrists and folded her arms behind her so that her hands grasped her elbows, she stood still, curiosity giving her patience she normally did not have. The rope slid along her arms as he bound them together and she smiled. Her pussy was soaking wet again. Each turn of the rope pushed her closer and closer to the edge. But she moved at his pace, not hers.

Daniel tied off the rope, being sure to use every inch available. Grabbing the back of the desk chair, he pulled it out and set it behind her. Lowering her onto the seat, he watched her face for any sign that he went too fast or in a direction she was not willing to go. But all he saw was a woman close to the edge. The sight made his cock twitch. He couldn't remember the last time he had come twice in one day. But seeing her sitting there, her eyes slightly out of focus as she tested her bindings, his cock hardened in anticipation.

Isabel wasn't paying attention to his cock. She was too intent on the myriad feelings flinging themselves against the ropes that held her. One part of her brain told her this was silly, she shouldn't be excited, she should be angry. Another part called her a lunatic for letting him tie her up without so much as a protest. The feminist side of her simply stared at the ropes, shocked and dismayed that years of struggle for equal rights should so easily be thrown aside.

And yet, all those voices dimmed as new ones took their places. Stronger voices that started with a whimper in her throat when she discovered she was caught fast. Her hands flopped uselessly, unable to reach the knots or move the ropes that dug into the skin of her arms. The whimper became a groan as her breasts jiggled against the loose loops that held them.

She wanted to come. She wanted to run full tilt to that edge and jump off the cliff. But with her hands bound, she could not reach around and touch herself. Frustration welled inside her and the growl turned again to a whimper of need.

"I can let you come, Isabel. If you want that, just say so. Or," Daniel paused and crossed his hands over his broad chest, "I can take you higher."

Isabel's face twisted in a grimace of indecision. Patience had never been one of her virtues. And yet, a higher cliff than the one she stood near now? Curiosity won out and she nodded. "I trust you, Daniel."

Her submission humbled him even as it empowered him. Going back to the shelf, he picked up another, shorter length of rope, hefting it in his hand as he returned. These were the only pieces he had available. There was the length that currently held some tools fastened to the shed outside, but Daniel decided what he had at hand was plenty for his purposes today.

Kneeling in front of her, Daniel ran the backs of his fingers over her tightly clenched legs. She had tucked her crossed ankles under the chair and he waited until she was able to relax a little before reaching under and pulling her right foot forward.

Isabel knew what was coming and almost pulled back. But with an intensity that surprised her, she wanted this. She wanted to let go completely and see where he took her.

Daniel looped the rope around her ankle, then tied it to the leg of the chair. When he had done the same to the other, he brought the extra rope up and forced her knees apart, tying them open. Now her sex was exposed to his gaze. Sitting on the bed, he leaned forward and pulled the chair around so he could indulge himself by examining her bound beauty.

Isabel's breath grew ragged. Embarrassment flushed her cheeks. Never had she been so open to a man's gaze. She squirmed a little, but a stern look from him stilled her. She couldn't move much anyway. The ropes around her legs held her open to his inspection and suddenly the vulnerability coupled with the lack of movement forced her arousal into high gear.

And he knew it. White cream oozed from her pussy to puddle on the twine seat of the chair. Isabel could hide nothing from Daniel and her moan filled the small cabin.

Daniel rubbed his hard cock as he watched the glistening puddle grow. He did not need to touch her now—she would come at a verbal command if he had played this right. She was so responsive that, with just a little urging, he knew he could bring her totally under his control. His cock throbbed painfully and he knew he had to do it now or he might not be able to hold back.

"Isabel, do you want to come?"

Daniel's voice, soft coolness in the fire that burned through her body, gave Isabel something to focus on other than the need that raged in every fiber of her body. "Yes," she managed to whisper.

"You cannot come unless I give you permission. Do you know that?"

"Yes." And she did. Her struggles had convinced her she could not climax by herself. She needed him to fulfill her.

Reaching forward, he slid a finger along her collarbone and down to her bound breast. Tweaking the nipple, he lingered there until her whimpers grew into cries of need. Sliding down, he paused at the mound of dark hair that signaled the entrance to her pussy.

And such a delightful pussy it was. The white juices begged him to taste and he scooped some on his finger, bringing it to his mouth. He waited until her eyes were fastened on him before tasting her. He dipped his finger for a second taste.

Isabel's head swam. No one had ever treated her in such a way. Never had she been tied to a chair like an object to be viewed and then touched as he saw fit. Her head fell back and she tried to bring her thoughts into focus.

But only one thought came to her mind. "Daniel, please. Please let me come!"

"You want to come now?"

"Yes! I cannot wait any longer. Please!"

He saw the tears in her eyes and took pity. "Come for me then, Isabel. Come hard." He thrust his finger into her pussy and felt the contractions take her as the sudden release racked her body.

She pulled against the ropes and bent toward the man who controlled her so thoroughly. Daniel's fingers were merciless, allowing her time to breathe only for a moment before sending the waves crashing over her again. She gave up and threw herself into his custody.

A jazz bassist slides his fingers along the smooth neck of his instrument, needing no frets to find the notes he wants. Plucking the vibrating strings, his heart soars at the improvised melody that sings into the night. Daniel's hands slid along the curves of her body, finding Isabel's notes and sending her music screaming through the cabin.

And when he had deemed he had played her enough, he gentled his fingers, slowing the melody as her body sobbed for breath against the ropes that bound her.

Isabel leaned back against the chair, whimpering as the remains of the greatest orgasm of her life continued to convulse her body with pleasure in slowing pulses until they finally stopped altogether. With an effort, she opened her eyes to try and focus on the man before her.

Daniel sat on the bed, leaning forward and watching her with great interest. Color rose into her cheeks as she realized he had witnessed her total lack of control. Smiling self-consciously, she ducked her head to let her hair hang in front of her face and cover her embarrassment.

Daniel reached forward and pushed her hair behind her ear before pulling her face back up. "You're incredible, you know that, don't you?"

A small frown of confusion furrowed her brow. "*I* am?"

"Definitely." His fingers lingered on her chin, letting his thumb run over the plump softness of her lower lip. He had plans for that lip later on. Right now he only wanted to bask in the power high she had given him.

Isabel's emotions were in a jumble. "I don't...I mean, I just sat here. You did all the work. All I did was come." The self-conscious smile came back. "A lot."

"That's what's incredible." Did she really not recognize how special she was? "Isabel, most women cannot come like you did."

"To be honest, Daniel, I've never come like that before either." She shook her head. "I think *you* were the incredible one."

He decided not to press the point. Very few women, in his experience, could give up control to the point where trust was totally given into another's hands. Literally. The rewards were terrific for both partners when it happened. The afterglow could last for hours.

Daniel saw her squirm in the ropes and stood, his semi-hard cock dangling only inches from her face. He saw her eyes avidly follow every movement he made. How could his male ego not respond?

Such a magnificent work of art, Isabel thought as his scent threw her tattered thoughts into disarray once more. She longed to taste him, to do for him what he had done for her. As she stared, the wrinkles of his cock slid into hard ridges as his arousal grew. So fascinated by the sight, she didn't feel the ropes digging into her arms as she leaned forward, mesmerized and wanting.

Who was he to deny her the pleasure she so obviously desired? Straddling the chair brought his cock level with her parted lips. He gathered her hair into his hand, watching as her tongue flicked out to take an experimental taste.

Isabel knew she wasn't very experienced in oral sex, but it had long been an avenue she wanted to explore. The somewhat salty taste that clung to him made her mouth water for more.

Tied as she was, however, that was difficult to get. She almost snarled in frustration as he pulled away from her.

Daniel shook his head to regain his focus. Having her tied and "forcing" her to come was one thing. Having her tied so she had no choice but to suck him was another. While it certainly was among his fantasies, Daniel wasn't ready to push his luck. He still wanted her speaking to him when all was said and done. If she wanted to give him a blowjob, then she would do it of her own free will. And in a much more provocative position.

"I want you kneeling before me," he explained as he quickly loosened the knots and helped her out of her bondage.

"Like a little slave girl?" Isabel's smile teased him.

"Just like a little slave girl." He grinned back at her, wondering if she understood just how close to the truth she had hit. Sitting on the edge of the bed, he leaned back on his hands and nodded to the space between his legs.

Isabel complied, trying and failing at adopting a humble demeanor. She was having far too much fun to be serious. Sliding sensuously to her knees, she made herself comfortable, grinning all the while.

But the sight of his cock, thicker than her forearm and rising before her face subdued her playful attitude. Intently, she examined every inch with her eyes, glorying in the straight, firm line that stretched from the magnificent mahogany sac to the rich, dark color of the cloven tip. She knew she had but to touch her tongue to that smooth surface and she would be rewarded with a salty drop of pre-cum.

But she was not a woman to hurry through a pleasant experience. Daniel had given her a gift of incredible proportions, she wanted to be sure he received equal value. Keeping her hands on her knees, she leaned in past his cock to place a tender kiss in the valley where his leg met his hip.

He groaned and she grinned. Perfect aim. Staying where she was, she teased him, flicking her tongue out to trail a thin line down along the valley and then pushing the top of her nose upward along the same track to dry the soft skin.

The heat of her breath was pleasant agony. As much as her teasing made him want to move, to take charge again and put her mouth around his cock, Daniel kept control and let her explore. Even when her lips caressed his balls, he didn't move. He watched her face, her eyes dreamy with desire that turned to dark mischief as she pulled the twin marbles into her mouth to roll them around on her tongue.

She liked the way his head fell back and the sound of the moan that came from the depths of his soul. So this was power. The same power she had let him have over her, he now gave to her. She was surprised at how humble it made her feel to know she had control of his orgasm.

A wicked grin slid up to her lips from the depths of her soul. Not one shred of doubt clouded her thoughts. With the gift he was giving her, she could move mountains. Still keeping her hands on her legs, she bent down again, this time teasing out one long lick from the base of his balls all the way to the tip of his cock.

"Oh God, Isabel, take me in your mouth and make me come."

Daniel's voice, shaky and rough, commanded her, but Isabel just grinned that evil grin and repeated the motion. This time, however, she wove her way to the top, sliding her tongue around his cock in a warm, wet caress. Deep moans punctuated by the writhing of his hips gave her great satisfaction. She knew where he wanted her to be, and deliberately took her time in getting there.

The sweet agony of her tongue inflamed Daniel's need. The little minx was having far too much fun tormenting him, he decided, when he caught a glimpse of the smile she made no attempt to hide. He recognized the look in her eyes— hadn't he had the same rush when he'd used her as the instrument he played to his satisfaction? And now her tongue had changed their positions. His groan became a growl as he felt the hot breath of her mouth hovering over the tip of his cock.

Making her mouth into a perfect "O", Isabel paused over his cock, fascinated by the noise he made. Taking pity on him, she closed her lips over the smooth tip, sliding her tongue into the cleft to scoop out the present that awaited her.

His hips thrust upward and momentarily sent her off balance. Dropping his cock from her mouth, she settled back on her heels until Daniel had calmed. He opened his eyes and looked at her, unfocused and in sensual pain.

"I want you to come, Daniel, but you have to let me do it."

"Then do it." His voice was barely a whisper squeezed out between gritted teeth.

Isabel knew her experience was limited in oral sex, but apparently Daniel enjoyed what she had done so far. Besides, she liked the little thrill of power that coursed through her at his words.

Once more she leaned forward to take him in her mouth, this time cupping his balls in the palm of one hand to gently squeeze them as her lips closed around the tip of his cock. Closing her other hand firmly around his incredible thickness, she set a slow rhythm.

Daniel floated in the fog, letting his mind wander along the paths her touch excited. A cliff face loomed before him and he flew along the base as her tempo maddened him. But when she quickened her pace, he soared quickly to the top edge. A woman stood there in a beautiful seafoam green gown, her arms outstretched to meet him. His heart leapt and he rushed forward to meet her as Isabel's tongue drove him to climax.

The last thing he remembered was the feel of the woman's soft arms around him, holding him close as the lights exploded behind his eyes and he came in Isabel's mouth. He felt her throat muscles contract around him, swallowing his gift and milking him dry. Then exhaustion claimed him and he fell back on the bed as Isabel licked him clean.

Chapter Nine

80

Daniel's first awareness was of a warm body curled up beside him in the bed. His second awareness was of the total contentment that seeped from every pore of his body. He shifted in the darkened cabin, throwing his arm over the warmth beside him and swore as his hand fell on a wet and furry snout.

Sasha simply nuzzled her master and put her head on her paws, promptly going back to sleep. Daniel sat up, peering into the darkness to find Isabel.

"I'm over here."

Her voice came from the direction of the stove. When she opened the iron door to throw another log in, her naked silhouette made him smile.

"What's Sasha doing in?"

"After I conked you out and got you under the covers, she started pawing at the door. I let her in and she went straight for the bed." Daniel heard her low chuckle. "I know better than to come between a man and his wolf...so I figured I'd best take the chair tonight."

Daniel reached over to run his hand over the wolf's head. When had she gotten so big?

"I'm surprised she came in. She hasn't slept with me since she was a pup. In fact, she doesn't like being indoors very much. I've been suspecting she's made a den around here somewhere."

"Well, it's started to snow again. Maybe we're in for another big storm and she wanted to be where she knew she'd get fed."

Daniel grinned. "Animal instinct, warning us of bad weather?"

Again the low chuckle carried softly across the room. "I'd trust her instincts over the weather forecaster any time."

Isabel shut the door to the stove and darkness filled the room again. He heard her settle into the chair and knew from experience she would be plenty warm enough with the extra blankets. But he wanted her beside him, to cuddle and touch.

"Isabel, come to bed with me. Sasha can sleep on the floor."

"Not on your life. She knew when I let her in where I'd been sleeping. She sniffed all over the room before choosing to settle there. I know when a woman is staking out a claim."

Daniel's hand still stroked the wolf's fur. Was Sasha being possessive? If so, he had some straightening out to do. But Isabel was probably right. The middle of the night was not the best time to do it. He stifled a yawn and fell back on the bed.

"I want to talk to you in the morning," he asserted even as he gave in to the two women that now seemed to rule his life.

"In the morning," Isabel managed around a yawn.

* * * * *

By the time the sky lightened, several inches of powdery new snow blanketed the ground and more fell every hour. Daniel eyed the pile of wood beside the stove and decided a few more hauls should give them enough to last a few days. Sasha followed him around as if she were a puppy again. Several times she got underfoot and he had to push the beast away. Finally the woodbox was filled to his satisfaction and he pulled the back door firmly shut.

"That's it. We're in now for a while."

Isabel snorted. "I've been in. Although I don't really mind it," she added when she saw his look of concern. "Really. No cabin fever yet." She muttered something under her breath as she turned away to finish the breakfast dishes, but Daniel couldn't make it out.

"What did you say?"

"Nothing."

"Yes, you did." He hated it when people mumbled and turned away. From his past experience of interviewing witnesses, he knew it was a truth they needed to utter, but didn't necessarily need anyone to hear. What was Isabel hiding? "I know you said something."

Her back still to him, and furiously drying the pan she'd just washed, she shrugged her shoulders and answered him. "I just said, 'unless you count the heat in here last night'."

He grinned. Now that was a truth worth hearing. She banged the pot as she put it away and Daniel decided that perhaps now was not the best time, however, to continue with this subject.

"What say we spend some more time on that basement?" Daniel eyed the trapdoor with some misgivings. How had so much junk managed to accumulate down there? Getting dusty and dirty in the basement was preferable to having her continue to make a ruckus with the dishes.

"Sounds good to me." Isabel finished the dishes and dried her hands. "I hesitate to bring this up, but your little shadow has been avoiding me."

"She hasn't growled at you or anything, has she?"

"No. Just ignored me."

"She's probably just hoping if she ignores you, you'll go away." Daniel sighed and rubbed the wolf's head between the ears. Sasha's tail beat a contented tattoo on the wooden floor.

Isabel studied the two of them. She smiled at the homey picture it made—a man and his dog. But the sight was bittersweet. The man wasn't her man and the dog was a wolf. "Only here, only now," she muttered under her breath, willing her heart to remain uninvolved. Daniel could take care of her libido, but her heart was locked away.

"Come on. Let's find some buried treasure today." Daniel pulled open the trapdoor and started down the rickety steps. Sasha remained in the cabin. When Isabel passed her, she held out her hand for the wolf to sniff, but Sasha made no move toward her. Instead she eyed Isabel with what she would swear was a weighing glance. Isabel dropped her hand and sighed.

"I promise you, Sasha. Soon as the snow stops and I can leave, I will. You have nothing to worry about. I promise."

For answer, the wolf just turned and curled up in front of the woodstove. Isabel descended the stairs, shaking her head.

The two of them fell into an easy camaraderie as they worked the better part of the morning, managing to clear a small chunk from the huge pile. Isabel kept finding intriguing new shapes that she could twist or tie or paint into being passable Christmas tree ornaments.

"You do realize Christmas is only three days away," Daniel reminded her as she set aside yet another bent spoon.

"I know. But Christmas is the first of the Twelve Days of Christmas, you know. So we can actually celebrate for another week and a half afterward."

Daniel eyed the small hoard she had stashed off to the side. "You're not going to give me twelve spoons all twisted, are you?"

Isabel laughed out loud. "Now that you mention it…"

He held up his hands in mock horror. "No, please…save me from dancing thingamabobs and twisted spoons!"

She couldn't hide her smile as she turned away to put the spoon under discussion with the rest of the pile. "No twisted spoons, I promise." But she said nothing of the present she already had ready to go under the tree after he fell asleep Christmas Eve.

As much as he enjoyed the banter, Daniel's gut kept pulling at him. He still found it hard to believe Isabel hadn't minded being tied up. But it was the woman from Isabel's dream that haunted him. He eyed Isabel as she straightened the pile of keepers. If he mentioned that woman in the green dress, she was going to think him a fool. But he really did need to talk about it.

"You know, we haven't talked about last night at all." He stretched as Isabel turned to face him, her cheeks blushing, but her voice firm.

"I'm not sure what there is to talk about. It was by far, the best orgasm I've ever had, bar none. And if I'm not mistaken, I did a pretty good job on yours as well…"

Daniel grinned. "Absolutely. But you're not going to get that kind of control very often."

Isabel paused, throwing him a puzzled glance as she bent down to pick up a broom handle with no straw attached. "Why not? I enjoyed it…you enjoyed it."

"Because you enjoyed sucking me off, I enjoyed it. You were having such a good time, I didn't want you to stop. And you have a very talented style, I might add."

"Thank you. But I still don't see why you don't want me to take charge like that every once in a while." Isabel paused to grin up at him. "The power trip was amazing."

"That's just it. The power trip *is* amazing…and not one I'm willing to share very often."

Daniel threw the challenge down, knowing if she couldn't agree to this, he couldn't push her. This was his deal breaker. Either she loved the power and needed it as much as he did, or it wasn't important to her and she would join him in the give and take of a power exchange. Anna hadn't seen that the power flowed both ways. She had only seen him as "an arrogant jerk", a "patronizing, pompous son of a bitch" and a few other choice words.

Isabel didn't answer him right away. Instead, she fussed with an old broom handle, twirling it in her fingers like a baton as she considered Daniel's preferences and he realized he wasn't going to get an answer right away. There was a certain faraway look her eyes got when she was thinking a problem through. He had seen it several times since he had taken her in. Turning back to the pile, he let her make up her mind as her fingers ran through drills learned a lifetime ago.

Isabel didn't even realize the intricate motions of her fingers. Her mind weighed the pros and cons of what Daniel wanted from her. Clearly this meant a lot to him. And it seemed more than just some stereotypical male need. There was something much deeper about his need to sexually dominate…something more primal than civilized. It wasn't like he was asking her to give up her coveted, hard-won independence. He was just asking her to let him control the way they had sex. Isabel realized her heart was pounding as she remembered the way he looked at her when she was bound—as if she was an artwork he could stare at all day long. As if she was nothing more than an object for his amusement.

The juices gushed between her legs and she dropped the broom handle as her fingers fumbled in the suddenness of her arousal. Taking slow, steady breaths, Isabel forced a smile, picked up the handle and leaned it against the wall as she watched Daniel emerge from the dark corner of the cellar where he had retreated when she'd obviously needed time to think things through.

The lantern threw long shadows into the dark corners of the room, but she could see his hair needed a trim and the red highlights shone in the soft light. His beard and mustache hid the sensuous lips that could bring her to her knees and Isabel knew her answer.

"So don't share it."

"What?"

"I don't need to have that power very often…just every once in a while." She reached over to take an oddly shaped piece of metal from him, since he seemed rooted to the spot. "I rather enjoyed being on the receiving end anyway. You do all the work and I reap all the benefits." She tossed the piece into the "get rid of" pile.

Daniel shook his head. "It really isn't that way, but…did I hear you right? You don't mind if I make all the decisions regarding our sex life?"

Isabel's eyes narrowed, but she made no attempt to hide their twinkle. "As long as one of your decisions is that we have sex every day, then I have no trouble accepting that."

Daniel stepped to her, taking her face in his hands as one would take a precious object and hold it close to examine it. "I do not understand what force brought you into my life, Isabel Ingandello, nor do I know how long you will be here, but while you are, I will make love to you every morning, every evening and every night!"

Pulling her into his arms, he kissed her soundly. Had Sasha's wild yapping at the top of the stairs not stopped him, he fully intended to take her up and into bed right there.

But the wolf's insistence would not be put off. Taking the lantern in one hand and enveloping Isabel's hand with the other, Daniel pulled her up the stairs.

"Sorry, Sasha, but you just need to learn how to share." Daniel dropped Isabel's hand and pushed the wolf toward the door. "Time for you to go outside, anyway."

The wolf paused at the open door and looked back at Isabel with what Isabel was sure was a wary eye, then bounded out into the falling snow.

"Still coming down fast out there, but not a lot of wind yet." Daniel shut the door firmly and eyed Isabel with a predatory look he had learned from the wolf. Several times during the morning he had glanced over at Isabel as she examined each piece he unearthed, weighing the possibilities of a new life for the old junk. And each time, he'd thought of a new way to tie her, a new wonderful torment for her body. And now that she had given him permission to lead? If he played his cards right and took things slowly, he could look forward to another three or four months of wonderful sex. He turned to his desk, intending to pull out the chair and tie her to it right now, but stopped when his grandfather's picture caught his eye. The haunting feeling came back. This time he could not ignore it. He tried to pass the feeling off as unimportant, even as he mentioned it to her.

"By the way, I meant to tell you...when I came last night, I had the strangest feeling."

Isabel grinned. "Good. Then I was doing it right."

Smirking in spite of his uneasy feeling, Daniel chuckled. "Don't get cocky, girl. You did all right."

"All right?" She turned to him, incredulity coloring her voice and making it rise several pitches. "As I recall, I did considerably more than 'all right'." Her grin broadened. "And I got some cock as well."

Daniel's laugh filled the cabin. "Okay, you win. You made me come harder than I have in a very long time...and you have a right to be proud of yourself." He eyed the picture again and hesitated.

His preoccupation got through to her and she realized something bothered him. A chill ran through her. "What is it? What did you feel?"

"That I wasn't alone."

She came to stand beside him. Together they stared at the picture on the shelf as the people in the picture stared back at them as if they looked at a mirror. Only the clothing was different. "He was with you."

Daniel nodded, then looked down at the woman at his side. "How did you know?"

"Because she was with me the first time I came yesterday."

"But not the second?"

Isabel grinned, but there was no mirth in her eyes. "But not the second. That one was only mine."

After a pause, Isabel looked up at the man beside her. "So do you believe me now? That in my dreams, I see her? Correction. In my dreams I *am* her."

Daniel's sigh was explosive and he ran his hand through his hair. "I don't know, Isabel. It all sounds so crazy. But I can't deny I saw her when I came last night. And I'm sure my grandfather was with me as I skimmed along the cliff face."

Isabel patted his arm, as there seemed to be nothing else to say. There was no logical explanation except mass hysteria, and while she wasn't ruling it out, it also seemed pretty farfetched. "Time will show us, Daniel. And that's one thing we have plenty of right now. Time."

The wistfulness in her voice brought Daniel back to the present. He turned, taking her in his arms. "I'm sorry you're stuck here, Isabel. I know you didn't really want this."

"I'm getting used to the idea. And to be honest…" Her voice trailed off as she looked into his dark eyes. How could she tell him she was having trouble with "Only here. Only now"? She had no idea what the future held. For either of them. She had no right to be falling in love with him.

"To be honest…" he prompted when she didn't continue.

"I'm not having such a bad time of it." She smiled and shrugged her shoulders as she stood on her tiptoes to buss his lips with a quick kiss before turning toward the kitchen part of the cabin to start making lunch.

Daniel watched her, wondering what she left unsaid.

Time. Everything would come out in time.

* * * * *

Christmas morning Isabel woke to feel Daniel's arm thrown over her waist, the weight of it spreading a comfortable feeling from her toes to her heart. She opened her eyes to find him still sleeping, his hair tousled, his face half squished…and beautiful. His beard, a bit straggly, was untidy and a small snore came from his parted lips. Wiggling even closer, she brushed his lips with hers and whispered, "Merry Christmas!"

He had been drifting through a cloud of white snow, the sleigh skimming over the drifts with a graceful ease as the team of horses pulled them along. The touch of her lips on his felt as warm as the sun that came out from behind the clouds to dazzle his eyes with a million sparkles. And then the warmth slid down to his stomach as she kissed him again.

The snow faded, replaced by a warm angel in the bed beside him.

"Merry Christmas," he managed when his eyes would focus. Her hair, mussed from sleeping, fell around her shoulders in disordered curls that bounced on the pillow like so many loose springs. Somewhere she had stopped trying to keep it straight, more and more allowing it to shape into the natural curls she had been given. Daniel smiled. He liked her hair much better this way.

Her eyes twinkled as she threw the covers back and bounced out of the bed. "Come on...we have to see if Santa came!"

Sunlight glittered off the myriad ornaments Isabel had made and hung on the tree. From her early attempts with springs and vacuum tubes to her latest creations involving bent spoons and ribbon made of paper, the homemade tree was the most beautiful Christmas tree Daniel had ever seen. And underneath, two presents lay side by side. Isabel stood, stunned.

"He did come! Look, Daniel...there's a present for me!"

Daniel laughed and pulled on a pair of sweatpants. "Isabel, my dear, get dressed and then you can open it."

So excited about it being Christmas morning, Isabel hadn't even realized she had bounded out of bed with nothing on. "Guess I'm a little excited." She ducked her head and grabbed for the oversized gray sweatshirt. In her sheepish grin, Daniel glimpsed the little girl who must've been the first one up on Christmas morning when she was younger.

Settled on her knees before the presents, Isabel gestured to Daniel to come join her. He threw a few logs onto the fire and put the water on first, however, thoroughly enjoying himself as he made her wait a few more minutes. He moved purposely slowly, his movements exaggerated and teasing.

Although her eyes flashed with impatience, Isabel sat quietly, as she had so many Christmas mornings as a child. Being an "only" meant waiting for her parents to finish their interminable morning routines before they would all sit down and open presents.

Finally Daniel stretched out beside her and she picked up the smaller of the two packages. She held it out to him. "You first."

He eyed the present, wrapped in old newspaper and tied with pieces of twine. Hefting the box to see if it made noise, he held it to his ear as he gently shook it. Isabel grinned and bounced, waiting for him to see what she had been working on in secret.

Untying the twine, he took his time unfolding the newspaper to reveal a box advertising cans of black olives. He raised an eyebrow at her as he set the wrapping aside.

"Hey, you don't exactly have a lot of gift boxes around here, you know. One must make do. I had to squish it some to get it in there, but I managed."

Opening the flaps, he peeked inside. Something dark green, soft to the touch...he pulled it out and a long scarf unfolded from his fingers.

"I made it from the sweatpants I took down," Isabel explained. "With this pair," she gestured to the pair that still lay where she had put them last night over the foot of the bed, "I just took tucks in them and haven't been able to get them comfortable. So with the other pair," she gestured to the scarf, "I cut away the extra fabric. I noticed you don't have a scarf when you go outside and when you come in, your beard is always frosty, so I decided to make you one!"

"It's wonderful." He wrapped it right around his neck to see how far it would go. There was plenty of material sewn end-to-end to make it long enough to circle his neck twice.

The stitching was close and neat on the hems. "It must've taken you hours to make this by hand."

"It did." She looked smug. "But I had hours to spend on it. I'm glad you like it."

Her look had turned a bit shy and Daniel leaned over to bring her chin up and kiss those beautiful lips. A scarf had been one of the things he had intended to purchase when he took her down the mountain. Actually, he had intended to go down the mountain much earlier, but her arrival had forced him to put it off. The snowstorm had made all those plans moot, however, and he had decided he'd just have to do without one.

"Here, your turn now." He pulled the other present over to her.

"It's heavy." She lifted it onto her lap, but the box was too large to lift and shake beside her ear. Like hers, it was covered in newspaper, but Daniel had fastened it with a long silk ribbon he had found in the basement and brought upstairs, snuck into the laundry to clean and then dried behind the stove so she wouldn't see it. The bright red of the ribbon had faded to a softer, deeper shade that would look beautiful twined in her dark hair.

Smiling, Isabel carefully untied the ribbon, pulling it off and draping it around her shoulders. The soft silk brushed against her cheek and she paused, rubbing it over her skin. "Mmm…thank you. I think I know how girls felt in the olden days, buying a ribbon at the fair."

"I will buy you a dozen ribbons when spring comes." Daniel pulled the ribbon off her shoulders and motioned for her to turn. Gathering her heavy tresses in his hands, he separated them and wove the ribbon in and around to form a beautiful braid.

"They won't mean as much to me as this one does." His fingers wove magic in her hair as he tied off the braid at the end with the remaining ribbon. "This one is special."

He kissed the hollow of her neck at the sweep of her shoulder, filing away for future reference the shiver she gave him in response. This was a spot he would taste again. But right now, he wanted her to open her present.

Unfolding the paper revealed a liquor bottle box. At her raised eyebrow, he explained. "Hey, I had to get moving boxes from somewhere!"

She grinned and opened the box. Inside, nested among crumpled newspapers, lay an old pair of mismatched men's boots. Puzzled, she pulled them out, setting the box to the side.

Daniel grinned at his own cleverness. "You've been stuck inside this house for, what is it? Six...seven weeks?"

"One day shy of eight weeks."

He shook his head. "You make my case for me. Being cooped up that long would drive me crazy. But you haven't said a word."

"Complaining about what one can't change is only a waste of energy." She continued to eye the boots, trying to figure out where he was going with this.

"Except I see you staring out the window sometimes, looking at the trees. Especially when the sun is out and it isn't too cold."

The guilty look she gave him confirmed he was on the right track. He continued.

"And I know you love going to the bathroom in that pail almost as much as I love emptying it every day."

She snorted and he pointed to the boots.

"I'm on my third pair of boots this year." He gestured to the pair that currently sat beside the back door. "Brought an old pair from home that were pretty much on their last legs when I moved out here, then wore out the next pair what with all the hauling and climbing onto the roof and all." He chuckled. "Taught me not to buy cheap boots. As each pair wore out, I threw them into the junk pile in the basement, figuring I'd deal with them later. I found them when I was down there looking for something else and thought of you. So I hid them, and made plans."

"You still have the mates? There was a garden tour I took once and a woman had put hens and chickens in an old boot. The babies had all spilled over the sides and it looked really picturesque. We could recycle the other boots as planters this spring."

The implication hung heavy in the room and Isabel shook her head. "But I'm not going to be here in the spring. I'm going home." Her voice, sterner than she'd intended, sounded determined and almost rude.

Daniel put his hand over hers, squeezing to let her know he understood her conflicting emotions. When he first came out here last spring, he hadn't intended to make this his permanent home. His body had needed the hard physical labor he had poured into the restoration just as his soul needed the retreat. But the more time he spent here with her, the more he thought of this as home.

"So, anyway..." He deliberately broke the tension by continuing his explanation. "I chose two boots that weren't as badly worn as the others, cleaned them up, aired them out and then lined them to make the insides smaller. You'll have to try them on and let me know if I need more stuffing...or less. I'm afraid I was just guessing at it."

"Really? They'll fit me?" Incredulous, Isabel stuck out her foot and pulled on a boot. The laces were tight, however, and she quickly loosened them so her foot could slide in.

"They're wonderful!" She danced around the room, clumping and clodding as she adjusted to their size.

"How are the insides?"

"The right one is perfect, the left one is a bit tight, believe it or not."

"Take it off and I can fix it right here."

"Not on your life! I'm headed out to use the pit you call an outhouse!"

She was three steps outside the door when she realized she had no pants on. The cold air hit her legs and she yelped, then grinned. Being outside and semi-nude heated her in a way she hadn't ever imagined. A shoveled path showed her where she needed to go and she took care of matters quickly. But big flakes drifted down like lazy feathers and she hesitated before going back in. Closing her eyes, she breathed in deeply, feeling the cold air sink into her lungs, cleansing and refreshing her spirit.

A cloud of vapor hung before her as she let the air out again. The sun peeked from behind the thin layer of clouds and light caressed her upturned face.

From the doorway, Daniel watched the beautiful woman he had become accustomed to, transform into an incredible, vibrant, sexy, earth goddess. She spread her arms and twirled, welcoming the air, the forest, the sun, glorying in their presence. He could almost see her spirit grow, expanding to encompass the entire area. And then a cold fist grabbed his stomach and clenched hard.

Behind Isabel, in the clear light of day, stood a woman wearing a seafoam green dress.

Chapter Ten

જી

"Isabel, turn around."

Daniel's whispered command caught Isabel's attention. Still wrapped up in the sheer joy of being outdoors, she turned slowly to face the phantom from her dreams. Far from being afraid, she felt relief that the woman had finally decided to appear.

But the woman did not notice her. Her attention totally focused on Daniel.

"Speak to her, Daniel. Say something." Isabel called softly.

"What do I say?" He felt the anguish in the phantom's gaze even over the distance that separated them. Spreading his hands in a helpless gesture he looked to Isabel for suggestions.

"Anything! Ask her name, find out who she is."

Daniel cleared his throat twice before calling out loudly. "Who are you? What do you want?"

Isabel winced at the harshness of the words, and yet they did not seem to bother the woman. She smiled at Daniel with the fond smile one reserves for children or pets. As if she noticed Isabel for the first time, she stepped in, raising her ungloved hand to brush against Isabel's cheek.

Unafraid of this woman who haunted her dreams, Isabel simply smiled back, a tacit understanding passing between them that needed no words. Isabel knew what the woman wanted, and who she was.

The woman inclined her head toward Daniel and Isabel nodded. Turning, Isabel closed the short distance to Daniel, sliding her cold fingers into his warm hand. A small grimace passed over the face of the phantom, as if recalling a painful memory, lasting only a moment before changing again to a more benign and beautiful visage. They watched as she turned away from them and stepped toward the trees. Later, neither one of them could say the exact moment she disappeared, only that she had.

Daniel's breath came out in a rush. "What the hell was that all about?"

"Inside, Daniel. I'm getting very cold."

"Sorry. That's what you get for not wearing pants out here in the snow." He teased to cover up the uneasiness he felt. But he didn't say another word until they were both inside and Isabel was snuggled under a blanket in the big chair with a cup of hot cocoa to warm her fingers.

"Had you asked me a week ago...heck! If you'd asked me an hour ago whether I believe in ghosts or not, I'd have answered with a smart-aleck comment and changed the subject." He sat down heavily on the stool before her, his hands also holding a cup of hot chocolate while his mind whirled. "But I saw her and so did you. And she..." his mind struggled with where she had gone, but decided the English language just didn't have the words for what she'd done, "disappeared. She just disappeared."

"Not exactly disappeared, more like faded away. Quickly."

"What did she want?" He ran his hand through his hair, trying to put the puzzle together. But somehow he knew they didn't have all the pieces yet, not by a long shot.

"To see you."

Daniel's head popped up and he stared at Isabel. "*What*?"

"Well, she really wanted to see your great-grandfather. But since he's not here, she contented herself with looking at you."

"Why?" Then realizing his question made no sense, he amended it. "I mean, why did she want to see my great-grandfather? I'm sure that wasn't my great-grandmother. I just know it."

"No, she's not your great-grandmother. I even looked at her hands. No rings of any sort."

"I don't know that that matters. But I feel it in my gut...she is no relation to me."

"But she is to me."

Again, Daniel looked up in shock.

Isabel leaned forward and set her empty cocoa cup on the edge of the nearest bench. Getting her thoughts together, she leaned back and pulled the covers closer.

"I never knew my great-grandmother from Italy. As far as I know, she never came to America. Not even to visit after her son emigrated. But her sister did. She came over, oh, I don't know. Sometime in the Twenties, I think. She was an old lady when I was born. Sat in a corner in a dark print dress and wore heavy shoes. Smelled of peppermint. But she had some great stories. I used to climb into her lap and listen to her talk about the old country in her fractured English."

Isabel smiled, remembering the times she had been scolded. "Now don't you tire out Aunt Maria. She doesn't want you running around and upsetting her." It hadn't taken Isabel long to know who was truly being upset by Isabel's more rambunctious behavior...and it wasn't her great-aunt.

"She told me a story several times. Always the same story, although sometimes she would embellish one part and the next time she'd tell it, she'd dress up a different part. But I heard it so often, I remembered it. Although I haven't thought of it in years." Her glance fell on the picture on the shelf above the desk and she pointed to it. Daniel stood and brought it over to her.

Taking it, she ran her finger over the woman seated on the chair. She wore the same dress in the picture that she did in Isabel's dream and that she had worn today. Was it only her mind playing tricks? Putting her into one dress because their minds had pulled that information from this photo?

When she didn't go on right away, Daniel prompted her. "Well? What was the story?" He settled onto the stool again, pulling it up close to her and running his hand over her arm where it rested on the chair.

She handed him the photo and leaned her head back. "My great-grandmother was fairly headstrong, according to her sister, her younger sister. She said she remembered how often her parents would yell and scream and tear their hair out over her because she had a tendency to slip away from her chaperones and go walking unattended. Apparently that just wasn't done."

"Don't think it was, especially among the more well-to-do families. Their daughters were precious commodities, remember, to be sold to the highest bidder." Daniel's tone was matter-of-fact.

"According to my aunt, my great-grandmother was involved in some scandal regarding a man she had met on one of her walks. Aunt Maria always told it to me as a cautionary tale to be a good girl and do what my parents told me to do. I remember questioning her one time toward the end of her life about the story. I asked her what was so bad about wanting to marry a man of her own choosing. I remember how she looked around to make sure no one was listening and leaned in close to whisper in my ear. She told me, 'The man was a foreigner!'"

Daniel frowned. "That was it? Don't marry a foreigner?"

"Don't you see?" Isabel sat up, her heart sure that her conclusions were right. "My great-grandmother created a scandal because she fell in love with a foreigner. Worse, she wanted to marry him. Back then, in Italy, if you were a good girl, you married the nice Italian man your parents picked out for you. Can't you see it? The arguments my great-aunt remembered? I'm sure they were all over this man."

"Isabel, I'm still not putting it together."

"Daniel, the man my great-grandmother fell in love with was your great-grandfather!"

"But my great-grandfather married a nice Irish girl. They emigrated to the States when they were in their thirties and had a family. Somewhere in there they built this cabin. Your ancestor did not marry mine."

"That's the point. Her parents won." Isabel slapped her hands on her lap. "It all makes sense! Why didn't I think of this before? Until I saw her today, I hadn't remembered my aunt's story. As soon as I looked at her, I knew." She shook her head when Daniel started to interrupt. "No, I'm sure of it. My great-grandmother fell in love with your great-grandfather. They tried to get permission to marry, but her parents wouldn't allow it. He left, went back to Ireland and married his own kind, just as she did. But they were still very much in love."

Daniel shook his head. "Call me the skeptic, but it seems to me to be pretty thin evidence. How do you know they were still in love?"

"Because of the dreams. Remember? Every time I hear his voice calling her. 'Come to me, Isabella.'"

"But my great-grandmother's name was Isabella. Not yours."

"My aunt always referred to my great-grandmother as "*Bella*". Since my grandmother called me '*cara bella*' — that means 'beautiful girl' — I thought it was just an endearment."

She leaned forward. "But what if it wasn't? What if Bella is short for *Isa*bella?" She grinned and leaned back in the chair. "Wouldn't that be a kick. He goes back to Ireland and finds a girl with the same name to marry."

"Like I said, the evidence is way too thin to present in court."

"All right, councilor. But I'll get my evidence, don't you worry."

Daniel stood, surveying the newspaper wrapping that still littered the floor. "I'm all for chalking up the woman in the woods as a Christmas figment of my imagination and having some Christmas breakfast that I can touch. What about you?"

Isabel held out her hand and he pulled her up, gathering her into his arms. "Give me a real, flesh and blood woman in my arms every time," he murmured, bending down to kiss her. Her lips tasted of chocolate and he lingered, but the events of the morning intruded on his thoughts and he let her go with a playful swat on the rear.

"Come on, let's make one hell of a Christmas breakfast."

Isabel watched him saunter off and smiled. If his great-grandfather had the same wonderful ass as Daniel did, it was no wonder her ancestor had fallen in love.

* * * * *

Daniel made love to Isabel again that night. In fact, he intended to make love to her every chance she gave him. All right, so his winter wasn't the enforced solitude and soul-searching he'd expected. With Isabel in his arms, he didn't mind putting off the decisions he knew he had to make.

"Take off those clothes before I blow out the light tonight." Daniel stood beside the table and laughed when

Isabel turned toward him, brashly singing an old striptease melody.

"Bah dum, pa, da." She bumped her hip to the right and she locked her eyes on his.

"Bah dum, da dum." Her hip swung to the left as a mischievous twinkle sparkled in her eyes.

"Bah da, da, da, Bah dum, dum, dum." Thrusting her shoulders forward on each of the last three beats, she shimmied for him, the toss of her breasts lost in the oversized sweatshirt. She looked down and slid her arms out of the sleeves on the next line of the melody and pulled it up and off on the last line.

"Bampa-dampa, bampa-dampa,

Badda-ta badda-ta bump da dum."

She circled the shirt over her head and repeated the last line before dropping the act and the shirt. Daniel applauded and whistled.

"More, more! All the way!"

Grinning, Isabel started the melody again, this time turning her back to him and slowly pushing down her pants, kicking them off at the end, bending over and wiggling her ass in his general direction.

Daniel's wolf whistle and applause lasted only long enough for him to cross the small space and scoop her into his arms.

"I like the slut in you." His hands slid down to cup her ass cheeks and pull her toward him, claiming her as his.

Isabel's cheeks grew red. "I have no idea what made me do that."

"I do." He pulled her up onto her toes, rewarded by her gasp. Her eyes widened at his possessive touch. "Here you have no reputation to worry about, no prying eyes to judge you. You've accepted that you can't run away from me, so the real you is coming to the surface."

Irritation flashed in her eyes as she struggled to lean back and look into his eyes. Daniel relaxed his hold on her, but didn't let her go.

"Are you saying that the real me is a slut?"

"Yes."

When she struggled, Daniel tightened his grip again.

"I'm not a slut, I'm a...let me go."

"I'm not going to let you go...and being called a slut is a compliment."

She suddenly stopped moving and stared at him as if he'd lost his mind. "What are you talking about?"

"Only sluts are secure in their sexuality. You are a sexy woman, Isabel. You know that. Well, part of you knows that. But you've been so conditioned by a society that denigrates a sexual woman that you've buried that part of you. Here, society doesn't exist. Only I do."

Isabel's voice wasn't above a whisper. "Only here. Only now."

Daniel nodded. "Exactly. So go ahead and explore that side of you. You're safe from prying eyes...and I like to see your sexiness."

A wry grin slowly spread across her face. "I bet you do."

He tightened his grip on her ass cheeks, spreading them slightly as he did so.

"Will you let me play with you tonight?"

She didn't trust her voice, but nodded instead, knowing the ecstasy he had given her before was a state she wanted to experience again and again.

"And you'll let me tie you up?"

"Yes." Her voice was stronger this time. "Please."

He let her go, moving abruptly away from her. "Stay there and close your eyes."

Isabel did as he told her, wondering what nefarious plan he had up his sleeve. Last time he bound her to the chair and played with her emotions as well as her body to create an incredible climax. What did he have in mind this time? She heard him rummaging around the cabin, but kept her eyes closed as she considered his words. What he said was true to a point, she decided. She did feel freer here than she did in the city. But was it because she had no reputation to worry about as he said? Or because she felt safe here with him? Or was it because she was falling in love...

Before she could deal with that thought, he was back, his hands on her shoulders, turning her to face the bed.

"May I open my eyes?"

"Yes, I'm going to bind your arms and hands so they won't get in the way later on. And I want you to remember the traffic signals. I intend to get more intense tonight. If I go too far, you tell me."

"More intense than last time?" She laughed. "I'm not sure how that's possible, but I'll remember."

Daniel placed her hands behind her back and tied them palm-to-palm. Throwing the rest of the length of rope over one of the cabin's beams, he gently pulled it taut, forcing her to bend at the waist as he pulled her bound hands up behind her.

"Spread your legs. You'll find it easier to keep your balance."

Isabel rocked from side to side, opening her pussy to him.

His fingers pulled at her nipples, tweaking them and making then hard. Gasping, she whispered "green" when he paused.

Daniel ran his hands over the ropes, checking to see that he hadn't tied them too tight. The warmth in her fingers reassured him. He let his fingers saunter down her arms toward her shoulders, smiling at the shiver his touch caused.

Satisfied, his movements became bolder, running his palm down to her hip and back to squeeze her ass. He listened as her breath quickened and a low growl escaped his throat. Pinching her nipples several times, he listened to the wonderful moans she made. And when he knew she was ready, he showed her the clothespin.

Pinching a small amount of her breast together, Daniel placed the first pin.

"Ouch! That..." Before she could complete her sentence, a new feeling surged through her and she stopped in surprise. How was it possible that her arousal should grow so strongly just because of a little pinch on her breast? She looked down and saw the ends of the wooden clothespin waggling in the air. Wiggling, however, produced new waves of pain.

"The more you move, the more it hurts." Daniel's voice floated down to her from somewhere up above her head. Knowing he watched her reactions so closely caused more cream to form in her already soaking pussy. Taking a deep breath, she calmed herself and forced her arousal to a manageable level. Her voice no more than a whisper, she gave him permission to continue. "Green."

Daniel now circled her breast with the pins, pinching the skin together then letting the pin do the work. Her moans had begun again, this time stronger. He shifted and created another sunburst of clothespins around her other breast, pushing her limits.

But she did not tell him to stop. And when both breasts were completely encircled, he went for the bull's-eye—a single pin right on her nipple.

Isabel's intake of breath was sudden, her eyes closed and remained that way. Holding her still with one arm, Daniel caught the other nipple between the two wooden slats of the pin and watched her reaction.

Pain rushed through her, making her cry out. The word "red" was on her lips, her indrawn breath forming the word to shout at him, when the pain eased into something...different. Her nipple throbbed with the beat of her heart and each pulse raced downward to the core of her being. A new sensation awakened in her and responded. When he pulled the other nipple between his fingers, once again she whispered "green".

Isabel felt like lights should be exploding somewhere. The pressure on her nipples was intense and when Daniel's fingers brushed against the pins, she thought she might cry. But she didn't want him to stop. Her pussy dripped with the proof of her arousal. Even when he let go and stepped back and her body bowed with the throbbing, she didn't plead with him. Instead, she gloried in the pain that quickly became pleasure.

But he had more torment in store for her. One by one, Daniel flicked the pins, and her face contorted as the pain increased her need.

"Oh my God, Daniel, please let me come." She closed her legs in an attempt to get the pressure she needed on her clit. Opening her eyes, she stared blindly at the floor, her breath ragged and uneven.

"Spread those legs for me, Isabel. You may not come yet."

With an anguished cry, she spread her legs even as one part of her mind tried to rebel. Damn it! She wanted to come now! Why the hell was she waiting for his permission?

Even as her wiggling waved the clothespins in the air and produced a fresh set of painful tingles, she knew the answer. She waited because he had proven that he could make it worth the wait. The last set of orgasms she'd had at his hand had been nothing short of incredible. Isabel decided to trust that what he had in store for her would provide more of the same.

Daniel moved behind her now, letting her breasts in their cages of clothespins alone for the time being. His hand caressed her ass, those twin hills perfect in their symmetry. Taking his time, he explored every inch with his fingers, from the skin stretched over her buttocks to the valley hidden between them. And when he was ready, he slapped her ass hard enough to leave a pink handprint on that beautiful white skin.

Isabel jumped. The ropes pulled on her arms and the clothespins pulled on her breasts. Daniel's hands on her hips prevented her from going far, but even the smallest movement caused her pussy to gush.

"What's this?" Daniel caught a drip of her white cream on his finger. "Looks like someone is enjoying this." He brought his finger around to show her, but her hair was in her face. Grabbing a fistful of it, he raised her head and showed her the evidence he had found.

"Do you like the taste of your own cum, Isabel?"

When she only groaned in answer, Daniel brought his finger closer. "I need a better answer than that. Taste yourself."

He put his finger in reach of her mouth, his cock hardening when she snaked her tongue out and licked it clean.

Isabel licked her lips when he removed his finger. "A bit salty."

Although her voice was raspy, the look in her eyes was a mixture of dark passion and total, sensual enjoyment. Without letting go of her hair, Daniel circled around behind her again, unzipping his jeans and releasing his cock as he did so.

But he didn't want to take her just yet. The torment in his own body mirrored the need evident in hers. His cock, huge and dark with blood, ached to sink into the depths of her wet pussy, but he held off. He wasn't quite done tormenting her.

Slapping her ass again, he watched the way her breasts jiggled in their clothespin sunbursts. But this time he didn't stop after a single spank. Raining a tattoo of slaps across her bare ass, he watched as her body began a dance under his hand.

Staying still was impossible. Even though each movement pulled at the pins on her breast, her body still strained to get away from the spanking he delivered. Her wordless cries filled the air as he played with her body, turning the skin on her ass a uniform pink all over her cheeks. He spanked her until his palm stung and the ache in his cock became unbearable. Taking hold of her hips with both hands, he poised himself at the entrance to her pussy and paused only long enough to claim her.

"You are mine, Isabel. You belong to me."

He thrust his cock into her hot and aching pussy in one quick lunge from behind. Her body didn't protest, but responded, pressing back to open for him, welcome him, embrace him.

His thrusts were hard, possessive, demanding her total submission to him. The first wave of her orgasm tightened her pussy around his cock and he almost came, managing to hold off his own pleasure only through a tremendous strength of will.

Feeling the contractions begin to subside, he leaned forward and unclasped a pin from her breast. She whimpered and he removed another, then more in quick succession.

Her pussy contracted again as she came a second time, her body's dance completely at his command. Again he held off coming, reveling in the power he had over her. His thick cock plundered her pussy without mercy until her dance slowed once more.

This time when he leaned forward, he removed all the pins quickly, except for the two still on her nipples. She was nothing but an animal now, the needs of her body ruling supreme. A feral growl came from the depths of her being as she came a third time, rutting against him without regard to dignity or pride.

He knew she was almost spent. But he had one more torment for her, one she could not avoid. At the very moment her body began to slow, he pulled on her clothespinned nipples, drawing them painfully taut. He increased his rhythm and thrust deep and hard as he gave himself permission to lose control. And just before he came, he unclasped the pins, letting the blood flow back into her nipples in a sexually painful spasm that created the largest and longest orgasm he had ever witnessed a woman experience.

Wave after wave of power surged through him. There was nothing to do but let the storm take him where it willed. He rose to the crest and crashed, rose and crashed and time had no meaning. Isabel became a part of him, their voices blended and became one melody. They sang and their music was of the heavens.

And when the waves lessened, Daniel stood, spent and exhausted behind her, barely able to remain upright. From some final reservoir of strength, he managed to untie his willing partner and carry her gently to bed. The last thing he remembered was her lips over his in a tender kiss.

Chapter Eleven

ဢ

Isabel woke still cuddled in Daniel's arms. Sunlight streamed through the windows, reflecting brightly off the pure whiteness of the snow. Running a light touch over her breasts, she was surprised to discover little residual soreness. Her nipples were tender, but that wasn't such a bad thing, since such a light touch aroused a very pleasant ripple of desire.

But it was a ripple of afterglow, not of need, she realized. For the first time in her life she felt sated. The sex of her youth had been hot and quick and, like a Chinese meal, satisfied her for a short time, but left her hungry for more an hour later.

Sex with Daniel was not of that sort at all. More like a seven course meal that would last her an entire day. Much more filling...and much more satisfying. There was something about this bondage stuff that definitely appealed to her.

Shifting in the bed, she propped herself up on one arm so she could watch her sleeping lover. His hair was untidy in sleep, the russet locks turning every which way. Resisting the urge to run her fingers through them, she memorized every feature of his face. In sleep, his eyes seemed more deep-set than they really were, but no lines of tension showed around them. She'd seen those lines a few times since she had come here as he chased his demons and battled them. Peaceful now, his face showed he slept in contentment.

Isabel grinned and stretched, careful not to disturb him. Taking her time, she left the bed, climbing out the bottom, and threw on her sweatshirt and boots, grinning as she did so. Sliding quietly out the door, she stepped into a world of white.

"It's really saying something, Isabel-girl, when going outside to take a leak can make you so happy." She laughed into the sunlight and practically skipped to Daniel's outhouse area. New snow had fallen, but the depression was still evident and Isabel colored the snow, thrilled with her freedom.

When she finished, Isabel lingered outside, half-expecting another visit from her great-grandmother. A hawk screamed overhead, a few hardy birds twittered in the trees and if she listened very hard, she could hear the bubble of the small stream that ran not far from the house. But her ancestor did not appear.

"There you are."

Daniel's frame filled the doorway to the cabin. Funny how she'd never noticed that before. His head came almost to the lintel and his broad shoulders were only inches away from the sides. And this gorgeous hunk of mountain man, with his incredibly sexy beard and marvelous command of her body, had taken her places last night she had never even dreamed of.

Isabel skipped over to him and bussed his lips with a kiss.

"Morning, big boy. Want some breakfast?"

Daniel caught the teasing minx in his arms and gave her a proper kiss. His hand rested on her ass cheek and he gave it a playful squeeze before he let her go.

"I could eat. You cookin'?"

"I'm always cookin'."

"Mmm…that you are. Any soreness today?"

Isabel shook her head.

"Lift your shirt."

Amused, she lifted her shirt, exposing her breasts to the bright sunshine. Daniel bent down and examined them, checking for marks.

"You have one small bruise right here." He pressed gently on the outside area of her left breast. "I'm sorry." Bending down, he kissed the tiny mark.

Isabel smiled. "Your kiss makes it all better." She shivered.

"Now, get inside and cook my breakfast, woman." He shifted in the doorway to let her through.

Isabel stuck her tongue out at him and pranced into the house. Daniel watched her go, his emotions roiling.

Walking out to the privy, he tried to understand exactly what he wanted in his life. He'd come here partly to get away from a woman who didn't understand him, and partly to deal with a whole lot of guilt for getting off a criminal who then went on to murder. The guilt he still dealt with. The woman...Daniel paused as he realized he hadn't thought about Anna in several days. In so many ways, Isabel seemed perfect for him.

He stopped that train of thought right there. She wasn't perfect for him. In a few short months, she would go back to the life she knew and he would have made the decisions he came up here to make. Their relationship was temporary, no matter how great the sex.

Making his way back to the cabin, he took a moment to look around. Satisfied that all was well and no ghosts lurked in the underbrush, he went to help Isabel with breakfast.

* * * * *

The phantom did not reappear, though Daniel looked for her every time he needed to be outdoors. As the beginning of the year approached, however, he relaxed, almost convincing himself it had been a dream.

He and Isabel made love often, although he did not attempt to reach the heights they had reached Christmas night. Leaving the ropes in the cupboard for the time being, he kissed her tenderly and took her gently, as if to make up for the rough way he'd used her.

The two of them made a great deal of headway on the pile of junk, and pulled some of the "get rid of" pile outside in order to make room in the basement. His remake of his old boots had proven to be a big hit with Isabel and she wore them every chance she got. The weather turned milder and she borrowed layer upon layer of Daniel's clothing to keep her warm enough to spend quite some time in the fresh air. Her cheeks took on a healthy glow he hadn't realized was missing.

New Year's Eve day dawned positively balmy with a thaw definitely in progress. Small streams of melting snow ran steadily from the rooftop to dig deep holes in the snow drifted against the cabin. The stream that ran nearby swelled and gurgled so loudly they could hear it inside the cabin with the door shut.

Daniel carried a load of wood in and dropped the logs into the woodbin he'd made, feeling very satisfied and contented. So far this winter he had finished several of the projects he had set for himself, cleaned out almost half of the basement and slept every night with a beautiful, sensuous, incredible woman. Could life get any better?

He surveyed the cabin. Signs of Isabel's presence shone in the nooks and crannies of the room, from the ornaments hung on the huge Christmas tree to the overall orderliness of everything. He had never considered himself a slob, but Isabel's hand in the cabin showed him a spotless existence.

He could get used to that. And, if he was being honest with himself, he could get used to her.

A wry grin crossed his face. Too late. He already *had* gotten used to her. And he liked that very much. He could still ignore the fact that the change of season would bring changes in his life.

A noise from the front porch caught his attention and he stuck his head out the front door. After that first big snowfall, he had stopped using this door. Because of the way the wind blew, the snow had piled up under the eaves and blocked it in. But now a wide path had been shoveled. At the end of the porch, gleefully swinging snow over the edge and into the yard, was the woman he loved. For several moments, he stood watching her, the layers of sweatshirts and sweatpants covering her slender form, the oversized boots clumping in time with her movements. As he watched, she broke into song.

"'Twas in the merry month of May,

When green buds, they were a-swellin'…"

Daniel laughed at the sight. "What are you doing out here, woman?"

Isabel jumped and turned around. "What? Oh, I'm shoveling…what does it look like I'm doing?"

Daniel surveyed the scrap of a porch that ran the length of the cabin. "Looks like an exercise in futility to me. Why are you shoveling the porch?"

She leaned her elbow on the shovel and shook her head. "I'm only shoveling a path from it so you can take me home."

His stomach tightened as if he'd taken a sucker punch to the gut. She wanted to go home. She was shoveling a path off the porch so he could take her down the mountain and out of his life. She didn't want to stay with him.

He'd gotten used to having her around and had figured she'd be here 'til March at least. Tomorrow was New Year's and tonight he had something special planned. Apparently she didn't share his enthusiasm. Turning to survey the field before him, he made a futile gesture toward the tree line as his mind reeled. "Isabel, you can't shovel your way all the way down the mountain."

Grinning, she turned back to her task, not noticing his sudden pallor. "Of course not, silly. But it's thawing and we can travel now. If I clear a path to those trees, it'll make the first part of our trip easier."

She wanted to go home. She didn't want to spend any more time with him here than she had to. He had been a fool. "Only here, only now." Hadn't he been the one to make up that rule? And he had been the first to forget it.

"I'll get the sled." He turned abruptly and went back into the cabin.

Isabel frowned at the closed door. After all the stuff he'd told her earlier about not being able to get off the mountain until spring, she expected to have to do a lot more arguing than that. He'd certainly given in a lot easier than she thought he would. Although he didn't need the sled. She could walk on her own with the boots he had given her. Her heart leapt into her throat as a new thought wormed its way in. Was it possible he didn't really want her? Had she misread all the little things that had passed between them?

Shrugging, she turned back to her shoveling. No, she was just being silly. "Only here, only now" had been their mantra, but she knew they were both ready to make it something steadier.

First, however, she had to go back to the city and close out her life there. What had happened to all her things? Had her parents given up on her? Why hadn't anyone come to search for her? All those loose ends bothered her and kept her awake many more nights than she was willing to confess to Daniel. Especially the last question. Daniel had gone a long way toward giving her back the feeling of worth she'd lost when no one had come looking for her. Okay, so she wasn't really lost. But no one in the outside world knew that. Between her mother's harping, the sour relationships and Eddie's abandonment, her self-esteem had taken a huge hit. Daniel and time had repaired much of that. But she still wanted answers.

She paused again and peered into the cabin through the large front window, examining the tidy room she had come to love. The gigantic Christmas tree took up a good chunk of the space and she grinned, remembering how she had expected a tiny Charlie Brown Christmas tree...and he had brought home a Rockefeller Center one instead. Okay, maybe she exaggerated. But his willingness to give her a home and to make it special helped her to know one thing from the bottom of her heart—she wanted to be here with him, forever. It was her place, she knew that now. Seeing her great-grandmother's spirit had put so much into focus. Now, instead of being troubled by dreams of the past, it was her old "city" life that haunted her and she needed closure to put it to rest.

Shaking her head to chase away the doubt, Isabel shoveled off the end of the porch and down the stairs into the sun. The snow wasn't as deep here where the wind had whipped it away. Still she kept to her plan, clearing a path just wide enough for them to hike single file. If Daniel wanted to bring the sled, there was plenty of room for him to just slide it along behind him. He probably wanted it so he could bring back supplies.

The tree line wasn't far from the cabin, less than a hundred feet away, but by the time Isabel made it halfway across the open meadow, she needed a moment to rest and catch her breath.

Shading her eyes from the bright sun, she got her first good look at the front of the cabin. "Just like a postcard," she murmured as she took in the roof that canted down, bending where it met the porch. The dark wood walls, seasoned by the decades it had stood here alone, spoke of comfort and warmth, as did the curl of smoke that drifted from the brick chimney at the end of the house. She wondered if the stove Daniel used was original or if there had been a fireplace at one point.

Dark green shutters, in a shade she had become very accustomed to, were fastened to either side of the one wide window that overlooked the meadow where she stood. Gazing on it now, she wondered how she could ever leave. While she and Daniel hadn't spoken of any permanent arrangements, she knew it was only a matter of time. Whether it was fate or kismet or any of those other fancy words that brought her to the mountain all those weeks ago, she didn't know. But if she saw Eddie right now, she'd probably thank him profusely for leaving her as he had.

Daniel appeared from around the side of the house, sled in tow. He slid it into the path she had made and suddenly her stomach gave a little lurch. There was a determination to his demeanor that unsettled her and she didn't know why. Perhaps it was just that she hadn't expected him to be ready to return her so quickly. He had acquiesced awfully fast. Why was he getting the sled out now? Did he mean to leave today? Turning her back to him, she continued to shovel her path across the clearing to the trees, little butterflies of uncertainty gnawing at her stomach.

At the cabin, Daniel saw Isabel turn from him and knew their brief time together was over. There had been a decided finality to that turn of her shoulder. Whatever emotions he felt toward her were obviously one-sided. After the first major storm, he had informed her he couldn't take her home until the weather changed. Well, it had changed and the week's thaw made it possible to get down the mountain. If nothing else, he was a man of his word. Taking one last look at her figure, the wonderful curves of her body buried under layers of his sweatshirts, he admitted the truth—he had hoped she might be willing to forget their "only here, only now" agreement. Clumping the snow off his boots, he turned away from the direction his thoughts were headed and went inside to put out the fire in the stove and close things up. Might as well get her down the mountain and safely to the Bernsens. The quicker he was rid of her, the quicker he could forget her and get back to his life.

Isabel finished shoveling her path at the entrance to the double row of pines she remembered from their first attempt down the mountain. Under the trees on this part of the mountain, the snow didn't seem so deep. Behind the cabin, near the outhouse, the snow piled four feet and higher. But here, barely a foot lay under the branches. She shook her head over Mother Nature's bizarre choices, shouldered the shovel and headed back to the house.

Daniel came out of the door to meet her since the sled blocked the path to the house. There was something bothering him, she could tell, but he said nothing and only held out his hand to take the shovel from her. "Daniel, what is it? What's wrong?"

"Nothing's wrong. I'll put the shovel on the porch and then we can leave."

"Just like that?" Her heart lurched.

"You wanted to get going."

A sudden fear gripped her stomach. She had thought perhaps they would go tomorrow. Not a cloud marred the brilliant sky, and the weather had already held for three days. Surely they didn't need to leave immediately? She opened her mouth to protest, but closed it again as she recognized the determined look in Daniel's eyes. He wanted to get this over with. He wanted her gone. She had done it again, gone and fallen in love with a man who didn't return her feelings. The alacrity with which he managed to get them organized was proof enough he wanted her out of his life.

Would she ever see the cabin again? This was happening all too fast. Wasn't there something she needed from inside? She shook her head and her nose tickled with tears that threatened to fall. No. She'd come here with nothing and would leave with nothing. She wore his clothes and his old boots. She would give them back once they made it to the city and she got home.

If she had a home. Apartment, rather. And her job. What did everyone think had happened to her? Had anyone even noticed her absence? When she hadn't paid the rent, had the landlord thrown her stuff onto the curb? With a rush, her newfound self-esteem plummeted ten degrees south.

Plagued by questions and unease, Isabel simply climbed onto the sled when he told her, "Get in." His careless toss of a blanket convinced her he took their agreement to heart. With her returning to the city, time would move on, and "only here, only now" was already a thing of the past.

Her knees grew weak as the reality of her leaving and the reality of Daniel's feelings for her, or lack of them rather, sank in and she slid into the sled, grateful she didn't have to walk beside him and look into his eyes. She doubted she could stand the hard glint she knew she would see in those beautiful eyes that had looked on her with such love only a few short hours ago.

They entered the double row of pines, leaving the cabin behind. Had either of them turned to look, they would have seen a dark-haired woman in a seafoam green dress standing on the porch, her hand uplifted in a pleading gesture, her eyes filled with tears.

The trees allowed only a narrow beam of sunlight that lit the snow like a beacon through the walls of pine. It had been near here that the blizzard had forced them back the last time.

But the sun shone on their journey today. Off to her right, Isabel could hear the stream and realized Daniel's path followed it. She wondered if the frogs sang by its side in the spring and with a pang realized she wouldn't be here to find out.

They traveled another fifteen minutes until Isabel's guilt about being carted around was stronger than her inability to look him in the eye. "Daniel, stop. Let me walk from here."

Dutifully, he stopped the sled and handed her out. His emotions were neatly tucked away and his actions were that of the perfect gentleman. She could not read what was going on behind those distant eyes. Not speaking a word to her, he turned and pulled the now-empty sled behind him, leaving her to follow on her own.

The snow wasn't too deep after the warmer days, but it was easier to walk behind the sled and step in his tracks than to blaze new ones beside him. Without a watch, Isabel wasn't sure how long they had walked, but judged it to be almost an hour since they had left the cabin. Daniel's route detoured several times as they came to drifts too high to go through, so she figured the path was actually much shorter. At last the path dipped down and when Daniel turned to follow a hollow that ran between the winter-naked trees, Isabel realized they had reached the road.

"So all we need to do is follow this?" His silence was beginning to grate. Since they had left the house, he had said barely a dozen words. She knew the answers, but asked anyway, just to get him to talk. "Is this the road that goes into town?"

"Yes."

His terse reply confused her. What was his problem? Isn't this what he wanted...for her to be gone from his life? How many times had he called her a nuisance? And yet, in recent weeks, she had imagined it to be a term of endearment when she kissed him at opportune moments, usually right when he was in the middle of doing something.

"Daniel, are you angry? If you don't want to take me, I can find my way from here."

"Oh, that would make a good story. 'Woman left on mountain by two different men finds her way back to civilization all by herself.'" He yanked the rope and pulled the sled up closer.

She stopped, puzzlement drawing her brows into a most unflattering frown. "What are you talking about?"

He shrugged and kept on walking. "We need to keep on going. I want you down to the Bernsens fast enough so you can get on with your life and I can get back to the cabin."

And get you out of my life. Daniel didn't say the words, but every mannerism shouted it to her. She was right. He *was* glad to get rid of her. "Fine, then," she spat back. "Be the macho man and show the little girl how to get home."

Daniel rounded on her and bit out the words. "I will take you to the Bernsens. After that, city-girl, you're on your own."

"Fine by me."

They stomped through the snow in silence for the next mile. Through the trees, Isabel glimpsed the dark wood of a large barn and knew they were close. Suddenly, she didn't want to go back. Ever. If they thought she was dead, then maybe she could stay dead. Why couldn't she drop out of "life" and live on the mountain? Standing still in the snow, she stared at the building with dread.

Isabel swallowed the lump in her throat and took a deep breath. It was really over. Was it only last night he had pulled her close in his sleep, her warmth under the covers all he needed for comfort? She must have dreamed it, she decided as she bowed her head and followed the tracks of the sled. Carefully, she put each foot into the print he left, fancying each step a farewell caress.

The Bernsens fell all over themselves welcoming the two of them. Like many couples married over thirty years, they finished each other's sentences, filling Isabel in on all the details surrounding her disappearance. The newspapers and TV stations had been full of it for weeks. Only recently had her story been relegated to the back pages as no new leads came forth.

"I was sure it was that Nowicki fella, myself," Mrs. Bernsen declared. "I thought for sure he was up to no good. Slimy sort of worm."

"Eddie's the one who left her by the old mine." Daniel explained to them as they sat at the kitchen table. Mrs. Bernsen passed him the plate of fresh cookies and he helped himself to another one as they talked.

Isabel shook her head. "Why didn't they just plow the road after the snowfall and come get me?"

"'Cause they wasn't looking on the mountain." Mr. Bernsen told her in his slow drawl. "They was looking in the city."

"Why?"

"According to the newspaper, your Mr. Nowicki told the police he took you home."

"He lied to the police? That scum! That son of a—" Isabel bit her tongue.

"It's all right, dear. You can call him what he is." Mrs. Bernsen patted her hand. "We've heard the words before." She giggled. "Even used 'em once in a great while."

Out of the corner of his eye, Daniel saw Isabel look at him for support. The fact that her date had lied to her parents, the police, to the world, had her shaking. Now they both knew why there had been no helicopters and no snowmobiles. The authorities had no idea where she really was. He drained his coffee cup, then sat frowning into the depths as if it held the face of the slimeball who left women and then lied to save his own skin.

But Isabel was no longer his problem, he reminded himself. She'd made it quite clear at the cabin that she couldn't wait to get back to her life. The Bernsens were good folk and he knew they would take her into town right away.

"What a wonderful New Year's present you'll be for your mother!" Mrs. Bernsen kept exclaiming.

They offered Daniel a ride into the city to see his folks, but he begged off. "Might as well get back before dark. The stream's pretty swollen and was up almost to the bridge supports where the road crosses by the big oak." Daniel pointedly did not look at Isabel as he said his goodbyes. "Need to get back before the water covers it."

"Does that every once in a while," Mr. Bernsen confirmed in his slow voice. "We'll see you in the spring?"

"You have my word on it." The two men shook hands and Mrs. Bernsen handed Daniel a parcel. "Some more of those cookies I baked up yesterday. Must've had a premonition we was goin' to get visitors."

"Thank you. You know how I love your cookies!" He grinned at the elderly woman and kissed her cheek. Only then did his eyes meet Isabel's.

Isabel blushed, suddenly flustered. The goodbye scene she envisioned evaporated in the steady gaze he turned on her. All the kisses she expected them to exchange to tide them over until they met again disappeared back into the dream world from whence they had come. Blinking back tears, she lifted her chin and kept her voice steady.

"Thank you, Daniel…for everything." If he didn't want her, she would not push herself on him.

"I'm glad I could be there to help." His voice — strained to the breaking point — was formal.

Neither of them noticed the Bernsens' puzzled glances, or Mrs. Bernsen cocking her head toward the inner door. So intent on protecting their own hearts from hurt, neither noticed when the older couple moved silently into the other room.

"Daniel…" Isabel reached out to touch his arm.

Daniel frowned and took her hand, shaking it formally. "What we had up on the mountain was great, but now you're on your way home. Have a good life, Isabel."

The tears she barely held in check now formed in her eyes. "That's it? 'Have a good life, Isabel?'"

Daniel turned away and walked to the door. "We agreed on 'only here, only now', remember?"

"Yes, but…" He didn't want her. How much more blatant did he need to get? She bit back the words and nodded instead. "Yes, Daniel. That was the agreement."

Isabel couldn't keep back the anger that crept into her tone. "You have a nice life, too."

She hadn't meant for them to part this way. She hadn't meant for them to part at all. Was it only last night she had enjoyed the warmth of his body as they cuddled in bed? How could he be so cold today? It all was happening too quickly. The Bernsens moved in the room beyond and she knew they were listening. Closing her eyes to compose herself, she tried again.

"Thank you, Daniel, for all you did for me."

The softer tone and hurt look almost did him in. For an uncomfortable moment, he remembered how she curled close to him in the cold night air, her back curving to fit against his chest. For just a moment, he closed his eyes and savored the clean scent of her hair, fresh-washed and air-dried before the fire.

Daniel hated being so abrupt, but knew in his heart it was for the best. Clean breaks didn't fester. Isabel was going back to the city and he was going back up the mountain. They had separate lives and he was not going to beg her to stay. If she could not choose on her own to stay, then she didn't belong to him anyway.

"You're welcome, Isabel. It was my pleasure."

Even to him the formal words sounded stiff and cruel. Leaving now was his best option before he said or did something stupid. Like going over and kissing that trembling lower lip. Shoving the thought aside, he turned on his heel and left just as the first snowflakes fell. Winter was returning.

Isabel watched the empty doorway for several heartbeats while her thoughts swirled and fluttered, confused and hurt. She bowed her head and a tear slipped down her cheek as she accepted the fact that Daniel had walked out of her life just as quickly as he had entered it.

"Well, now, let's get you down to the authorities, shall we? I'm sure your mama has suffered enough."

Isabel let herself be swallowed up by the Bernsens' kindness. They asked her no questions about her time on the mountain, and Isabel offered no answers. Letting Mrs. Bernsen mother her, she did as she was told and held her feelings at bay. It didn't hurt so much that way. Within minutes, Mr. Bernsen had the car out of the garage and the three of them bumped down a muddy road that was quickly disappearing under a blanket of white. She didn't look back.

Chapter Twelve

අ

"So are you going to the Valentine's Day dance at the church on Friday night? Isabel? Isabel! Are you still there?"

Isabel jumped and stared at the phone in her hand. "What?"

"I swear, woman, you've been wandering off ever since you got back. Where does your mind go?"

Isabel shook her head. Not even her best friend was going to pry that information out of her.

"Nowhere, Beth. What did you ask me?"

"I asked if you were going to the church's Valentine's Day dance. Paul and I are going...why don't you come, too?"

Isabel heard the concern in her friend's voice, masked by the cheery invitation. Briefly imagining herself as the third wheel at a dance for lovers gave her a chill and she begged off as she had with so many invitations lately. "No thanks, Beth. I have work to do at the library."

"That damn library! You spend practically every night there. What work is your boss making you do after hours and in a musty old library?"

In spite of herself, Isabel laughed. "It isn't for work. It's research on my family tree." And his, she added silently.

"Well, don't know who you're ever going to pass the information on to if you don't get out, get a date and get settled."

"Now you sound like my mother." Isabel knew she was being ungrateful, but the last time Beth set her up with a guy, he'd left her on an abandoned road at the top of a mountain. She was better off staying home.

The two friends talked a bit longer, and Isabel hung up with a promise to go out soon on a "girls' night out". Staring at the phone after she put the receiver back in place, Isabel's mind wandered again, turning over the events of the past six weeks.

The police had been glad to have their case solved for them by her reappearance and then had gone after Eddie for giving them false information. Apparently he had found her apartment keys in her purse, used them to gain entrance and gallantly left her purse on the coffee table where she would be sure to find it. Then he'd left, leaving the place unlocked so she could get in. Isabel had been surprised when the police had told her all that. She had pegged him as a total cad and would have thought he'd throw away her purse in spite.

When she hadn't shown up for work after two days and no one answered the phone at home, Beth had come over to check up on her. Finding the purse and the keys and an unlocked door, she'd leapt to the same conclusion everyone else did—that Isabel had simply gone out for a walk and hadn't returned. The search centered on her own neighborhood first, then in ever-widening circles as they looked first for her, then for her body.

The police told her she could probably press charges on harassment, but that Eddie hadn't really done anything illegal to her. Making advances and then leaving her on a mountaintop might be offensive, but it wasn't against the law. Isabel told them all she no longer cared. All she wanted was to pick up the pieces of her life and put them back together. All the same, she got a perverse satisfaction over the lawsuit the city slapped on him. The Powers That Be wanted him to pay restitution for all the time they had spent searching in the wrong places. Hitting the guy in the wallet was a much more satisfying justice than making him sit in a jail cell.

Isabel turned and surveyed her apartment. The landlord hadn't thrown her out. Not out of any sense of mercy, but because her parents had paid the rent. They couldn't, or wouldn't, believe their little girl was dead. Isabel's reunion with them had been filled with tears and pleas to return home for a while. There was a part of her that wanted that very much — to return to the womb was a natural instinct, according to the hospital psychiatrist the authorities had urged her to see. The doctor told her not to indulge herself in that fantasy for too long a time, however. Spending a small amount of time regrouping was healthy, but too much would make her eventual return to her routine difficult. Isabel assured both the doctor and her parents that all she wanted was for everything to be the same as it had always been.

For a while, little things were momentous. The first time Isabel entered her parents' bathroom and flipped the light switch, she smiled in perverse satisfaction. All through her first long, hot shower she reveled in modern technology and the comforts science had wrought. She flushed the toilet and grinned. She brushed her teeth and examined herself in the bright lights above the mirror, surprised there really had been no outward change to her appearance. She certainly felt different inside. Older, more mature. As if she had gone through a great hardship and emerged alive, unscathed, and free.

Not until she bent over to comb out her hair did she miss the cabin. There was no stove here to warm her as she worked the tangles out of her long tresses. No gentle yellow light glowed and softened the lines of her face. And no one splashed or sang in the tub beside her.

Even getting her period a week after coming down the mountain had reminded her of Daniel. She remembered his concern that he hadn't used protection and how she had been relatively sure the timing was such that it didn't matter. Now that she had the proof of that, however, a reluctant wistfulness settled within her.

Shaking her head, Isabel banished the cabin and stared at her reflection in the bathroom mirror. "You are not going to romanticize the place…or the man, Isabel-girl. See it for what it was and get on with your life. Your *real* life." The image in the mirror didn't speak to her.

So she'd spent a week with her parents more out of a sense of moral obligation than anything else before venturing back to the city to her apartment. If they noticed her restlessness, they chalked it up to her desire to get back to the life she'd lived before her "incident", as they called it.

That restlessness found an outlet in an unlikely place— the local history division of the library. Increasingly, Isabel spent more time with the newspaper clippings and photos of a bygone era as she dug through the archives to find stories from the past.

It had taken her a while to organize the information she gathered, mostly because at first she had no pattern to her searches. She looked up information on a variety of topics and took notes, made copies indiscriminately, never knowing if the information was useful or not. She felt as if she were gathering all the pieces…but she didn't know what the picture was or even if all the pieces belonged to the same puzzle.

But after a few weeks of random poking in the library's local history division, a pattern had begun to emerge. Pushing herself away from the telephone, Isabel stepped over to the nondescript desk she had found last week at a thrift store. Her mother would cringe when she saw the battered piece of furniture, but Isabel rather liked its dark, coffeeringed top and gouged sides. There was something fitting about using an old desk for her research into old memories.

Three neatly stacked sets of folders and matching spiral-bound notebooks sat in a row across the top of the desk. Mentally, she reviewed the information in each as she turned over the pieces in her head again, trying to find the picture that eluded her.

The first pile held all the information she could find on the case that had sent Daniel to the mountain. His firsthand report had spared her the grisly details that the papers delighted in. From what she read, there had been little left of the woman's body for identification after her husband had gotten through with her. And that poor twelve-year old boy who had hidden in the closet after the first few blows? What kind of emotional and mental damage had the act done to him? Isabel shuddered. No wonder Daniel was having a hard time dealing with the fact that he had helped this guy beat the first set of charges.

She had filed all the case information in the green folder with a matching green spiral-bound notebook for her own scribblings on the matter. Beside that pile, the yellow set held information on her family tree. Although she hadn't had a single nightmare or visit from her great-grandmother since her return to the city, Isabel's curiosity needed satisfaction. While home, she quizzed her father on his memories of his grandmother, but found they were few. He had only seen her once when he had gone back to Italy with his parents. She was an old, wrinkled woman who wore dark flower-print dresses. That was about all he could remember. So she turned to Italian history books, learning about the culture of Calabria and hoping it might give her insight. She touched the bright yellow notebook as she thought of the woman in the seafoam green dress.

And that led to the third set of notes. Daniel's family tree. The police had asked about the mysterious mountain man who had rescued her and Isabel had given them vague replies. He wanted privacy, he'd get privacy, she'd told herself with a spite she hadn't really felt. The Bernsens had spoken publicly for her rescuer's character as well, and Isabel was grateful the couple understood that Daniel wouldn't want his name dragged into the public eye again. The press would only dredge up the old case and he'd be forced to relive the whole thing all over. The gains he'd made in finding peace would be shattered. The police admitted they didn't really need to talk to him and the papers took to simply referring to her rescuer as the "unnamed Good Samaritan".

Isabel was convinced there was a connection, however, between her ancestor and Daniel's. Even if he never wanted to see her again, she had to find the answer for herself. And so she spent her evening hours in the library, becoming one of the "regulars" known by the staff.

By day, she went back to work. Getting her job back hadn't been difficult, either. In fact, Isabel was surprised by how easy it had been to slip back into her old routines. While her company had reassigned her office, they had been able to find a good-sized cubicle out on the floor for her and she dove into her client's needs in an attempt to wash away the memories of fresh air and snow on a mountain. Except that several times she found herself staring blankly at the white printed sheets, their columns of numbers marching down the page in neat rows of black that shifted and became bare, black arms of trees reaching out over a snow-covered field.

Tonight, fingering the folders and notebooks, she came to understand her daytime attempts to forget the recent past were similar to her nighttime forays to dig deeper. Both were attempts to substitute work for the memory of Daniel's face in the lantern-light, attempts to forget the warmth of his presence in bed, attempts to forget the caress of his hands on her body. She tried to imagine Daniel at a St. Valentine's Day dance and failed. He didn't belong in her world any more than she belonged in his.

"But I *could* belong in his, that's the point!" The words exploded into the silence of her apartment. "That cabin..." Her voice caught and her eyes filled with tears as they did every time she thought of how she'd left the mountain...and him.

Rather than face the boring routine that had been her life before and now was hers again, she scooped up the notebooks and folders and threw them into a bookbag she had picked up on some conference or another. Dropping in several pencils and a roll of change for the copy machine, she grabbed her winter coat and headed to the library.

* * * * *

Two weeks later she was ready to give up. No matter what source she used or how much information she found, she still could find no information at all that would connect her great-grandmother with Daniel's great-grandfather. All she had been able to unearth was corroborating evidence that Daniel's ancestor had, in fact, married a woman named Isabella and that they had emigrated from Ireland during the late 1880s. Census records showed the names of their children. By tracing those and the places they lived, she suspected she knew as much about them as Daniel did. But nowhere in the cold, hard data were the warm stories about their lives...or whom they might have loved and lost.

She'd been somewhat more successful with her own family. Census records, coupled with birth and death certificates gave her a path that confirmed her great-aunt's recollections and that her great-grandmother's name was Isabella. Except that left her right back where she'd been when she started. Daniel's great-grandfather had married an Irish woman and her own great-grandmother had never come to these shores. So what was an Italian woman doing walking around a mountain here in America...and what was a picture of her doing in Daniel's great-grandmother's sewing basket?

Admitting defeat, she pushed her chair back from the secondhand desk and stood. Papers strewn over the desktop fluttered in the breeze she made. "That's it. I can't find any connection because there isn't one. I imagined the whole thing. There never were any dreams, I've never seen my great-grandmother's ghost and for that matter, I probably only dreamed I was ever living in a mountain cabin with a handsome, rugged, logger-type, God-I-want-to-see-him-again guy."

Spinning from the desk, she snarled at the nondescript apartment. "I hate this place. I hate my job and I hate Daniel Patrick Sullivan Fox!"

She grabbed the phone and punched in Beth's number. "Beth, I need ice cream. With lots of chocolate sauce and whipped cream and I don't care that it's still winter outside." A reply came from the other end. "Right. Meet you at the parlor in ten minutes."

* * * * *

The ice cream and conversation had done her a world of good. Isabel waved goodbye and sauntered home through the drifting snowflakes. The forecasters had warned of another blizzard on the way...what did that make? Three of them for the season so far? The one early on that had gotten her stuck on the mountain, another had started just as she'd left to come back to the city with the Bernsens. And now the third, expected to begin tonight.

Once back in her apartment, she methodically sorted the papers she had strewn about trying to find that elusive piece that would solve all the mysteries of the universe. She had only eaten ice cream and yet felt slightly tipsy. "You know what it is, Isabel-girl. You're over him. You're over the whole darn thing, that's what's got you feeling so lightheaded. I mean, hearted. Light*hearted*."

Pulling open a drawer in the desk, she dumped the entire stack of color-coded notebooks and their corresponding folders into the recess, slammed it, and went to bed.

* * * * *

Her alarm did not go off in the morning. Neither did the timed electric pot in the kitchen. Isabel's first realization that something was wrong came from a steady cold breeze across her nose. Opening her eyes, she saw an opaque light coming through the window of her bedroom. A long, graceful curve arced from one corner of the glass pane to the middle of the window and the winter wind whistled as it found a way into her room.

"Damn." Pulling a blanket around her nudity, she stumbled over to inspect the window more closely. The crack was recent and frost had already covered much of the pane. The lace curtains she had on the window did little to prevent the wind from coming in, so Isabel reached up and pulled down the shade.

Frowning, she looked at the shade in her hand. "Must've been more out of it than I thought last night. Usually put that down *before* I go to bed." She pulled the blanket closer and threw a glance at her nightstand clock. For several seconds she stood there, staring at the blank face as her mind processed the information. It was a measure of how quickly she was waking up that it only took a few seconds. "Hey, the power is out!"

The apartment wasn't all that big, just the bedroom, an eat-in kitchen, and the living room. None of the rooms had power. Isabel picked up the phone. The familiar hum of a dial tone calmed her. She wasn't totally out of touch. Civilization was only a phone call away.

Back in her bedroom, her eyes fell on the oversized sweats she had worn at Daniel's. She'd washed, folded and set them on the straight-backed chair in the corner of her room two months ago, the old boots neatly placed side by side under the chair — all ready to be returned to Daniel once spring came.

The plow went by and Isabel scraped a small section of her broken bedroom window to see what she could. The big, thick flakes continued to fall, already filling in where the snowplow had cleared. Nothing else moved. This was an all-day storm, for sure.

Isabel went back to the phone and called the office to find out if she really needed to come in. The night janitor answered the phone and told her the whole place was empty. Power was out not only in the building but in half the city. He couldn't get home, so he had made himself comfortable and was now telling everyone who called to stay home.

Isabel grinned at the thought of the night janitor becoming chief cook and bottle washer of the entire company for the day. She wished him well and made a mental note to bring him something special when she could get back in. In the meantime, she had the day to herself.

Back in the bedroom, she eyed the sweats. Picking up the pants, she fingered the stitches she'd sewn with the old thread that had broken often. A little farther along the seam, the newer thread peeked through in a brighter color. She slipped them on, snuggling into the memories as much as she snuggled into the clothing. The taken down pants, the oversized top and the snow storm seemed to go together. She put the teakettle on the gas stove to heat water for cocoa, her thoughts drifting back to the cabin. She imagined Daniel puttering around, doing the same things she did...only pumping his water instead of turning on a tap. And loading wood into the stove instead of turning on a burner.

The memory of watching him chop wood and haul it into the cabin turned her knees to jelly. She remembered his big, muscular hands grabbing the end of a log to pull it up and drop it into the waiting bin. The same calloused hand that could encase her entire breast in its grip. Isabel's eyes closed and she leaned against the counter as her memories of their incredible night of lovemaking overtook her...

The ropes had been tied differently this time. Her hands, palm-to-palm and tied behind her back, rested comfortably on her tush as she stood before him. Because he'd used only a portion of one of the ropes on her hands, he had plenty left to throw over one of the cabin's beams, forcing her to bend at the waist as he pulled her bound hands up behind her.

"Spread your legs and you'll find it easier to keep your balance," Daniel had suggested to her.

Isabel smiled at the memory as her hand rubbed her breast through the fabric of the large sweatshirt. At the time, she hadn't considered it a suggestion, but rather a command, and had opened her legs.

The rush of cool air against her pussy combined with the awkward position of her body to cause a dramatic upsurge in her arousal. She whimpered a bit and shifted her weight until she was more comfortable in her helplessness.

Daniel pulled at her nipples, tweaking them and making her knees weak. But the pressure on her arms meant she couldn't give in. Forced to bear it, she whispered "green" and let the violent arousal he caused in her simmer, just on the edge of erupting into a rolling boil.

And then he showed her the clothespin. A simple object...two pieces of wood kept together by a plain metal spring. How often had she clipped the clothes to the line over the past few weeks and not really paid any attention to the pins she used? Yet in his hand, they became a nefarious...evil...wonderful tool to torment and delight her onto higher planes of existence. Pinched heat ran directly to her pussy, flooding the entrance with her arousal.

Isabel's eyes closed as the memory of his touch inflamed her. In the silence of her apartment, she lightly pinched the skin of her breasts.

She moved and slivers of excitement sliced through her control. A sunburst of pain encircling each breast radiated internal heat that collected between her legs in a pool of white cream.

She pinched her nipple under the shirt, her nails digging in as her mind transported her back to the cabin, back to his touch...

The first slap startled her into a sharp movement that caused the clothespins to pull in every direction. Daniel stood behind her, his finger finding evidence that she not only enjoyed this treatment, but reveled in it. His roughness made her stomach flip over and she almost came when he grabbed her hair and showed her his glistening finger.

"Do you like the taste of your own cum, Isabel?"

She tasted herself on his finger, licking it clean, wanting to please him, the musky scent filling her nose and the salty taste sending her deeper into a wonderful state where all that mattered was his use of her.

And then he spanked her again. Hard. And he didn't stop. She danced her body away from the blows, only to have it reined in by the ropes pulling on her arms. Fire spread over the skin where his blows landed. The remnants of control shredded and she became an animal, wanting only to rut with her mate.

"You are mine, Isabel. You belong to me."

She was his. He owned her. Her body was his to control...

In the silence of her apartment, Isabel's moans went unheeded. Her fingers slipped inside the cut-down sweatpants and she found her soaking clit. In her mind, she remembered the moment Daniel took the pins off her nipples, how he had warned her the pain would be fast and deep, and that it would send her off the edge again. Her free hand reached protectively toward her nipple as the remembered pain shot through her and the cries of her orgasm echoed off the walls of her apartment as she once again soared and danced to Daniel's touch.

Daniel had taken her places no lover had ever come close to. Was that why she had fallen in love with him? Gasping for breath and sagging against the kitchen counter, Isabel sobbed for air as she came back to reality. A reality that did not include a handsome mountain man.

"No!" She shouted into the empty rooms. "I am not in love with him. He practically threw me out, why would I want a man who lives on a mountain anyway? I'm not going there!"

Her voice broke as a sob welled up inside her throat. She shook her head back and forth as her heart warred with the words she uttered. "No, I can't be in love with him. I won't be! I won't!"

Pushing herself off the counter, she stood firmly on her own two feet. Clenching her fists at her sides, she stared at the bottom drawer of her desk as if Daniel himself were there. "Listen up, Daniel. I'm going to forget about you. I'm going to forget the way your hands warmed me. I'm going to forget how your eyes looked at me with respect and, yes, love. You did love me, even if it melted with the snow.

"But I'm done with you now. Do you hear me? Done!"

She knew she sounded like a hysterical lunatic and didn't care. Grabbing her coat and lacing her feet into the sensible boots she had bought upon her return to the city, she slammed a hat on her head and headed out into the snowstorm for a long walk.

* * * * *

Within a block, the biting wind had reddened her cheeks and Isabel welcomed the cold. It drove the memories from her mind as she trudged through the deepening snow, grateful for the respite. Lights shone from the corner grocery and she ducked in to warm herself for a moment before heading back home, the ghosts finally at bay.

"Isabel! What are you doin' out in dis weather?"

Isabel recognized the accent of the elderly Italian man who ran the store and smiled as her eyes adjusted to the bright lights. "Ran out of milk, Mr. Napoli. And if I'm going to be snowed in, I might as well have some of your homemade cannoli to ease the anguish."

Mr. Napoli's mustache curved when he grinned at her. Wagging his finger, he admonished, "Well, if you is gonna come out for something, my cannolis is a good thing to come out for. Here, you take extra. You need some weight after what you been through."

She didn't bother protesting. Mr. Napoli was always trying to fatten her up and she loved him for it. Food was the old Italian's way of saying "I care about you" and she appreciated it. Digging the bills out of her jeans pocket, she was handing over the money when her eyes fell on the morning newspapers piled on the counter. Her heart thumped inside her chest and she couldn't breathe. Her eyes, fastened on the front page, blinked several times as the picture registered in her mind.

"Hey, Isabel. What is it? You see a ghost on my papers?"

"No, I…here, add one of these to my bill, all right, Mr. Napoli? I need something to read since I'm going to be snowed in."

"Yeah, sure. I add." Mr. Napoli's concerned look did not go away, but he added the paper to the total and gave Isabel her change. Wrapping the paper in a separate plastic layer, he put everything into a double plastic bag against the storm. "You gonna be okay getting home?"

Isabel forced a smile. "Yes, Mr. Napoli, I'll be fine. It's only two blocks."

The wind hit her full force as she left the grocery with a quart of milk she really didn't need, three cannolis wrapped in wax paper, and the newspaper that stole her breath.

The wind's force, however, was a gentle summer breeze compared to the whirlwind in her heart. Bending and twisting her body away from the worst of the snow, she mentally cowed away from the truth revealed to her in today's paper.

Not until she was home, had put away the milk and downed an entire cannoli in spite and growing anger, did she open the newspaper to confront the picture and the headline blazed across the day's side story. "Lawyer Honored for 40 Years of Service". Beside the story was a photo of a tall, broad-shouldered, gray-haired gentleman shaking the hand of another distinguished-looking gentleman, both in three-piece suits. But Isabel's eyes ignored them for the figure standing at the lawyer's shoulder, obviously the man's son, despite the fact that his face was covered in a neatly trimmed beard and mustache. Isabel knew how his eyes, dim on the page, twinkled when he was happy and how they darkened when he was angry. She knew how the beard tickled her face when their lips met.

The storm in her soul settled into hurt as she struggled to read the short article about Daniel's father. The Chamber of Commerce had honored the elder Mr. Fox at a small dinner last night and the mayor had even made a speech.

She stared at the picture as the pain welled. Last night, Daniel had been in the city and hadn't called her. He had been only ten blocks away. So close to her, yet her phone hadn't rung.

Silent tears slid down her cheeks onto the newspaper. She felt so stupid. How could she have been so wrong about it all? How could she have thought Daniel might love her back?

She looked down at the sweats that had so many memories and in a sudden fury, tore them off. The newspaper fell unheeded onto the floor as she stood, ripping off the shirt.

"I won't! I won't sit here feeling sorry for myself. So I'm not married. So I don't have a boyfriend and the man I finally allowed myself to love doesn't love me back." She kicked the clothes as the tears fell. "I don't care. I don't." Her voice caught as a sob overwhelmed her. "I don't."

Collapsing onto the floor beside the desk where the sweats had landed, she pulled the clothes into her arms, hugging them to her heart as she cried out her hurt.

"How can he do this to me? Doesn't he care at all?" The thoughts spun in her head, not making sense. Why had he been so distant on the day he brought her back? And why had he not called her now?

Gathering the clothes in her arms, she shuffled into the bedroom and crawled under the covers, feeling more lost and alone than she had after Eddie left her on the old road. Curling up, she fell asleep, hugging the sweats.

Chapter Thirteen

ೲ

A warm breeze greeted Isabel when she came out of the office building and she lifted her face into its caress. As the winter snows had melted, she'd gathered her routine around her like a cloak, wrapping herself in it and muffling the hurt and pain of lost love. Each week she had spent fewer and fewer hours in the library, until eventually she had stopped going at all. The notebooks and folders remained in the bottom drawer. Bit by bit, she regained her old life as she convinced herself she was moving on.

The snow had all but disappeared. Black piles still lined the streets and dark rivulets of snowmelt filled the gutters. The soft blue of the sky in the city would never reach the brilliant blue she'd gloried in at the cabin, but Isabel didn't look up very often anymore. Her jaw had taken on its familiar set, clenched with the stress of work and life in the city. Near her apartment, a single, brave crocus lifted its purple splendor to announce spring was near.

She knew she had to go back. The clothes she had borrowed from Daniel were back in their proper place on the chair, cleaned and folded. The part of her that wanted to keep the clothes as a reminder of him became a little smaller each day and she finally accepted that getting rid of them would be the final nail in the entire incident. After all these weeks, she was ready to face him, ready to say goodbye with grace. The pants would be of no use to him, but he would want the two sweatshirts she had worn down the mountain during the brief thaw.

And yet she dallied. Two more weeks went by as the clothes tormented her by their existence. She made excuses. How could she find the place? Sure she could drive up the road, but then what? Would the Bernsens know how to get there? And what would they think of her? She snorted at the last. The question was, did she care?

But she did…and that was the truth holding her back. Not about the Bernsens' opinion of her, but Daniel's. Every day he entered her thoughts in some form or another. Sometimes it was the way the delivery man loaded packages in the same way Daniel loaded firewood. For several weeks she took to haunting a particular gas station because the attendant in the little glass booth had a beard and mustache the same color as his. If she looked into her heart, she knew she still loved Daniel Patrick Sullivan Fox.

So she didn't look very often. And the clothes continued to remind her.

The last day of April fell on a Saturday and Isabel resolved to wait no longer. In the morning light, she stood staring at the gray sweats. "You're a grown woman, Isabel Ingandello. And he's just a man. Go give him back the clothes and be done with it, for crying out loud."

Screwing her courage to the sticking point, she marched herself out of the apartment and into her car. Her determination got her as far as the Bernsens before she quailed. Might as well stop in to see them. Get directions and all.

But the Bernsens were on their way out. Mrs. Bernsen gave her landmarks to look for and they were off to see their daughter. Isabel drove slowly up the mountain, suddenly unsure of what she would say when she found Daniel.

Beside the road, the returning birds twittered in the newly leafed trees. A robin flew by, showing his bright red chest and Isabel made a quick wish before he disappeared.

"First one I've seen this season," she whispered. "Please make my wish come true."

But the wish itself she would not give voice to. Only in the silence of her heart did she dare even think it.

Slowing, she neared the spot where the Bernsens had told her Daniel usually parked his truck if he was hauling stuff to the cabin. It was easy to miss, Mrs. Bernsen had told her, not much more than a wide spot in the road between two old oak trees. From there, she would find the path that led to the cabin itself.

Half-afraid and half-wishing, she watched for the pull-off. Would Daniel's truck be there? Or was it still down at Bernsens' farm? She pursed her lips as she drove around a large hole in the dirt road. She should have peeked into the Bernsens' garage so she knew what she was getting into. Then again, what if she came all this way and he was out hunting? Would she stay? Where was Sasha?

Right where Mr. Bernsen had told her they would be, two oaks in their yellow-green new leaves stood guard on either side of what used to be a driveway, if Isabel used her imagination. Planted close to twenty feet apart, the two stood out from the maples and birch that surrounded them, marking the area as special. Isabel pulled her car over to the side of the road and turned off the engine.

In the sudden silence, the sounds of the mountain came through her closed window. Returning birds sang happily as they built new nests for the coming warm season, flirting with each other in song as they flitted from ground to tree making their homes. Isabel gathered Daniel's clothes in her arms, holding them protectively to her chest as if they could keep out the hurt she was about to inflict on herself. As she got out of the car, a light breeze lifted her hair and she turned into it, letting it play over her face as she stalled, not wanting to face Daniel's indifference.

"This is silly. You're a grown woman. So he doesn't love you. Get over it already, will you? He made you no promises. Just walk up that path, say hello, give him back his clothes with a smile and a thank you and go home."

Funny how she had fallen back into the habit of talking to herself in recent weeks. She'd gotten out of that habit when living with Daniel. Resolutely, she set her foot on the path, taking one step, then another. The trail was well-worn and fairly wide. Daniel had told her this had been one of his first jobs in restoring the cabin—clearing a path to it so he could get supplies in. "Wonder why he didn't make it wide enough to pull the truck right up to the cabin," she mused.

Several wild dogwoods, in full blossom, stretched their short limbs toward the sunlight that filtered through the canopy of bare branches and new leaves. Their stark whiteness contrasted with the dark tree trunks and Isabel found her eye drawn to them again and again. In the darkest recesses of the forest, small patches of snow still clung to the shade, reluctant to give up and admit spring had arrived.

The path wound on, bending around the larger trees. Slowly the sound of running water grew louder, until finally Isabel glimpsed the stream, still swollen with last week's spring rains mixed with the last of the snowmelt. Her heart thumped harder. The cabin must be near.

Her steps slowed and she gulped in several deep breaths to steady herself. Above her, a squirrel admonished her for being too close to his nest and in spite of her nervousness, she grinned. "Welcome home to you, too," she called up to him, then bit her tongue. The cabin wasn't home to her. Not anymore.

In front of her, the familiar double row of pines gave way to the clearing in front of the cabin. Isabel stepped into the sunlight and her breath caught. In her last memory of the small building, Daniel's home was surrounded by drifts of pure white snow that covered much of the area surrounding the dark cabin. Now the dark wooden slats blended with the trees behind and to the side of it, making it appear like a small fairytale hut. Isabel glanced around for Sasha. The wolf's appearance would be right in character.

But there was no movement under the trees and Isabel crossed the open field with a light heart. In a few more steps, she would see him again, and even if he didn't love her, that didn't mean she didn't want to see him. Bypassing the porch for the well-used back door, she practically skipped around the short end of the house.

The small lean-to stood just as Daniel had built it this winter past, although small weeds sprouted along its base now. The woodpile still marched along by the near tree line, looking untouched and aged. She didn't see the sled he usually kept by the back door, then shook her head and grinned. "Silly. By now it's put away 'til next winter."

At the door, she paused before knocking. Through the window beside the door, she could see the 1950s print kitchen curtains still hanging in place. "Those really do have to go," she muttered as she waited.

No one answered. Deciding he might be in the basement, or even out hunting, Isabel tried the handle and wasn't surprised to find it unlocked. She never once remembered him locking the door when she was here. Pushing it open, she stepped into the familiar room.

Too familiar. She frowned at the Christmas tree still secured against the wall, a carpet of needles scattered underneath. Several ornaments had fallen from the drooping branches and rolled in various directions.

She glanced at the bed. The familiar quilt covered the bed and it looked as if she had just made it. No dishes in the drainer, but then she did the dishes after each meal. On a hunch, she opened the door to the stove. The old, musty scent of the ashes confirmed there had been no fire inside for a very long time.

Puzzled, she set the sweats on the dusty table and surveyed the cabin, trying to understand. Daniel had left her at the Bernsens and returned here. At some point, he had come back to the city for his father's award. Had he stayed? The heartache had been bad enough when she thought he'd been in town for only a weekend. But to realize now that he had been there for several months without ever calling her…with a quick intake of breath, she steadied her suddenly trembling lower lip.

"There you are, girl!"

Isabel twirled to face the now-closed kitchen door. She heard the yelp of the wolf and her heart pounded as she realized the greeting had not been meant for her. In panic, she glanced around for somewhere to hide, but her legs refused to move. Daniel's voice came through the door as he played with the wolf.

"Hey there, did ya miss me?"

A shadow fell over the window and Isabel saw Daniel's frame silhouetted against the curtains. Not even realizing she was doing it, she wrung her hands together, kneading her fingers in her nervousness.

His attention on the welcome from Sasha, Daniel's head was down as he opened the door. He carried a gym bag and transferred it from one hand to the other as he entered. Not until he had taken several steps into the cabin did he see Isabel standing in the center of the room, frozen in shock.

Isabel couldn't move. She drank in Daniel's leaner frame as if her eyesight were perishing from thirst. His shoulders were just as broad as she remembered, but he had lost weight. There were hollows in his cheeks that hadn't been there before. His hair was closer cropped, and his beard now a shade darker, which, in turn, only accentuated the paleness of his cheeks. Apparently Daniel had spent the winter months indoors in the city, not out here in the fresh air and sunshine.

For the space of several heartbeats they just stared at one another before Daniel managed to state the obvious.

"You're here."

Isabel attempted to answer him, but the words stuck in her clogged throat at the sight of him standing in the open doorway. He didn't seem happy to see her. It was worse than she'd expected. Clearing her throat, she forced the words out. "I came to return your clothes."

Daniel's first instinct had been to rush to her and crush her to him. He wanted to press kisses to every part of her body and get reacquainted with every inch. But the stiff formality in Isabel's voice threw cold water on his spirit and drowned out the pounding of Daniel's heart in his ears. Covering his shock at finding her in the cabin, he dropped his head to hide his sudden disappointment, taking another step in and closing the door behind him while his thoughts grappled with her tone of voice. Isabel's manner was diffident and cold. She hadn't changed her mind. For three eternal months he had given her the space she needed, letting her have her old life back, hoping she would eventually miss him and return.

Daniel glanced at the folded sweats on the table and gave a noncommittal nod. Silence stretched between them in the closed air of the cabin. In the heat of their lovemaking, he had told her he had fallen in love with her, but their "only here, only now" agreement had prevented him from putting any claim on her. And apparently she didn't want it, anyway.

Desperately, he cast around for something to say. "Is that your car parked down by the road?"

"Yes."

She was twisting her fingers as if she were nervous. At a loss, he watched her jam her hands into the pockets of her jeans in an effort to stop fidgeting. What did one say to a woman who had so blithely walked out of one's life?

The silence lengthened between them. Outside, Sasha whined. When Sasha whined a second time, Isabel finally spoke. "Better let her in."

"She doesn't really want to come in. She just wants attention."

Daniel tried to marshal his whirling emotions as he strode over to the bed and dropped the gym bag on top of the coverlet. There were changes in Isabel. She had gone back to straightening her curly hair and it hung stylishly to her shoulders, where only a hint of its true nature was allowed expression in the small flip at the ends. She looked odd in jeans and a turtleneck sweater. He was used to seeing her in the sweats that now lay on the table. The ramrod had taken its place in her back again. She was once again the controlled, uptight woman she had been when she first awoke those many months ago. He shook his head and took his disappointment out on the wolf, who whined again outside the door. "Sasha, stop it. I will come out and play with you later."

"She misses you." The words slipped out before Isabel could stop them.

"And what about you, Isabel?" Daniel's voice was deadly quiet. "Did you miss me?"

"What?" Anger flashed in her eyes. "You have to be the most insufferable, conceited ass I've ever met. Did I miss you? What the hell difference does it make if I missed you or not? Did you think I was just going to sit there all winter in my apartment, waiting for you to come down off your mountain? Why didn't you call me? You went home for your father's award ceremony and you didn't even care enough to call and ask me how I was doing. And you want to know if I missed you?"

Deliberately he kept his voice cold. "I went home long before that."

The words were like a splash of icy water on her anger, turning the fire in her eyes to hurt. "You were in the city all winter, weren't you..." It wasn't really a question and she didn't ask it as one.

The pain in her eyes confused him. She was the one who had wanted to leave the cabin so much. Why should it matter that he hadn't called? Shrugging, he unzipped the gym bag and began to unpack. He kept his voice neutral as he filled her in on the unexpected events that had prevented him from returning to the cabin before today.

"I started back up here after the Bernsens took you home, and then decided to get a few supplies while the weather was good." He snorted. "I should've known how fickle the mountain is. By the time I got back to the Bernsens it was dark and the snow had started blowing. I waited 'til morning, and that was too late. I ended up spending the rest of the week with them until the plows came and dug out the road up to their driveway. Then I bade them goodbye and went back to my parents."

"And never called me."

He heard the unmistakable ice in her voice and his anger flared. "Of course I never called you. You were so busy with your network interviews and your 'I just want to get my life back' attitude, the message was loud and clear. You made it quite obvious the day you left that you couldn't wait to get off the mountain...and away from me."

"Away from you? What?" Isabel frowned. "I wasn't trying to get away from you. I wanted... I wanted..." Her voice faltered and she turned away from him, clenching her hands into fists as she pressed her lips closed. How could she tell him she'd wanted to stay here, forever? How could she admit she had broken their agreement? "Only here, only now." What rubbish! Breathing deeply to calm herself, her jaw clenched as she fought for control of her scattered emotions.

"What, Isabel? What did you want? 'Cause I sure as hell couldn't figure you out. Hot as fire in bed the night before and cold as ice in the morning. Making love to you was like grabbing a live wire or trying to ride a wild horse. You were incredible every time. And then bam! One morning it's all joy because the snow had finally melted enough for you to leave." The anger in his belly grew cold and his voice reflected it. "I thought you were happy here."

Isabel stared at him, her eyes wide and uncomprehending. "I *was* happy here. Daniel, you made me feel alive for the first time in my life. And the way you touched me...hell, I let you tie me up and make love to me and found it blew my mind. I didn't want to go back to the city, but I knew every day I stayed would make it that much harder to explain to people. I had an opportunity to go home and I had to take it. Otherwise, how could I tell my parents, 'I could have come home and eased your concerns, but I was too busy having the best sex I've ever had with a man who's stolen my heart?'

"Don't you see, Daniel? I had to go back. I had to give those interviews and make those reports. I wanted to. I wanted to get them out of the way so I could be free again. Free to come back because you made me feel wonderful, because you didn't just look at my boobs and think, 'There's a good lay'. And then you were in the city and didn't call me. What was I supposed to think?"

His anger flared and hot words poured out of his soul. "Of course I didn't call you. How many times did I watch you on the news, or read some interview in the paper? And every time you looked..." he groped for the word and found it, "relieved to be home. Not once did you mention me in all your interviews, not once did you thank me for taking you in. And now you show up in my cabin like a bad penny."

"I didn't mention you because you told me you value your privacy so much. That is why you ran away last spring, isn't it? Because you didn't want to face real life?" She hated the bitter words that flew from her tongue, but didn't pull her punches. He had hurt her and she lashed back. Snarling, she gestured toward the bundle on the table as she stalked toward the door. "I only came to return your clothes."

"No, you didn't."

She whirled around, her eyes flashing as his words cut her to the bone.

"You came because you're what I always thought you were. A tease who lets men get only so close, then pushes them away."

Daniel crossed his arms over his chest, trying to stop his heart from hurting. She looked stricken at his words. It was all he could do to keep from crushing her to him. But the hurt went both ways.

Her voice was unsteady as she answered him. "You were the one who insisted on 'only here, only now'. I can't help it if I was stupid enough to fall in love with you. Obviously, I read more into your actions than was there." She hated that her lower lip trembled. She bit it, trying to make the dam stronger, but the tears fell anyway. "I hate the city. I hate my job and I hate—" She couldn't say it. She didn't hate him. She loved him and he didn't love her back, just like all the others. Only one option was open to her and she took it, opening the door and fleeing from the man she loved.

Stumbling around the end of the cabin, the tears slowed her down. Sniffling and wiping her nose on her sleeve, she dashed the tears from her eyes and focused on the pines that marked the path to her car. Even as she lurched away from the porch, her ears listened for any sound that he might call her back. This wasn't how it was supposed to be.

But he didn't call her name, and she heard no movement. Sobbing, she crossed the open field and entered the double row of pines.

Daniel stared at the door where she had been as his mind worked through what had just happened. How often had he envisioned seeing her again? Countless times he'd played it over in his head, sometimes imagining they'd meet in the city, sometimes here at the cabin. Never once had it ended like this.

Sasha howled from outside somewhere and Daniel pulled open the door, ready to take his anger out on the wolf. He stalked into the yard and stopped when something caught the corner of his eye. Slowly he turned and saw the seafoam green dress of Isabel's great-grandmother. He didn't want to meet her eyes, but forced his gaze to face her.

She did not speak to him—she didn't need to. The look of sorrow on her face said it all. Daniel knew she wanted him to run after her great-granddaughter and make up to her. He wanted it too, but pride got in his way. Shaking his head at the spectre, he turned away as she faded.

"You do know you're being a fool."

Daniel's head whipped up. On the far side of the yard, over near the woodpile, stood a barrel-chested man in old-fashioned clothes. His foot was propped casually on a log and he leaned on his knee, taking Daniel's measure.

"Who are you?"

The man straightened. "One who let his pride get the better of him a long time ago. Learn from my mistake, son, and go after her before she gets herself lost again."

"Not until you tell me who you are."

"You already know. Bring her back and make her yours. My dark-haired Isabella will never be mine, you should at least have yours. Go."

Daniel didn't wait another second. Ghosts from the past seemed perfectly normal all of a sudden. Turning on his heel, he whistled for the wolf and dashed toward the row of pines.

Isabel couldn't find the path. Where it emerged on the forest side of the pines, it wasn't much more than a deer track, but she'd managed to find her way *to* the cabin, why couldn't she find her way from it?

"Damn it, I can't be lost. Not again!" Her voice startled a covey of partridges that flew up, startling her in turn. She screeched, then clamped her mouth shut. *I will find my way out of here all by myself,* she thought grimly. *I don't need him for anything.*

A blur of white beside her came to rest in front of her and Isabel stopped. Sasha planted herself in her path and bared her fangs.

"Now, come on, Sasha…it's me, Isabel. Let me go back to my car and make a decent exit, will you?" Isabel took a step forward and the animal growled. "Okay, I'll go a different direction. Is that what you're trying to tell me?" Isabel turned to the right and took two steps before the wolf was in front of her again. This time the animal howled and Isabel realized what the wolf was up to.

"Oh, no. You're not going to corner me like some wild animal for Daniel to come here and capture. I'm not lost. I just can't find the path. I'll get to the road in my own way, thank you very much. Now let me get past you!"

Isabel started around the wolf again, and again the wolf bared its teeth and growled. Deciding she was all show,

Isabel continued, her heart pounding with so many emotions she was surprised it didn't echo through the woods. But Sasha wasn't so easy and wasn't going to let her prey get away. Grabbing Isabel's pants leg in her teeth, the wolf pulled Isabel to a halt as Daniel crashed through the underbrush behind her.

His heart exploding, Daniel closed the distance between them in two long strides. He clasped Isabel's face in his broad hands and pulled her up to him, his thumbs drying the tears still spilling from her eyes. "Isabel, I let you go once, I'm not going to let you go again."

"I'm a nuisance, I'm in the way of your private angst." She sniffled.

"Not anymore. Somewhere along the line, I fell in love with you. I told you that."

"In the cabin, in the heat of lovemaking, you told me that."

The breeze wafted a stray hair into her face and Daniel gently tucked it behind her ear. "I did," he admitted. "And I meant it. When I said it then, and when I say it now. I love you, Isabel."

"Oh, Daniel, I love you too. I never meant to hurt you when I went back. I just wanted to put everything in order...and all I ended up doing was making a mess of things. I'm sorry."

"And I'm sorry, too. I should have called you every day and told you I wanted you to come back." His lips hovered over hers, prolonging, anticipating the sweetness of their kiss to come.

"Daniel," she whispered, "kiss me. Please?"

He complied. Gentle and tender as the morning breeze that caressed them, their souls met and the ice between them melted.

"Come back to the cabin with me?"

"For the day."

He looked at her in surprise as he took her hand to lead her back through the trees. "Just today?"

"I have to work tomorrow, remember?" She smiled and called to Sasha.

"So you do, so you do. Well, we're going to have to do something about that." He held back a branch so she could pass, then let it thwap behind.

"And just what do you propose to do?" Isabel bit her tongue. She hadn't meant to use such a leading word. There were far too many details to work out between them before either of them could think of marriage.

"I propose," Daniel accented the word to tease her, "that you quit the job you hate and move up here with me."

"And what will we do for money?" She stopped as they reached the path. "Did you go back to lawyering?"

His laugh, loud and deep, rolled through the woods. "Nice word. I think you just made up a new one." He sobered, however, as they walked beside each other through the row of pines, his fingers entwining with hers. "No, I didn't go back to 'lawyering'. We won't need much, if we make the cabin our home. I was planning to put in a kitchen garden this spring. And I can hunt."

"A return to the old days?"

"Yes. Could you do it? Could you live without a light switch and indoor plumbing?"

"You have indoor plumbing…it's called a pump. But I'd need an outhouse. A real one, with heat. And maybe a bathhouse?"

He laughed. "One thing at a time."

She paused as they came to the clearing in front of the cabin, eyeing it critically. A broad swath of new green grass covered the field like an Emerald City carpet. Wild violets in purple and white dotted the green with small spots of color.

"I don't know, Daniel. You're thinking you can be self-sufficient up here. Grow your own vegetables, hunt your own meat and all. And that's fine. But what about other things? Like going to the movies? Or shopping at a mall? I don't want to live in the city anymore and suburbia drives me nuts. But I'm not sure I could become a hermit."

"I'm not sure I could, either. Living here doesn't mean never going down to civilization. Only in the winter are the roads impassable." Daniel took a long look at the small cabin and tried to imagine raising a family there. "My great-grandparents built this as the first room to a much larger house. I still don't know why they never built here, but I've been thinking of making this a real home."

"But that takes money, Daniel. I have some savings, and you must, too, but you've already spent a bundle in lumber just to make what's here livable. How could we ever add on?"

The pronoun change spread a warm feeling throughout his soul. But the question she had asked was one that deserved an answer. It was time he 'fessed up.

"Um, Isabel…"

He had the look a little boy gets when he's about to confess his hand was in the cookie jar. Isabel's eyes narrowed and she pulled her hand from his, crossing her arms in front of her and taking on a mock scolding tone.

"Yeeesss?"

"Did I tell you how much of the mountain my grandfather left to me?"

"No, Daniel, I don't think you did."

"It's quite a lot."

"Oh?"

"My grandfather left me the entire mountain."

"The entire mountain." She pursed her lips and looked around. To her right the trees sloped upward toward a summit she couldn't see from here. Behind her, the mountain sloped downward for over a mile before coming to the Bernsens' driveway. "All sides?"

"All sides." She seemed to be taking this remarkably well, he thought.

"And how big is this mountain?"

"About four thousand acres."

"Four thousand acres?" She tried to imagine such an amount of land, but her city upbringing had no frame of reference. "What about the mine up near the top?" She frowned as she remembered what had brought her to the mountain to begin with.

"The mining company owned that area at one time. But when they went out of business, my grandfather bought up the land."

"So you own a lot of land. That doesn't make you self-sufficient. Or rich."

Daniel looked away.

"You are. Rich. Aren't you?"

"Well, I'm pretty well-off."

She narrowed her eyes. "How rich?"

He shrugged. "Does it matter?"

Her hands planted firmly on her hips, she faced him down. "Daniel Fox. You're asking me to live with you in a tiny little cabin in the middle of the forest on some forsaken mountain. Now I want to know whether I'm ever going to get that outhouse or not."

He grinned. "Isabel, I promise, you will get your outdoor privy. And more."

She stepped closer and put her face up to him. "I'm pretty low maintenance. A roof over my head, a warm fire when it's cold, and a pot to pee in is all I need." She grinned. "And the occasional night in town at a fancy restaurant wouldn't hurt."

Her perfume filled his senses and ignited his passions. Bending down, he pulled her into his embrace and kissed her soundly.

"Come inside before I take you right here."

Laughing, she pulled away from him and raced him to the cabin. She reached the door only a second before he did and ran inside, where the dried scent of the dead Christmas tree met her. She paused to gaze at it fondly, even as Daniel's hands turned her around to face him.

"The poor thing. Up here and unappreciated, untended all these weeks."

Daniel pulled her sweater over her head. "Forget the tree. What about me? I've been pretty unappreciated...and untended, too!" The sight of her shape, emerging from the layers of clothing was like setting a flame to a pile of dry kindling. The need of the past few weeks threatened to overwhelm his control. He bent to kiss her before she removed anything else and let his tongue plunder through her lips to possess her mouth. He grasped her to him, lifting her small frame, feeling her legs wrap around him and pull him closer.

"I want you, Isabel. Now."

"Then take me, Daniel. Now."

Their pent-up passions careened out of control as both released their misconceptions and accepted the truth. Isabel's turtleneck joined the heap on the floor beside Daniel's coat and jeans. They tore the clothes off each other like wild animals, grinning at each other in their race to be naked and in each other's arms again.

Spring air filtered through the windows as they fell onto the bed, the quilt and sheets tangling as they rediscovered the joys of the other's body. Together they relearned the tweaks and touches that elicited squeaks and whimpers, deep growls and gasps of ecstasy.

Daniel pinned Isabel's arms over her head, enclosing her wrists with his own massive hand, attacking her neck with kisses, nipping and running his tongue over the ticklish skin. He loved how she tasted of fresh air and springtime, with just a hint of the garlic she had last night for dinner. He slid his tongue over her breasts, greedily indulging himself in his explorations. Her satisfied moans beneath him sang the music he'd missed.

Isabel gloried in his power. The weight of his muscular body pressed her down into the bed and she could barely breathe. Her squirms were not designed to get away, but to take full advantage of his thigh between her legs.

She arched her back and rubbed her clit against his leg, her body hungry for his touch. "Daniel, please...oh, please..."

"Ask." His voice, rough with desire, barked the command.

"Please let me come!"

"No." He poked his head up from her delicious nipples. "This time, we come together." Sliding his arm around her waist, he rolled her over so she straddled his legs, then pulled himself up to lean against the headboard.

"Come to me, Isabel."

The words of her dream! Her heart beating wildly, she answered the summons.

"Oh, Daniel, any time you want…" She rose, embracing him in her arms as she poised herself over his cock. His hands guided her hips and slowly she sank down, feeling his cock enter and enlarge her.

"You are mine, Isabel. I claim you."

His kiss plundered her mouth as he took possession of the woman he loved. Fervent and hot, their tongues met, entwined, danced as their bodies rocked in a timeless rhythm.

Her greedy hands slid over his body, twining through his hair, digging into the muscles of his shoulders, pulling him to her in a tight embrace. She spread her legs wider, inviting him deeper and moaned in pleasure when his cock hit home. Isabel gave herself to Daniel with every movement, every whimper and every moan she made.

Daniel thrust into her pussy, setting a steadily increasing rhythm as they claimed each other. His hands, hungry and insatiable, squeezed her breasts, cupped her cheeks, guided her hips. Unable to hold back any longer, he wound his fingers in the silkiness of her hair and pulled her back to look her in the eye.

"Open your eyes." He growled the command. "Come with me."

She couldn't refuse. She would refuse him nothing. Trying to focus on his face, her eyes blurred and steadied as her lungs heaved for breath. Quickening the pace again, he repeatedly slammed into her, stretching her opening to fit his wide cock. "Now," he growled as the first of his seed shot into her.

Their music filled the cabin, a cabin that had been silent far too long. The bed added a rhythmic squeak to their chorus and outside, a white wolf howled. Time had no significance as their bodies contracted in tandem, the entire world consisted only of themselves.

Isabel soared among the clouds, secure in the knowledge that Daniel flew beside her. Together they floated hand in hand, basking in the afterglow of lovemaking as springtime sunshine streamed through the window to light their entwined and spent figures. Isabel breathed deeply, inhaling the mingled scents of fresh air and old pine and love. She lay with her head on Daniel's chest, rising and falling with each breath he took and listened to the steady beat of his heart. She smiled. She was home.

Chapter Fourteen

෨

"On my count, heave!"

Isabel, covered in dust and cobwebs nodded, saving her breath for the big push. Determined to get to the back of the junk pile, the two had worked all morning, cleaning the basement. Now just one huge block of stone stood between them and the last few pieces.

"One, two, three...push!"

Daniel's face turned red with the effort. The stone moved, incrementally at first, then finally fell onto its side, giving the two of them their first good look at the oldest junk in the pile.

"Daniel, look! I told you we'd find buried treasure." Isabel grabbed the flashlight and shone it on the trunk that stood revealed, the curved top covered with decades' worth of dirt and dust.

Stretching out the kinks, Daniel reached for the Italian beauty beside him. He still couldn't believe their misplaced pride almost kept them apart. When she smiled and put her dirty hand in his, the warmth that spread through him wasn't entirely due to the workout he'd just had.

Isabel had given her boss and her landlord her notice. In two weeks, she would be living with him full-time. But first, Daniel wanted the rest of the pile in the basement out of the cabin to give them more room.

"I think this stone has always been here," he announced, grimacing at the size of the thing. Its irregular shape was close to two feet across and almost four feet long. Made of solid granite, it stood on its end, blocking the back corner. Underneath was the other end of the board neither of them had been able to budge.

"No wonder," Isabel had exclaimed when they saw the edge of the board buried beneath the behemoth. "Looks like someone tried to move this in the past."

At first they both thought it was a part of the foundation. But it was angled wrong. Determined to find out what, if anything, lay behind it, they had pushed and shoved and dug and at last toppled it onto its side, revealing the old trunk behind it.

"I think someone went to great lengths to keep this hidden, Daniel." Isabel grabbed the rag she had used to dust off several of the "keepers" they'd found and rubbed it carefully over a corner of the rounded top. "Bring the light over?"

A knot had formed in Daniel's stomach. What family skeletons were they about to dig up? Pursing his lips, he shone the light as she directed. Bit by bit, her cloth revealed a stamped tin top, the raised stars dark with spots of rust.

"There's no lock on the front," he observed as she got rid of the worst of the dust. He took a deep breath. "I'm ready if you are."

Isabel nodded and stepped over to bring the kerosene lantern closer. Somehow this didn't feel like a moment for a battery-operated flashlight. Daniel's smile was thin as he clicked it off, understanding her train of thought.

Stooping his large frame, he bounced on his heels a moment, then put his hands on either side of the lid. It groaned and protested when he tried to lift it, but gave way under his determination. With a gentle clunk, the lid fell back.

Two wooden boxes lay side-by-side. Daniel picked up the smaller of the two. In the soft light, he could easily see the

Cuban woman on the top. "Apparently, someone in my family smoked cigars." His voice fell heavily into the close air of the basement. Was it his imagination, or did he feel his grandfather in the room? He didn't want to turn around and find out.

Instead, he opened the box.

The sweet scent of honeysuckle filled the air. Isabel breathed deep. "Her perfume."

"But which one? My great-grandmother's? Or yours?" Daniel cocked an eye at her, but Isabel only shrugged and motioned to the box as she hung the lantern above them so she could see better.

Daniel nodded and lifted out the fine linen handkerchief that rested on top of other items, unfolding the fragile fabric as he lifted it. Beautifully embroidered initials graced one corner, their brilliant scarlet still vibrant after all these years.

Beneath it, several items that must have had meaning to his great-grandfather lay in ordered rows. A pebble, a seashell, some old Italian coins all lay as if purposely set in an order no one now understood. A small, black velvet box stood alone off to one side. Daniel lifted it gently, setting the cigar box back into the trunk so he could look inside the tiny box.

"I think I know what's in here." Daniel looked at Isabel and she sank to her knees beside him.

"Oh, Daniel...do you think...I mean, do you suppose it had gone so far?"

His heart beating in his ears, Daniel opened the box. The silver glitter of a diamond winked back at them. The teardrop shape of the stone set upon a ring of gold told them just how in love their ancestors had been.

Neither of them spoke. Isabel laid her head on Daniel's shoulder as sorrow for the doomed lovers washed over her.

"Their cultures were just too different then. Their families couldn't see that love was far more important than upbringing."

"But I can." Daniel shifted his weight, coming down on one knee and turning to Isabel.

"What?" She knelt back in the dirt, puzzled by the sudden decisiveness in Daniel's voice.

"Isabel Ingandello, my great-grandfather let a woman go once because he didn't have the sense to set his pride aside. I let you go once for the exact same reason and that's not ever going to happen again." Out of the corner of his eye, he imagined he saw his great-grandfather's image form in the dark corner of the basement. "Will you marry me?"

Isabel's heart leapt into her throat as Daniel took the beautiful diamond ring from the velvet box and held it out to her. The light glimmered on the multiple facets, showering her with small sparks of light. Without looking, she knew her great-grandmother was near.

"Yes, Daniel Patrick Sullivan Fox, I will marry you."

And as she flung her arms around his neck, her heart beating high, she sent a mental "thank you" to her wonderful great-grandmother, wherever she was.

Epilogue
ಹ

Isabel and Daniel sat amid the old papers strewn across the table. The larger of the two boxes sat at one end, empty now of all its contents.

"I still can't believe your great-grandfather wrote a rough draft of all his love letters...and then kept them!" Isabel shook her head over the correspondence their ancestors had shared.

"Neither can I, but I'm glad he did. Look what a complete picture we have of the two of them." Daniel finished reading one of the fragile pages and set it down carefully with the others.

"I think this is a newspaper clipping about him in Italy, but we're going to have to find someone who reads Italian." Isabel sorted it into a separate pile. "It appears my theory was correct. The two of them met when your great-grandfather was doing the Grand Tour in 1885. They fell in love, and would have married if her family had not raised so violent an argument."

Daniel picked up one of the letters. "At least her brothers didn't break any bones. But it does sound like he got a pretty bad beating before they stuck him on the boat for home."

"And that's where the letters stop." Isabel sighed. He must have gone back to Ireland and given her up." She picked up the photo that had started the two of them on their quest. "I'd still like to know why this was in the bottom of your great-grandmother's sewing basket."

Daniel held out his hand and stared at the couple in the picture for several minutes when she handed it to him. "I have a suspicion, but I'm not sure I want to unearth any more skeletons."

"You're thinking she knew?"

"About my great-grandfather's Italian Isabella?" He dropped the picture down among the other papers. "Yeah, I think she knew. And then hid this photo from him so he would forget."

Isabel considered. "Except he never did." She sat back and surveyed their treasure. "So much we still don't know…"

Daniel shook his head. "I doubt we'll ever know all the details. I'm just glad they married their own kind."

Isabel sat up, shocked. "What? You don't wish they'd had a happy ending?"

"No." Daniel grinned that mischievous grin she loved so much. "If they'd had their happy ending, we wouldn't have ours. We'd be related."

A contented feeling spread through her as she reached across the table and took his hand. "We will be related, right after the preacher says, 'I now pronounce you man and wife.'"

Daniel pulled her up and came around the end of the table in three long strides. Gathering her into his arms, he leaned down to kiss the lips he loved to taste.

"You will always be mine, Isabel."

"I never wanted to be anyone else's, Daniel."

A soft sigh came from the corners of the room as their lips met, but Daniel and Isabel were oblivious. Their eyes were only for each other as a dark-haired woman in a seafoam green dress and a giant of a man in an old-fashioned suit clasped hands and faded from sight.

Enjoy An Excerpt From:

Table for Four

They ordered and David told her what he'd accomplished while she was 'busy' elsewhere. He was very careful not to refer to her private fetish in public—to do so would violate another taboo. Lissa, however, was grateful for his discretion, it had taken her a long time to tell the person she most loved in all the world; there was no way she wanted anyone else to know.

Indeed, part of the arousal of the afternoon was listening to the life teeming around her; life that had no idea what little secret lay behind the open balcony door just above their heads.

The diner filled quickly and when the little bell over the door rang again, David looked up as something or someone caught his eye—and stared. Lissa frowned and nudged his foot under the table, but it seemed to have no effect. Turning her head slightly, she saw what held his fascination.

A man and a woman had entered and were making their way down the aisle toward them. With her straight, long blonde hair and svelte figure, the woman was a walking goddess. Her dark heels were at least six inches high—which just about matched the length of her navy blue skirt.

But while Lissa acknowledged the beauty of the woman, it was the man who followed that held her eye. Even though the woman's heels made her tall, the male behind her still towered a full head above her, his broad chest and commanding bearing daring Lissa to look away. His neatly trimmed wavy black hair fell in small curls just long enough to give a girl something to run her fingers through. His round face sported a small goatee and neatly trimmed mustache. The very image of a Gypsy king come to life.

The diner was full and every eye watched the couple as they made their way along the narrow aisle. No seats were left and when the waitress apologized and told them they'd have to wait, the gentleman, without turning his gaze from Lissa, told the server in a smooth voice, "That won't be necessary. I'm sure this nice couple will share their booth with us, will you not?"

There was a faint accent in his quiet, baritone voice, but Lissa could not place it. She tore her eyes away to signal 'no!' to David, but he was already moving over and letting the woman slide in next to him. The blonde made an odd little movement, then settled next to Lissa's husband and smiled across the table at her. Lissa smiled weakly in return, while glaring at her husband. What was he doing?

"Please, by all means. We are happy to share the table." David tore his eyes away from the blonde beauty just long enough to dismiss the waitress. But anything further was cut off as he watched the goddess readjust her seat, and flip up her short skirt to place her naked rear end on the vinyl seat cover. He knew he was ogling, but he just couldn't stop. It wasn't every day that a beautiful woman just walked into your life and showed you her ass.

David's entranced absorption of the blonde goddess' actions made her male companion smile. He watched his partner and when her soft blue eyes met his and she nodded, he knew she wanted to play. While he spoke English extremely well, he let his rich baritone affect more of an accent than usual as he made his apologies to the couple whose booth they had invaded.

"Thank you, sir, you have saved my lovely Adora from having to stand so long in her shoes. They make her sexy, do they not?" He put out his left hand and Lissa caught sight of a large gold signet ring on his forefinger—but no wedding band a little further along. The woman he called Adora smiled at him and placed her hand in his. The image of her slender and delicate hand in his larger and rougher one made

Lissa's heart skip a beat as she recognized their poetic contrast: he was night; she was day.

David's mouth was dry and he hurriedly sipped from his water glass to cover the fact that this man's girlfriend had given him a hard on—an amazing accomplishment, considering he had just had sex with his wife not an hour before. "Yes," he finally managed. "Yes, her shoes, I mean, your shoes are very sexy." He tried not to look down, but the woman's tight shirt barely covered her bosom and her cleavage just cried out to for a quick glance.

"Oh, David, really!" scolded Lissa, totally embarrassed by her husband's obvious fascination with the blonde, but more embarrassed by her own internal reactions to the man beside her. Her panties were soaked and her pussy was open and aching, right there in the restaurant. For crying out loud, she was a married woman!

"Methinks my Adora likes your husband's attentions, even as you are not sure you appreciate mine, my dear woman. Permit me to introduce myself. I am Master Richard."

If the man were not sitting so close to her and so obviously exuding sex appeal all over the place, Lissa might have laughed at the Hollywood movie tone the man affected. And what was up with the Master title? All the man needed was an opera cape with red satin lining and the picture would be complete. He already was dressed in the suit. All right, so he wasn't wearing a white tie and tails, but a nice three-piece, well-cut, black, very sexy suit.

His left hand occupied with Adora, Richard now held out his right to Lissa, palm up in a gesture of peace. He noted how the woman beside him shrank away, careful to not touch him with any part of her body, and waited until she extended her own hand, noting she was unable, or unwilling, to meet his eyes. Master Richard gently took her hand in his, turning it and bringing it to his lips. The kiss on the back of her hand intentionally put her off balance.

Lissa knew she should not sit here and hold hands with a perfect stranger, no matter how sexy he was. Even knowing she should pull her hand away, she remained still, letting him touch her.

"Pleased to meet you," she murmured, more out of habit than real pleasure.

Richard decided to let the pretty dark-haired woman off the hook, turning to the gentleman across from her. "Sir, you have met Adora, my beloved. And I have introduced myself. Is it not the custom for you to now introduce your wife and yourself?" There was a hint of amusement in his voice, since the man was still entranced with his companion.

"Oh! Erm, yes, of course." David cleared his throat and shook his head, trying desperately to bring his mind back under control and focus on something other than the extremely sexy woman beside him. "I'm David Patterson, and this is my wife, Lissa."

"Enchanted." Richard released Adora's hand, but still held Lissa's; he turned it over to place a tender kiss on her palm. His eyes held hers, never leaving her face; Lissa felt her soul was open to the man's inspection. An absurd thought ran through her head that perhaps the man really was the King of the Gypsies and she smiled at the absurdity.

"Ah! Your lady smiles and the world lights with happiness."

The waitress brought their dinners and saved Lissa further embarrassment. Her cheeks burning a bright pink, she withdrew her hand to take her dinner plate from the waitress' hand. Since the new arrivals had not yet ordered, the server now turned her attention to the handsome couple. Richard's voice was different when he spoke to the waitress; he ordered for the two of them in clipped tones that brooked no nonsense. It occurred to Lissa that she had yet to hear the woman speak.

As the waitress hurried away and Master Richard turned his attention to David, Lissa tried to calm the heartbeat that thundered in her ears. What was it about the man beside her that caused her stomach to flutter as if she were a schoolgirl? Clearly David appreciated Adora, and Lissa knew that she should be jealous—he certainly hadn't looked at her like that in a very, very long time.

Too bad she and David had already had their Saturday night sex; she certainly needed to give vent to the arousal that had continued to build inside her all through dinner. She thought of herself as she had been earlier, spread upon the bed; open, wanting—only the man who walked through the door to release her was not her husband, but Master Richard.

Why an electronic book?

We live in the Information Age—an exciting time in the history of human civilization, in which technology rules supreme and continues to progress in leaps and bounds every minute of every day. For a multitude of reasons, more and more avid literary fans are opting to purchase e-books instead of paper books. The question from those not yet initiated into the world of electronic reading is simply: *Why?*

1. ***Price.*** An electronic title at Ellora's Cave Publishing and Cerridwen Press runs anywhere from 40% to 75% less than the cover price of the exact same title in paperback format. Why? Basic mathematics and cost. It is less expensive to publish an e-book (no paper and printing, no warehousing and shipping) than it is to publish a paperback, so the savings are passed along to the consumer.

2. ***Space.*** Running out of room in your house for your books? That is one worry you will never have with electronic books. For a low one-time cost, you can purchase a handheld device specifically designed for e-reading. Many e-readers have large, convenient screens for viewing. Better yet, hundreds of titles can be stored within your new library—on a single microchip. There are a variety of e-readers from different manufacturers. You can also read e-books on your PC or laptop computer. (Please note that Ellora's

Cave does not endorse any specific brands. You can check our websites at www.ellorascave.com or www.cerridwenpress.com for information we make available to new consumers.)

3. *Mobility*. Because your new e-library consists of only a microchip within a small, easily transportable e-reader, your entire cache of books can be taken with you wherever you go.

4. *Personal Viewing Preferences.* Are the words you are currently reading too small? Too large? Too… ANNOYING? Paperback books cannot be modified according to personal preferences, but e-books can.

5. *Instant Gratification.* Is it the middle of the night and all the bookstores near you are closed? Are you tired of waiting days, sometimes weeks, for bookstores to ship the novels you bought? Ellora's Cave Publishing sells instantaneous downloads twenty-four hours a day, seven days a week, every day of the year. Our webstore is never closed. Our e-book delivery system is 100% automated, meaning your order is filled as soon as you pay for it.

Those are a few of the top reasons why electronic books are replacing paperbacks for many avid readers.

As always, Ellora's Cave and Cerridwen Press welcome your questions and comments. We invite you to email us at Comments@ellorascave.com or write to us directly at Ellora's Cave Publishing Inc., 1056 Home Avenue, Akron, OH 44310-3502.

ELLORA'S CAVEMEN
TALES FROM THE TEMPLE

Try an e-book for your immediate
reading pleasure or order these titles in print from

WWW.ELLORASCAVE.COM

COMING TO A BOOKSTORE NEAR YOU!

ELLORA'S CAVE

Bestselling Authors Tour

Cerridwen, the Celtic Goddess of wisdom, was the muse who brought inspiration to storytellers and those in the creative arts. Cerridwen Press encompasses the best and most innovative stories in all genres of today's fiction. Visit our site and discover the newest titles by talented authors who still get inspired - much like the ancient storytellers did, once upon a time.

Cerridwen Press

www.cerridwenpress.com

Discover for yourself why readers can't get enough of the multiple award-winning publisher

Ellora's Cave.

Whether you prefer e-books or paperbacks,

be sure to visit EC on the web at
www.ellorascave.com

for an erotic reading experience that will leave you breathless.